'You are a rogue, Jack Dilhorne, a very rogue.'

He leaned forward to whisper conspiratorially to her, 'You should do that more often, Marietta, it becomes you.'

She was so unused to such compliments that she said abruptly, 'What…what did I do?'

'Laugh,' he told her, solemn now. 'You should laugh more often. I must think up some jokes.'

'Oh, Jack,' she riposted, 'you are a living joke.'

'In that case,' he shot back, 'you should be favouring me with a laugh all the time instead of rationing me so severely.'

Well, Jack Dilhorne knew how to flirt and no mistake! Which was perhaps why she was suddenly doing all those flighty things which she had never done as a young girl.

Dear Reader

Some years ago I did a great deal of research on the lives of those men and women who, for a variety of reasons, lived on the frontiers. Re-reading recently about life in Australia in the early nineteenth century, it struck me that an interesting story about them was only waiting to be told. Having written HESTER WARING'S MARRIAGE, it was a short step to wonder what happened to the children and grandchildren.

Hence *The Dilhorne Dynasty*, each book of which deals with a member of the family who sets out to conquer the new world in which he finds himself. The Dilhornes, men and women, are at home wherever they settle, be it Australia, England, or the United States of America, and because of their zest for life become involved in interesting adventures.

Paula Marshall

Recent titles by the same author:

AN INNOCENT MASQUERADE*
A STRANGE LIKENESS*
HESTER WARING'S MARRIAGE*
THE QUIET MAN

*The Dilhorne Dynasty

HIS ONE WOMAN

Paula Marshall

*All the characters in this book have no existence outside the imagination
of the author, and have no relation whatsoever to anyone bearing the
same name or names. They are not even distantly inspired by any
individual known or unknown to the author, and all the incidents are
pure invention.*

*First published in Great Britain 2000
Harlequin Mills & Boon Limited,
Eton House, 18-24 Paradise Road, Richmond, Surrey TW9 1SR*

© Paula Marshall 2000

ISBN 0 263 82337 7

*Set in Times Roman 10½ on 12¼ pt.
04-0201-69851*

*Printed and bound in Spain
by Litografia Rosés S.A., Barcelona*

DILHORNE FAMILY TREE

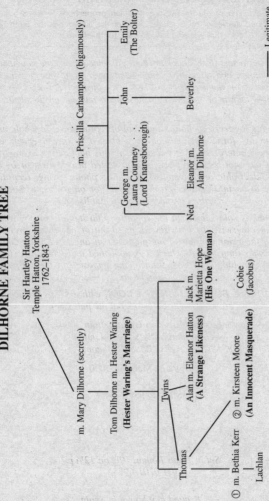

Sir Hartley Hatton
Temple Hatton, Yorkshire
1762–1843

m. Mary Dilhorne (secretly)

m. Priscilla Carhampton (bigamously)

Tom Dilhorne m. Hester Waring
(**Hester Waring's Marriage**)

George m.
Laura Courtney
(Lord Knaresborough)

John

Emily
(The Bolter)

Ned

Eleanor m.
Alan Dilhorne

Beverley

Twins

Thomas

Alan m. Eleanor Hatton
(**A Strange Likeness**)

Jack m.
Marietta Hope
(**His One Woman**)

Cobie
(Jacobus)

① m. Bethia Kerr

② m. Kirsteen Moore
(**An Innocent Masquerade**)

Lachlan

———— Legitimate
· · · · · · Illegitimate

Chapter One

Washington, April 1861

'Are you still working, my dear? I thought that you had promised to escort your cousin Sophie to the Clays this afternoon. I do not like to see you constantly at your desk. You deserve a little pleasure in your life; it should not be all hard grind.'

Marietta looked affectionately up at her father, Senator Jacobus Hope.

'Visiting the Clays with Sophie is not my idea of pleasure,' she told him, 'and I needed to catch up with your correspondence—which I have now done. Aunt Percival has gone with her in my place.'

Her father sighed and sat down opposite to her. Marietta thought sadly that he was beginning to look his age. For the last seven years she had been his faithful assistant, ever since she had decided that she would never marry after four years of being pursued by every fortune hunter in America's northern states. Now, at twenty-seven, she was her father's mainstay:

no man could have been more useful to him, and, had she been one herself, he thought that she would have made a superb senator—but, being a woman, all such doors were closed to her.

Knowing this, the Senator felt the most bitter regret at having to tell her his unwelcome news, but in fairness to her he must. He ought not to delay any longer.

'Marie, my dear child, I am sure that you are aware that age is beginning to affect my ability to perform the duties of my office efficiently, and only your invaluable assistance has kept me on course for the last few years. I have been wrong to lean on you so much, but you are the beloved child of my old age, my last memory of your mother. I was sorry when you refused Avory Grant seven years ago. I know that you thought him a flighty boy, but the years and marriage seem to have sobered him, as they sober most of us.

'Knowing this, it grieves me to tell you that I shall not seek office again when this term ends in 1864. Had I not been certain that war was coming, I would not have stood for the Senate in 1860, but, since I had long warned that war was inevitable, I decided that I must play my part in it when it did arrive.

'I have no regrets, I have had a long and fulfilling life, but what does trouble me is that you have given your life and your youth in service to me and before my term is over I wish to see you married. I do not want to think of you as a lonely spinster when I am gone.'

Marietta put up a protesting hand at this. 'Oh, Father, you have many years yet, I am sure.'

Her father shook his head. 'The doctors do not think

so, my dear. It is even possible that I shall not live out my term. I repeat, I would wish to see you married.'

Marietta answered him as lightly as she could. 'But who would marry me, Father? I am twenty-seven now, past my first youth, and I am not even pretty.'

'Marie,' he said, 'you must know that there are many who would want you for a wife—'

She interrupted him for once. 'Fortune hunters to a man, Father. I know that.'

Indeed, all the world was aware that, as the Senator's heiress, Marietta stood to inherit a vast fortune in dollars, land, property and investments.

'Yes, Marie, but not all men are fortune hunters, and you are a clever woman—I would trust to your judgement to choose the right husband. I blame myself for not encouraging you to marry after you refused Avory, but you were adamant and I was selfish. Go more into society, my dear, and the suitors will come running.'

'You mean when I am available for sale in the market again,' she said bitterly. 'I don't want that, Father.'

'It would be preferable to a lonely old age. Do you wish to be like Aunt Percival, Marie? Even your dollars would not sweeten that fate.'

He could see that she was rejecting his advice, well-meant though it was—but he could also see that he had touched an unwelcome chord. He sighed, and turned to go, but before he left her to attend a Congressional committee, he murmured, as gently as he could, 'I beg that you will consider most carefully what I have just told you, Marie.'

The door closed behind him.

Marietta rose, and sank into an armchair beside the empty hearth. Unwelcome thoughts raced through her brain. Had she been foolish, not clever, when she had rejected Avory Grant? He had seemed so young and callow, and she had wanted someone to whom she could talk, who would share her inmost thoughts, and Avory had certainly not been that ideal man. Had she been too discriminating, too certain that he had been marrying her for her money and not because he had felt any real desire or affection for her?

Alas, she had no illusions about herself. She was Marietta Hope, the only plain member of a bevy of beautiful Hope cousins, all of whom sported the blonde ringlets, pink and white faces, and hour-glass figures which mid-century Americans considered to be the acme of female desirability. Instead, she possessed a face which was clever rather than pretty, glossy chestnut-coloured hair, and a body which was athletic rather than curvaceous.

But what she lacked in beauty she made up for in intellect and commonsense, which she dismally knew was not what young men looked for in their future wives.

'Good God, never say she's cousin to the Hope beauties,' had been the first remark she had heard when she had attended her come-out ball at the age of eighteen—whispered behind her back, of course. 'What a sad disappointment she must be for her poor papa.'

'Oh, never mind that,' had been the unkind answer.

'All his lovely dollars will make her plain face seem pretty.'

Useless for her father to tell her that she *was* pretty—after a fashion which, alas, was not now in style. After two years of misery in ballrooms where her cousins were enjoying themselves, she had retired from frivolous society in order to be her father's companion and, until now, she had never regretted doing so, for his political career had given her life meaning and point.

In three years, perhaps sooner, that life would be over, and what would be left for her then? She would become Aunt Hope, the spinster sent for when needed or, if not that, she might become one more of the wealthy and eccentric old Yankee women who toured Europe, bullying their servants.

No, she would not think of the future—other than to contemplate what the evening's duties held for her. She was due to attend yet another White House reception in company with her father and her young cousin Sophie, to whom she was acting as temporary chaperon. Well, at least she had avoided this afternoon's tedium at the Clays, and that was something for which to be grateful.

She pulled out her watch. Time for tea—and not in the study. The room suddenly seemed oppressive. She would go downstairs and play at being an idle lady, a role she would have to take up when her father retired. She would sit on her own, and Asia, the new black maid, would bring in tea and cakes, English fashion as Aunt Percival liked. She would indulge herself for once and not think of maintaining her admirably firm figure. Perhaps becoming plump might make her fashionable!

But her desire to be alone was destined not to be fulfilled—an omen, perhaps—for when she entered the front parlour there was a strange man standing before the window, his back to the room, until he turned to see her as she came through the door.

They faced one another, both surprised. Marietta walked towards him, her face a question mark—a polite one, to be sure, but still a question mark.

'I see that we have a visitor, sir. You came to see me—or my father? If so, you were not announced.'

He bowed.

'I believe that there must have been some mistake, madam. I came to visit Miss Sophie Hope, but the little maid who admitted me left me here some time ago, and has quite abandoned me.'

Marietta sighed. 'Asia,' she said cryptically; as one of his eyebrows rose, she added, 'Our new maid: she is only half-trained, I fear. Alas, I must disappoint you. My cousin is out for the afternoon, and so Asia should have informed you.'

He had moved from the window and she saw him plainly now. He was tall, but not remarkably so, being barely six feet in height, she guessed, and well built. He was, after a strange fashion, handsome, with laughter lines deep around his mouth and eyes. His eyes were remarkable, an intense blue. His hair was ordinary, being sandy and straight. His carriage was as good as his clothes, but his accent was strange. He appeared to be in his late twenties or early thirties.

She was a little intrigued by him. What was he doing, this unknown man, calling on Sophie at tea time?

He seemed to read her thoughts. 'I am, perhaps, a little beforehand,' he explained cheerfully. 'I have met Sophie on several occasions in the last fortnight, the latest being last night when she asked me to call, but gave me no fixed date. Since I had no engagements this afternoon, I decided to accept her invitation.

'My name is John Dilhorne, madam, and I will take myself off with my apologies,' and he bowed again.

Marietta surveyed him, and his undoubted self-possession, coolly. 'The apologies are due from us for wasting your time.'

She made a sudden surprising decision: a decision which was to alter her life and his. 'Since my cousin Sophie is out calling, with our Aunt Percival, and you are here, and I was contemplating afternoon tea on my own, then I would take it as a favour if you would join me.'

It was his turn to assess her. This must be the plain cousin, the bluestocking, of whom Sophie had spoken last night. Senator Jacobus Hope's daughter, secretary and good right hand, now almost a recluse, Sophie had said, forswearing normal social life. She had left Aunt Percival to escort her last night, which was a blessing, Sophie had remarked with a laugh, since her aunt was not as severe as Cousin Marietta.

He had first met Sophie at a grand ball given by the Lanceys and, attracted by her looks and vivacity, he had pursued her with some assiduity. He was now a little disappointed that he was to be entertained by the only plain Miss Hope, for so he had heard her called.

Not, he thought, that she was remarkably plain. She made little of her striking hair, and her expensive but dark clothes did her no favour, being more suitable for a woman of fifty rather than one of not yet thirty.

Where women were concerned Jack Dilhorne was both fastidious and discriminating, and the thing which he valued most in a woman was a good body. Unfortunately, the fashions of the day often denied him the opportunity to discover whether those he met possessed one. On more than one occasion he had found that a pretty face was allied to a lumpy or flaccid figure.

His assessment of Miss Marietta Hope told him that—despite her severely classic face—by her carriage and walk she possessed this valuable attribute. On the other hand, by her expression, manner and reputation, however, it was plain that no gentleman was ever going to have the privilege of seeing her unclothed!

At the moment she was busy making him welcome with extremely cool formality, pulling the bell to summon the servant, ordering tea for them, and recommending him to a large armchair.

'My father's,' she told him. 'But he is out, attending a committee on the Hill.'

When his eyebrows rose at this remarkable statement, she told him that the Hill was shorthand for Congress where the Senators worked. 'He will not be back until late. It is the coming war which exercises us, Mr Dilhorne, as you have doubtless noticed. You are from abroad, are you not?'

'From Sydney, Australia, Miss Hope. I have business here.' He did not explain what it was. 'I am staying at Willard's Hotel until I find suitable rooms. So, you are sure that there will be a war?'

'No doubt of it all,' she told him firmly. 'Now that Mr Lincoln is President, and the two sides being so intractably opposed to the degree that seven Southern states have already seceded from the Union, how can we doubt it?'

'How, indeed?' said Jack, amused. Yes, she was a bluestocking, and doubtless as well informed as any man. She was quite the opposite of little Miss Sophie with her ardent seeking of his opinion on everything. Miss Marietta Hope was used to speaking her mind— but it was as though she were able to read his.

'Come, Mr Dilhorne, you did not visit my cousin to talk politics with her. Pray speak to me as you would have done to Sophie.' Her face was alight with amusement when she came out with this.

'Oh, I do not think that would be wise, Miss Hope. You would not be entertained by it.'

'Now, why should you suppose that, Mr Dilhorne,' she parried, 'seeing that you have only just met me? Sophie and I might well be intellectual twins.'

So saying, she briskly wielded the heavy tea-pot which a repentant Asia had just brought in, handed him a cup brimful of tea, and offered him English muffins, and sandwiches, as well as Aunt Percival's best pound cake. None of which he declined, and it was surprising how slimly athletic he was if this were his usual appetite.

Seeing her eye on him while he was eating, he grinned at her a little. 'But you are mind-reading, too, Miss Hope. Yes, I like my food. I was taught to.'

Perhaps food had been short in his childhood, Marietta concluded—but he looked as though he had been well fed from birth.

'You have not answered my last question, Mr Dilhorne, nor carried out my express wish for idle conversation.'

Marietta was overcome by surprise to find that she was flirting with an attractive man whom she had only just met.

'Do call me Jack,' he said through his muffin, which exploded ungracefully, splashing him with melted butter. 'Sophie does.'

'Most incorrect of her,' said Marietta severely, 'since I deduce that you have not been formally introduced.'

'For that matter, neither have we,' said Jack, elegantly retrieving the remains of the muffin and depositing them on his plate.

'No more we have,' returned Marietta, who was beginning to enjoy herself. 'So licence reigns supreme.' She further added, after watching him struggle, 'As your way with muffins would seem to suggest.'

'They call them English,' said Jack, cleaning his sticky fingers on his expensive lawn handkerchief rather than on the Hopes' equally expensive damask napkin, 'but I have not seen an English muffin like this one. Ours do not explode.'

'Oh, you have mannerly muffins, like the English themselves, I suppose. But a bit weighty, perhaps?'

'I own that I was wrong,' said Jack, accepting a sandwich and warily inspecting it before taking a bite, lest that, too, should cascade about him. 'You are even more adept at light raillery than Sophie, but you do have the advantage of the muffins. Ballrooms and receptions have fewer diversions; conversation there must be sustained without such useful props.'

'Try the pound cake,' suggested Marietta, waving the plate at him, her face alight with an amusement she had not felt for years. 'Or do you call pound cake something exotic in…New South Wales, is it not?'

'Bravo!' exclaimed Jack as he took a piece. 'You are the first bona fide US citizen I have met who knows where Sydney is situated. No, unless our aborigines bake this delicacy, I have not met it before. It is well named, a most filling concoction. You may help me to another slice.'

'And your cup needs refilling,' said Marietta, putting out a hand for it.

Jack watched her concentrate on pouring out the tea—aware of his gaze on her and that she was a little entertained by him.

'Since you will not engage in froth and fun with me, Jack—you see, I take you at your word—we may be serious. Pray, what is the business which brings you to Washington? That is, if you wish to inform me.'

He stirred his tea vigorously. 'No reason why not, Miss Hope—'

'Oh, Marietta, please,' she said softly.

'Marietta,' he continued, 'but ladies are not usually interested in my speciality. I will not say that it is dry, since it concerns the sea, but one might call it heavy. I ran the shipping side of our family firm until recently. Now my situation has changed and I may pursue my engineering bent. Among other things I am interested in such remote matters as the design of metal warships or iron-clads—hardly tea-party entertainment, I fear—but the States is the place to be these days for matters of invention.'

'Indeed,' she said, her eyes mocking him a little. 'And screw-propelled ships, too. You are interested in those as well as iron-clads, I presume? I can see that Mr Ericsson is your man.'

Jack put down his delicate cup with exaggerated care. 'Lest it, too, explode,' he offered when he saw her smile. 'Well, now, Marietta, you do surprise me. Most gentlemen around here do not know of such arcane matters, let alone pretty ladies at tea.'

'Pray do not flatter me, Jack. A gentleman of such profound knowledge about design will know how lacking I am in it, even in a different line,' she flashed back at him, for daring to describe her as pretty. 'But there is a simple explanation for my surprising expertise. I am my father's secretary and he is on a Congressional committee which deals with shipping of all kinds. What shall we discuss, sir? I am ready for you. Explosive shells, not muffins, and their effect on wooden ships?'

Jack's laughter was unforced. 'If you like,' he said. 'I warn you, once you start me going, you will not be able to stop me. On these matters I am a very bore.'

'Oh, I doubt that, Jack. I doubt it very much. I am sure that Sophie does not think you are a bore.'

'Oh, but I do not discuss iron-clads, and their future peaceful use, with Sophie,' he said, waving away further proffered cake. 'I see that you are determined to sink me, Marietta, with your broadsides.'

'Difficult to achieve, I think,' said Marietta, who had not enjoyed herself so much for years. He undoubtedly knew how attractive he was, but he displayed little conceit. He had a wicked look now and then, and she was subtly flattered that he was favouring her with it. He reminded her, while he talked with great enthusiasm of his passion, of a small boy, excited among his toys.

Marietta was surprised to find herself disappointed when he suddenly looked at the clock, and said, 'I am remiss, Marietta, I have talked the afternoon away. I must not strain your patience.'

'No, indeed,' she told him. 'You could not do that, Jack. You must come again for tea, and soon. I promise to serve you no exploding muffins next time.'

He rose. 'Perhaps we shall meet this evening. Sophie said that you would be attending the White House reception. I am working with Ezra Butler, and he is taking me with him.'

'I shall look forward to that,' she replied, meaning her words for once, and they parted with more warmth than either could earlier have deemed possible.

An intelligent and amusing man, was Marietta's

verdict, while Jack thought that Marietta might not be conventionally pretty, but she had a good mind and an engaging manner. Nothing like Sophie, of course, whom he had been sorry to miss, but he had spent a pleasant hour all the same. Miss Hope was not quite the dragon of report.

Not long after he had gone, Sophie came rushing into the room, her pretty face aglow. 'Oh, Marietta, was that Jack Dilhorne I saw leaving as we came home?'

On Marietta nodding assent, she gave a great pout. 'Oh, how annoying. I knew that it was a mistake to go duty calling with Aunt Percival. And now I have missed him. Did he stay long?'

'We had tea together,' said Marietta quietly.

'Oh, even more annoying,' exclaimed Sophie disgustedly. 'Jack is such fun. What on earth did *you* find to talk about with him?'

'Explosives and marine engineering,' said Marietta repressively.

'Explosives and marine engineering! How exquisitely dull for the poor man. I might have guessed that *you* would bore him stiff.'

'I don't think that Jack…Mr Dilhorne, that is… found explosives boring,' said Marietta, remembering the muffins. 'On the contrary.'

'Oh, he has splendid manners for a backwoodsman,' said Sophie. 'It's only his clothes which are a little odd, but I don't suppose that *you* noticed that. All the girls are wild for him,' she added, and then said proudly, 'but I am the one that he is interested in.'

'Apart from his passion for marine architecture, that is,' said Marietta unkindly. She had had enough of Sophie's open patronage of her lack of attractions.

'Oh, Marietta, you have no sense of humour at all,' said Sophie, dismissively, 'you are so solemn. Now Jack has the most enormous sense of the ridiculous.'

'Then he should get along with me, should he not?' said Marietta savagely. 'Seeing that you all consider me to be the most ridiculous thing in Washington.'

She swept out of the room, leaving Sophie behind with her mouth open, since Marietta rarely bit back, however much she was provoked. It was one of her collection of amazing and boring virtues.

Goodness me, she thought, whatever had caused that? Well, she would tease Jack about his misfortune in being exposed to Marietta's earnest and learned conversation at tea.

Explosives and marine engineering at four o'clock in the afternoon. What next?

Marietta thought that her father looked tired when he came in later. He was overwhelmed, he said, with work and with place-men. His senses, however, were as acute as ever, and while they waited in the hall for Sophie, before leaving for the reception, he said, 'I shall be glad when my brother and sister-in-law arrive in Washington to take her over, even if I have to endure their presence here. She really is most excessively spoiled. Whatever can have caused her tantrums this evening?'

Sophie had been making her displeasure at missing Jack quite plain to all and sundry, and so Marietta explained to the Senator.

'Hmm, Dilhorne. An odd name, and the second time that I have encountered it today. An Australian, you said, so they can scarcely be related.'

This was cryptic, even for the Senator, who frequently left out the connections in his chains of thought, expecting his daughter to pick them up, which she usually did—as today.

'You mean that you have met another Dilhorne?'

'Yes, an English MP and his aide. Alan Dilhorne and Charles Stanton. Dilhorne says that he does not represent the British Government, but you may be sure that he does. A handsome and devious fellow: one must listen carefully to what he says, or be misled.'

'A little like mine,' said Marietta.

'His friend, though, is quite different,' pursued her father. 'A quiet dark man, a marine engineer, but a gentleman, patently.'

'And that is another coincidence,' said Marietta. 'For my Dilhorne is a marine engineer.'

'I do not like coincidences,' said her father peevishly. 'Coincidences make life difficult to control.'

'But exciting,' said Marietta, who had lately found this ingredient sadly lacking in her life. 'Will they be at President Lincoln's reception tonight?'

'Of course,' said her father, 'and yours?'

'Mine, too. Ezra Butler is taking him.'

'That figures,' said her father. 'Butler has shipping interests in Australia. It will be stimulating to meet your man, and you must meet mine—although he is happily married, I understand.'

So her father was determined to matchmake. But she would not be pushed into anything, and, if she married, it must be someone whom she respected. Plain and twenty-seven as she was, love was too much to ask for.

Chapter Two

The drive outside the White House was thronged with carriages and bobbing flambeaux there to light the way for Mr Lincoln's guests. Marietta, who was used to such events to the point that they bored her, was handed down from the Hopes' carriage, Sophie following her. Sophie was looking particularly charming in young girl's white. A wealth of gauze rosebuds decorated her hair and her pink sash emphasised her tiny waist. She was carrying a bouquet of crimson and white hothouse carnations from which trailed filmy lace.

Marietta, for once not in a dark dress, was wearing lavender and was becoming increasingly conscious that it did even less for her than her usual colours, whatever her maid had said when she had helped her into it. She looked extinguished and knew it. The pale mauve gave her creamy complexion, one of her better points, a bilious cast.

Sophie, coming into the hall just before they had left, and still resentful of Marietta for having entertained Jack that afternoon, had said, sweetly unpleasant, 'Are you well, Marietta? Your colour is poor tonight.'

Even the Senator—usually unaware of Sophie's frequent brutality towards her cousin, whose lack of looks she thought was a good foil for her own delicate beauty—was alert to the insult, so pointed had it been.

'I think that you look very well, my dear,' he'd said, frowning at Sophie whom he disliked. His praise had done little to comfort Marietta. Her glass had told her only too clearly the truth about her appearance.

Before her father's words that morning she would have shrugged off Sophie's unkind remarks, but the armour which she had worn for the seven years since Avory Grant's proposal had suddenly disappeared, and she was as vulnerable as she had been as a girl. Yesterday she would have ignored, or even been amused by, Sophie's spite. Today, though, the words had stung—but she did not allow her distress to be visible.

Once inside the White House, Sophie was less interested in her short meeting with the President and Mrs Lincoln than in looking around her for Jack Dilhorne. Marietta thought that Mr Lincoln looked tired, which was not surprising in view of his country's desperate situation: civil war was almost upon them.

Mary Todd Lincoln was, as usual, overdressed, and Marietta wondered how he had come to marry her: they seemed a most unlikely pair. This thought worried her, for she suddenly seemed to have marriage on the brain, and before tonight such a thing would not have occurred to her.

Senator Hope's party walked on through the crowds of eagerly chattering people, most of whom Marietta knew through her father's work—but she was suddenly aware that none of them knew her because she was Marietta Hope, but only because she was her father's daughter. This was another new thought, and not a pleasant one.

A long mirror presented her with her ill-dressed self. I look forty, she thought, I really must take more interest in dress. No wonder Sophie laughs at me. I hope that she finds Jack soon; I cannot bear much more of her tantrums. I shall slap her, or scream, if she complains again.

Marietta betrayed none of this while bowing and smiling at those around her. The foreign diplomats who filled Washington were all present and she spoke pleasantly to them in her schoolgirl French. The elegant representative from Paris inwardly regretted that Miss Hope's looks and general appearance were not so good as her brains.

A subdued scream from Sophie suddenly announced that she had seen Jack Dilhorne, and she began wildly semaphoring in his direction.

'A little more decorum would be fitting, Sophie,' said Marietta repressively, unable to resist, for once, the temptation to pay her cousin back for her earlier unkind remark, 'or the world will think you a hoyden.'

'Oh, pooh, we are not all old maids,' said Sophie spitefully. 'I particularly wish to speak to Jack, having missed him this afternoon.' She waved her little bouquet again, narrowly missing a footman who was carrying a tray of drinks.

Jack had seen her and was threading his way through the packed room to her side. He looked even more handsome in his elegant evening dress, and even more in command of himself, if that were possible, than he had done that afternoon. He bowed to both Marietta and Sophie and was presented to the Senator.

Before the Senator could speak to him about his unusual name, twice encountered that day, Sophie took command of the situation.

'Oh, Jack, what a bore that I was out this afternoon. I do hope that you were suitably distressed by my absence!'

What could the poor man say but 'Oh, yes, indeed, Miss Sophie,' thought Marietta satirically, as Jack promptly did so, with an apologetic smile at the Senator for their interrupted conversation. Unluckily he then added, 'But Marietta looked after me most efficiently.'

'Marietta...' pouted Sophie prettily, '...but you call me Miss Sophie.'

'Then that must be remedied immediately, Sophie,' said Jack, quite the gallant.

Really, thought Marietta, he is too ready. Such charm is almost offensive. He even wasted it on me. For practice, one supposes. To have her own unkind thoughts immediately rebutted by Jack carrying tactlessly on by saying, 'You see, Sophie, having the misfortune to miss you, I found another Hope cousin ready to give a poor stranger comfort and cheer.'

This was not what Sophie wanted at all. He should have been devastated at missing her, not congratulating himself on having his afternoon rescued for him by a plain Jane. She was provoked into being more publicly unkind to Marietta than was wise.

'By discoursing to you of weighty matters, I hear. But then, Marietta is always so solemn. I hope that it did not sink the tea,' she said, sarcasm plain in her voice.

Jack was no fool, and the false notes he could hear reverberated in his head. It was flattering that Sophie was jealous, but he did not care for such open spite. It presented a different picture of her from the pretty kitten Sophie usually showed to the world. A slight set-down might be in order.

'On the contrary,' he said cheerfully, directing his winning smile at Marietta, and noticing while he did so that the Senator disliked his niece, for Jack, like his father, was always keenly aware of such nuances of behaviour, 'matters were most unusually light. So much so that even our muffins nearly flew away. Was not that so, Marietta?'

Marietta gratefully returned his smile with one of her own, and Jack wished that she would do it more often. It quite transformed her.

'Indeed, Jack, although I must admit that your muffins were more affected than mine.'

Such banter from Marietta did not surprise Jack after taking tea with her, but it surprised the Senator and Sophie. Jack did not miss the surprise, either, nor that Sophie was annoyed by Marietta's response to him. For the first time he thought that she was a little spoiled.

Sophie, suddenly aware that she was not presenting herself to Jack in a favourable light, first tried to remedy this by being as charming as possible, and then by allowing him to resume his interrupted conversation with the Senator. He had been joined by several of his colleagues and they were busy discussing the latest news from the South, which seemed to indicate that the Confederates, as they were known, were on the verge of attacking Fort Sumter. If they did, it would almost certainly plunge the Union into war.

Standing by Marietta, Jack listened with interest, and even joined in the lively discussion himself. On the Senator informing his friends that Mr John Dilhorne was something of an expert in the current revolution in shipping, his advice was sought on its implications for naval warfare.

Marietta saw by the expression on Sophie's face that this was by no means what she had hoped for from the evening, but the prospect of war occupied everybody's minds these days and Sophie, like everyone else, must learn to live with it.

Jack had hardly finished speaking when his attention was drawn by the entry into the room of two men: one was a large fair gentleman, impeccably dressed, and the other was smaller and dark. A look of the utmost surprise crossed his face. He turned towards the Senator, saying, 'I must beg you to excuse me, sir, but I do believe that…no, no, it cannot be possible…'

The Senator followed Jack's gaze and smiled a little.

'I deduce, sir, that you have just seen Mr Alan Dilhorne enter. I deduce, too, that you must be related. You have the distinct look of one another.'

'By all that's holy,' said Jack eagerly, 'it *is* Alan!

What an astonishing thing to meet one's big brother in another country's capital city. You will excuse me, sir, if I go to him. We rarely have the opportunity to meet, he being settled in England and I until recently in New South Wales.'

'You have my permission, young man,' replied the Senator, amused. He had already decided that he liked Mr Jack Dilhorne, not least because he seemed to have a proper appreciation of Marietta. He watched him cross the room and clap the large gentleman on the shoulder before engulfing him in a bear hug. The Dilhorne brothers were reunited. Marietta, watching them from a distance, found their evident affection for one another touching.

'Let me look at you,' said Alan, standing back. 'Good God, little brother has grown up! How like the Patriarch you are—you have his look exactly.'

He turned to his companion. 'Charles, this is my little brother, Jack, of whom you have heard me speak. Jack, this is Charles Stanton, who is in your line of work. He is a famous engineer back home who has come to see what's happening here so that we may do it better.'

Charles smiled and put out his hand. He was a silent man, quite unlike the articulate and jovial Alan, who was indeed very like Jack, only bigger in every direction. Now in his late forties, he looked younger than his age, and was, everyone who met him in Washington agreed, an extraordinarily handsome man.

'And what are you doing here?' asked Jack when they had both finished exclaiming over the odd coincidence of their meeting and Charles had discreetly retired to leave the brothers together.

'Oh, I am on a kind of mission for the Foreign Office,' said Alan easily. 'No one in England quite knows what our policy ought to be when war starts. If it weren't for slavery, all Europe would support the South. But slavery sticks in most people's throats,' and he shrugged. 'Despite that, most in England do favour the South a little—apart from the working classes, that is. I'm supposed to look about me, talk to everyone and then report back home. Vague, isn't it?'

Vague it might be, thought Jack, but if Big Brother was involved in it, something very real and to the point would be taken back home to England. Alan suddenly became serious, took his brother's arm and walked him off down a corridor, away from the noise of the room.

'I must speak to you, Jack, even here. It cannot wait,' he said suddenly. 'I find it difficult to believe that the Patriarch has gone. I know that he was very old, but it was a great shock when I received Mother's letter. He seemed immortal somehow.'

'Yes,' said Jack simply. 'I know. Did Mother tell you how he died?'

'No details,' said Alan, 'only that he went quite suddenly at the end.'

'He was very frail for the last eighteen months of his life. He'd never really been ill before. He had a bad chest complaint in the winter and he never quite recovered from it completely. Oh, his mind was as sharp as ever, but his body had gone. He hated that, as you might guess. Mother said that he was over eighty and wanted to be thirty. He was confined to the Villa and the gardens, and, much though he loved them, he hated to lose his freedom of movement.

'One day he persuaded Mother to let him be driven into Sydney. On the way back he asked for the carriage to be stopped at The Point, overlooking the Harbour. They sat silent together for some time, she said, until he kissed her cheek, took her hand and gave a great sigh, and when she looked at him he had gone— just like that. Typical of him, wasn't it?'

The two brothers were silent, thinking of the Patriarch, their father, whose last sight on this earth had been of the vast ocean across which he had been transported from penury and great hardship to unimagined wealth and happiness. Who had died with his hand in that of the wife who had brought him his greatest joy.

'He was in his mid-eighties,' said Alan. 'I found that out in England, but he never cared to know. And Mother, how did she take it?'

'Well,' said Jack simply, 'very well. She just said that he'd had a long and happy life after a dreadful beginning and that in the end he had decided to let go, and she could not grudge him that. She knew that he could not bear to become helpless and mindless. Father always said that she was a strong woman.

'It was Thomas—now known as Fred—who took it badly. Before he went to the gold fields he was never close to the Patriarch, but afterwards they were inseparable. Mother feared that Fred was going the way he did when his first wife died—but Kirsteen soon stopped that!'

'She would,' said Alan. 'Another strong woman.'

'She and the Patriarch got on famously together. Mother said that she dealt firmly with him just before the funeral. She reverted to type—you know what a fine lady she became. "You can just behave yourself, Fred Waring," she shouted at him. "You're not going to put us through all that again. We're not having stupid Thomas Dilhorne back, I can tell you. And if you haven't the wit to see that it was the way your pa wanted to go, you aren't fit to be his son." That did the trick, Mother said. It brought him to his senses immediately.'

Alan laughed heartily. 'She's been so good for him. She washed out his starch and God knows where *that* came from. None of the rest of us have it. The girls don't—lively pieces all.' He paused. 'I've learned what I wanted to, and I respect the Patriarch more than ever now I've learned exactly how he died.'

'He set me free, too,' said Jack confidentially. 'He left it so that I could go my own way or stay with Dilhorne's as a roving representative. He said that I needed a holiday—I'd never had one. So, here I am. I'm working for the firm with Ezra Butler and looking out for what's new in my line.'

'American know-how.' Alan grinned. 'They keep talking to me of it. Now let us go to pay our respects to the Senator. I hear that the daughter is plain, but that his niece is pretty and reasonably rich. I suppose you're after her, you dog. Going to settle down with the one woman soon, are you?'

Alan was referring to the joke about the Dilhorne men, beginning with the Patriarch: however rowdy each one's early life, once he was married to the one woman he settled down and was faithful to her. It had certainly been true of their father and the twins, Thomas and Alan, thought Jack. He wondered whether it would be true of himself.

He and Alan made their way back to the Hopes, to find that Sophie had temporarily departed with another admirer, and so Alan had to be presented to the Senator's strong-minded, if witty, daughter. Sophie would have to wait for another time.

Alan Dilhorne fascinated Marietta. He was so undoubtedly Jack's brother, and there was so much of him, all of it overpoweringly handsome. He was, as her father had told her, devious, and the four of them engaged in a lively conversation about all the matters which were engrossing Congress at the moment.

He was tactful, too, over such issues as slavery, but showed plainly that he thought that it was the main cause of the coming war— 'After the economic divisions between North and South,' he said, 'although old English gentlemen such as myself aren't supposed to know about such things.'

Later, it was plain that Senator Hope had been greatly impressed by him. 'Those fools on the Hill,' he said, 'are taken in by his manner and think him another effete English gentleman. My colleagues think that I am wrong about him. Time will show which of us is right.'

He asked both the brothers and Charles Stanton to dinner before they left Washington.

'But before then,' said Marietta who was enjoying herself hugely, and who had seen approval of her in

Alan Dilhorne's bright blue eyes, so like Jack's, 'you must come to tea. I believe that Jack here is in a position to recommend it.'

Jack looked solemnly at his brother. 'Most certainly—and I promise you that the conversation is better than the food, good though that is. Muffins again, Marietta, and pound cake, I trust.'

'Yes, indeed, and I promise you Sophie as well. She will be sorry to have missed your brother and Charles.'

The entire party were now on Christian name terms and the Senator was delighted to see his daughter sparkle and blossom in the company of three attractive and handsome men who appeared to have no female appurtenances to get in the way.

After they had paid their respects to Marietta and the Senator, the Dilhorne party left to spend the rest of the evening at Willard's Hotel. Alan was staying with the British Envoy and Charles with a cousin who worked in the Envoy's office and had a small villa outside the capital.

Predictably Sophie was furious when she discovered that she had missed Jack's return. 'But I have invited them all to tea,' said Marietta. 'His brother and his friend as well as Jack.'

'Oh, I don't care about *them*,' said Sophie inelegantly. 'It's Jack I mind missing. I trust that you won't monopolise him when he next visits us.'

Marietta's hand itched to slap her, and she was greatly relieved when Sophie's wounded feelings were soothed by the arrival of yet another beau, a naval

officer this time. Indeed, on looking around the room
Marietta saw that more uniformed men were present
than ever before, and she hoped that they would as-
suage Sophie's greed for attention and admiration.

Unfortunately, the Senator soon tired and decided
to leave early. Sophie complained all the way home
at her evening being cut short, until even his courtesy
was frayed to the point where he was ready to reprimand her.

Marietta put a gentle hand on his arm to restrain
him and said to her cousin, 'Sophie, if you say one
more word I promise you that I shall not escort you
to another function, never mind give tea parties for
your admirers. Your uncle is tired and needs to rest.'

This silenced Sophie, but added another to the long
list of wrongs which Marietta had committed against
her, and for which one day, Sophie promised herself,
she would be paid back in full.

Two days later Jack, his brother and Charles Stanton came for afternoon tea at the Hopes'. Sophie had
thought that she would enjoy herself in the company
of three attractive men, but she didn't. They appeared
to direct their conversation almost exclusively at Marietta.

This wasn't true, but appeared so to Sophie. They
spoke first of what occupied the minds of all Washington—except Sophie's, of course: the coming war.
They were all quite certain that it *was* coming—only
the question of when it would arrive remained. In
other circumstances Sophie would have found Alan
Dilhorne attractive, but not when he droned on about

such boring subjects. Marietta was hanging on his every word—but then she would, wouldn't she? Goodness, politics was all she had to talk about, poor thing, but did she need to monopolise three…well, two attractive men so determinedly?

Charles Stanton seemed to be irreparably dull. He was even more solemn than Marietta, if that were possible. He was only interested in subjects of such profound boredom that Sophie found it difficult not to yawn in his face.

For once, even Jack was dull. He certainly cracked his usual quota of jokes, but, most uncharacteristically, they were incomprehensible. What in the world was amusing about muffins and iron-clad ships? Iron-clad ships? What drearier topic of conversation could be found than that? But they all pounded away about them as though they were men-of-war themselves. Marietta even had the face to be amused by Jack's silly jokes, and to look enthralled when the conversation moved on to screw-propellers and Charles's and Jack's interest in them.

Give the large and handsome Mr Alan Dilhorne his due—he did come to Sophie's rescue. He talked about more interesting things, such as the nature of Washington's social life, but, after all, he was in his forties, already married to some Englishwoman across the Atlantic—horse-faced, no doubt—so there was little point in talking to *him*. Even then, in the middle of it, he broke in on Jack and Charles, who were talking to Marietta about walking and riding.

Walking and riding! They were two things which Sophie particularly hated. Horses were such tricky creatures and she was too frightened when on them to be able to look alluring. As for walking! Sophie never walked when she could ride in a carriage, and one of the reasons for her intense dislike of Marietta was all the exercise that she was compelled to take with her.

'You'll get fat if you sit about so much and eat so many sweet things,' Marietta had had the gall to say to her severely at least once a week. Fat! Well, she would rather risk that than be a beanpole like Marietta.

To make matters worse, Alan Dilhorne now began to talk of the difficulty he had found in obtaining enough exercise in Washington.

'We must go riding together,' he said to Marietta. 'I am sure that Miss Sophie and yourself can advise me on how to go about finding suitable stables and some useful mounts. I shall get fat if I sit about all day on the Hill, eating and drinking,' and he made a comical face.

The Dilhorne brothers were good at comical faces, thought Sophie resentfully, unlike Charles Stanton who seemed to possess a permanently glum one. Not that she found either of them very comical on this particular afternoon.

'Are you missing your sparring, Alan?' Jack asked his brother, adding to Sophie and Marietta, 'Big Brother here was quite a bruiser in his time. He could have made a name for himself in the ring.'

Could he, indeed? thought Sophie nastily. I thought that he was supposed to be a fine gentleman with a big house in Yorkshire. Some fine gentleman he must be if he were almost a bruiser once!

Charles Stanton, who, for all his quietness, was no

fool, read Sophie's slightly shrugging manner correctly.

'Gentlemen box in England, you know,' he said, trying to be helpful.

'No, I don't,' said Sophie off-puttingly. She thought nothing of Charles. He was apparently only some secretary dragged along by Big Brother in order to prose about dull matters and take Jack's attention away from her.

Jack was now engaged in discussing railway lines with Marietta, and their importance in the coming war. Railway lines! Who cared about them?

She gave poor Charles her shoulder, ignorant of the fact that he had felt sorry for the pretty young girl who was so patently bored by the conversation of her elders and had tried to include her in it.

Marietta was well aware that, for once, she was not considering Sophie before herself by bringing her out and turning the conversation towards matters that would interest her. She was finding her male guests both interesting and amusing—and was enjoying herself for a change, rather than always thinking of others. Sophie was the third of her cousins whom she had introduced to Washington life.

She decided that Jack and Alan were more alike than she had originally thought, both in looks and intellect. Alan might, at first, give off the impression of being a bluff and open Englishman, but her father's appreciation of him as a devious and clever man was an accurate one. Jack resembled him in that for, when first met, he gave off the impression of being a charming idler, and this was what had caused Sophie to be attracted to him. But this impression was not a correct one. He was both knowledgeable and shrewd, reminding her of some of the men she had met on Capitol Hill who concealed their ability beneath charm and good manners.

She liked Charles, too, and was sorry that Sophie was being so openly rude to him in her disappointment at the turn which the tea party had taken, which was giving her little opportunity to display her kittenish charm.

Fearful that Sophie might be provoked into displaying even more bad manners, she steered Jack's and Alan's interest adroitly towards her and began to talk to Charles herself. She found him as interesting a man as Jack and his brother. Unlike them, his manner was diffident, but he was well informed, and even a little surprised to discover how knowledgeable Marietta was. It was also evident that he hero-worshipped the large Mr Dilhorne, who was plainly fond of him.

Everyone enjoyed the promised tea and Jack's jokes while they ate it. Everyone that was, but Sophie, who, seeing Marietta's eye on her, ungraciously refused a third muffin. 'Marietta will threaten me with growing fat if I eat another.'

'Quite right, too,' said Alan cheerfully. 'I have to watch *my* weight, alas,' and he, too, waved a muffin away. 'We are fellow sufferers, Miss Sophie, and must comfort one another.'

Despite this offered sympathy, Alan had decided that he did not like Miss Sophie, and wondered a little at Jack for pursuing her. The cousin, though not the prettiest of women, was a much better bet. She had a good mind and possessed an excellent body beneath all the clothing which women were forced to wear. Must be the exercise she takes, he decided. It would pay Miss Sophie to take more.

Sophie would have been horrified if she had been privy to Alan's thoughts, but, devious man that he was, he gave her the false impression that he found her as charming as Jack did and had quite won her over before the visit ended.

'We shall certainly abuse your hospitality by coming again soon,' Alan told Marietta before they left. 'Where else should we find two such charming ladies, such an excellent tea and such entertaining conversation? Pray pay our respects to the Senator when he returns.'

Marietta and Sophie watched them go.

'I'm sorry that I couldn't return all the large gentleman's compliments,' said Sophie harshly once they were safely away. 'And why in the world did he bring such a dull stick as his office boy along with him? Surely Charles Stanton has enough pen-pushing to do at the British Envoy's office without inflicting his boring opinions on us.'

Marietta looked at Sophie. She had learned something during her conversation with Alan which was going to upset her cousin more than a little.

'I'm sorry that you disliked Charles,' she said quietly. 'But Alan could hardly leave him behind when he came to visit us. Besides, I doubt whether he does much pen-pushing. Charles does not use his title in private life, but he is here as the representative of the British House of Lords, and is properly Viscount Stanton. He is also an expert in his line of engineering and is a cousin of Alan Dilhorne's wife.'

Sophie blushed an unbecoming red. A real live lord! A viscount, no less! Sophie over-estimated this—her knowledge of the British peerage, her knowledge of everything, was small—and she thought that a viscount was even grander than he was. Alas, she had snubbed him so mercilessly that, however kind Charles was, there could be no chance of her ever retrieving her position with him.

'How dare you keep that from me?' she burst out. 'I suppose that you wanted me to make a fool of myself. How was I to know that such an inconsequential little man was even grander than Jack's brother?'

'Since I only found out who he was a few moments ago, and purely by accident,' returned Marietta quietly, 'I could hardly have informed you before their arrival. May I remind you that your own good manners required you to be civil to him, and from what I saw you were sadly lacking in them.'

'I will not be prosed at by a plain old maid,' said Sophie, disgusted by the whole wretched business, what with hardly speaking to Jack, and being bored witless. 'If you're so all-fired clever, Miss Marietta Hope, how come you're on the shelf, and like to remain there for all your fine conversation about ships and submersibles?'

Marietta looked steadily at her cousin. She had always known that Sophie disliked and despised her—the first of her cousins whom she had helped through their début in Washington society to do so. She thought that she knew what had brought this outburst on, but she had as much right to enjoy herself as Sophie did. She had found their guests to be out of the common run, and their patent admiration of her knowledge and her intellect had been most flattering. Englishmen were not supposed to like clever women, so they must be exceptions.

Of course, Jack was not English, and his brother little more so, and it was plain that Charles was also a remarkable man behind his quiet exterior, so she could not take them as true representatives of the English tribe. She could only hope that they would visit her again. She could not resist indulging in a small smile at the sight of Sophie flouncing upstairs in disgust.

A real live English lord and she had been rude to him!

Marietta, on the other hand, had not enjoyed herself so much in years. She refused to admit to herself that it was Mr Jack Dilhorne whom she particularly wished to see again.

The brothers and Charles walked back to the British Envoy's office along Washington's filthy and unpaved streets. There had been a fall of rain earlier in the day and the three of them were amused to see the heavy wagons, drawn by mules, struggling in the thick mud. However magnificent Washington was going to be in the future, when its buildings and boulevards were finally completed, at the moment it was a ramshackle and sketchy town. The Capitol, high upon the Hill, dominated everything, as it dominated Washington's social and political life.

The dirty streets were crowded with people. Alan had been told that all the Southerners and Southern sympathisers had earlier left in droves once war seemed to be imminent. They had been replaced by a mass of office seekers and entrepreneurs determined to make a good thing out of the coming conflict.

'To say nothing of the military and naval presence,' Charles said. 'I like the plain Miss Hope,' he added reflectively, 'but I think little of the pretty cousin. She has no regard for others' feelings.'

Jack had been thinking this himself, and was saddened by it. He had met Sophie on a number of occasions without Marietta being present, and had been greatly attracted by her looks and charm. She had spoken often and dismissively of Marietta, so he had assumed that she must be an unpleasant, middle-aged harridan, there to guard a high-spirited girl and carrying out her duties with a heavy hand.

On meeting Marietta, however, he had been surprised to find that the older Miss Hope was comparatively young, and had proved to be a lively and amusing companion. He thought that Sophie's manner to her verged on the unpleasant, particularly since it seemed to be quite unjustified. He felt, however, duty-bound to defend Sophie, of whom he had previously spoken warmly, when Alan supported Charles in deploring Sophie's conduct.

'I thought that you liked her,' he told Alan. 'She's usually a charming little thing, and one cannot expect her to be interested in the weighty topics which engage her elders.'

'No, indeed,' said his brother. 'But one might expect her not to show her displeasure quite so plainly. She was openly rude to Charles, and to Marietta, more than once. My regard for Miss Marietta led me to try to placate the young miss, even at the expense of losing some good conversation. It is not for me to advise you, Jack, but I should go easy in that direction if I were you. Spoilt young beauties are likely to turn into shrewish women when their looks begin to fade.'

Charles nodded at this in his thoughtful way, while Jack said easily, 'I think that you're both making heavy weather of the poor little thing,' but when they mounted the steps to the Envoy's office, he was thoughtful himself.

It was a good thing for Sophie, he decided, that Marietta was so patient with her. It might encourage her to improve her company manners if she were to follow the sterling example her cousin set.

He looked forward to seeing them again in the near future. He had promised to support the stall which they were running at the coming Bazaar to raise money for an orphans' home. He would try to persuade Charles and Alan to accompany him. Hard-working Marietta deserved all the support she could get, what with being the Senator's right hand and Sophie's duenna as well.

He would make sure that he provoked that attractive smile again: when offering it to him, she no longer seemed to be at all plain.

Chapter Three

'Jack says he's bound and determined to support me at the Bazaar this afternoon,' Sophie told Marietta in as patronising a manner as she could. 'I don't suppose that you will want to come, will you? Not your sort of thing at all. Aunt Percival and I are perfectly capable of running the stall without you.'

'On the contrary,' said Marietta coolly. 'Seeing that I have done the lion's share of the work needed to gather together enough *bric à brac*, needlework, bibelots and trinkets to make a good show, I have no intention of being deprived of the pleasure of selling them. Besides, I should like to meet Jack again—I found him a most interesting companion.'

Sophie's pout was a minor masterpiece of displeasure.

'Oh, I'm sure that *he* would like an afternoon when he didn't have to waste time discussing boring topics with you,' she said sharply. 'Besides, if you do come, you will have so much work cut out making change for our customers to spend much time talking to any-

one. You know that Aunt Percival and I aren't very
good at sums.'

'In that case, you really will wish me to accompany
you—seeing that I will be useful after all.' Marietta
smiled.

She was beginning to enjoy wrong-footing Sophie,
whose spite was becoming unendurable. Aunt Percival
had berated her the other evening for 'allowing Sophie
to walk all over you' and had advised her to stand up
for herself a little more. 'You are doing her no favour
by letting her use you as a doormat,' she had ended,
trenchantly for her.

Well, I wasn't a doormat this morning, far from it,
thought Marietta, looking around the crowded church
hall to see whether Jack was present. He had apparently told Sophie that he would arrive early, but it was
already four o'clock and there was no sign of him.

Nor was there any sign of Sophie, either. After two
hours of waiting for Jack, she had flounced off to take
tea in a back room, telling Aunt Percival to be sure
to fetch her if he should suddenly arrive. Aunt Percival's answer to that, once she had gone, was to remember a sudden necessary errand which she needed
to run, leaving Marietta alone in blessed peace at the
stall.

She had just sold an embroidered pocket book to
Mrs Senator Clay when she saw Sophie returning with
a man in tow. She was chattering animatedly to him,
even though he was not the missing Jack. He was
someone whom Marietta had once known very well

and whom she was surprised to see at this unassuming event.

'Guess who I found?' bubbled Sophie at Marietta. 'He says that he knew you long ago when you were young.'

Marietta looked at the handsome blond man who was bowing to her before offering her a faint smile. 'I don't need to guess,' she said quietly. 'It's Avory Grant, isn't it? I would have known you anywhere.'

Marietta had not seen him for seven years and those years had changed them both. There were grey streaks in his fair curls and lines on his classically handsome face, even though he was still only in his early thirties. She wondered what he saw when he looked at her.

'You haven't forgotten me, I see,' he said quietly, bowing to her.

'No, of course not,' she told him, smiling at him. He might once have proposed to her and been refused, but that was no reason for them to be uneasy with one another.

He smiled. 'And I would have known you, even though you have become handsome after a fashion which must cause heads to turn in your direction these days.'

'Now, Avory, you must not flatter me. You know as well as I that I am past my first youth.'

He shook his head. 'I meant what I said. I am delighted to see you again, and to find you looking so well.'

She did not tell him that he had not changed, for he had, even though he was essentially still the young man who had asked to marry her—something which Sophie did not know.

'I arrived in Washington yesterday and my aunt told me that I would find you here this afternoon—and so Miss Sophie confirmed when I encountered her.'

Sophie slipped a proprietorial arm through Avory's, and her smile for Marietta was that of a crocodile hanging on to its prey. 'Avory and I first met when Pa invited him to dinner this time last year,' she announced sweetly.

Avory nodded agreement, adding, 'I am having a short holiday in Washington, renewing old friendships, before I join the Army of the Potomac—'

He was not allowed to finish. Sophie exclaimed, 'Oh, no—do not say so. It is not even certain that there will be a war.'

'Would that that were so,' he told her indulgently, 'but I am afraid that war is now inevitable.' He turned to Marietta. 'I am sure that the Senator would agree with me. May I compliment you again on your appearance, Marietta—it is as though no years at all have passed since we last had the good fortune to meet.'

Marietta's thanks for this compliment were coolly polite but genuine. For the first time in months, nettled by Sophie's constant criticism of her, and a little on her high ropes because of the Dilhorne party's open admiration of her, she had dressed herself with some care.

She was wearing a fashionable green velvet gown decorated with gold buttons and a certain quantity of discreetly placed gilt lace which showed off her glossy chestnut hair to advantage. More to the point, she had abandoned her normally severe coiffure in favour of one which allowed her glorious locks to hang loose a little before they were confined by a black velvet bandeau round her forehead. In the centre of it she had pinned a small topaz brooch. Her mirror had told her how much this unwonted care had improved her appearance.

Sophie tossed her head a little. Plain Jane had no business to be receiving praise—that was for her. 'Oh, Marietta always looks the same,' she said, as though that were some major fault. 'I suppose that your wife is still recovering from your journey from Grantsville and would find a visit to a Bazaar too exhausting.'

Marietta threw Sophie a glance so withering that even that careless kitten quailed before it, while Avory, his face shuttered, said in a low voice, 'My wife died suddenly six months ago—the news has possibly not yet reached you.'

To save her cousin at least a little face for having forgotten what she must have been told, Marietta said, 'Sophie has been living in the country until she came to Washington early this spring and consequently would not have been informed of your sad loss.'

'Oh, yes, indeed,' stammered Sophie. 'May I offer you my belated condolences, Avory?'

Despite Marietta's kind intervention, she shot her a look which was poisonous—but which Avory did not see. He inclined his head towards her and said, 'You may, indeed. I thank you.'

He addressed his next remark to Marietta. 'I should wish to pay you a more formal visit before I leave

Washington. I take it that you are still at your old address.'

'Yes, we shall be pleased to see you.'

Sophie announced in a distracted voice, 'Oh, look— Charles Stanton has just come in, but Jack isn't with him. Wherever can he be?'

Her brief moment of remorse for her thoughtlessness was over, and she was ready to resume her exciting social life. As on the night of the reception at the White House, she waved her hand above her head to attract attention, only this time it was holding her fan, not a bouquet.

She had already forgiven Charles for having caused her to insult him by not using his proper name, and when he arrived at the stall her pleasure at seeing him was unfeigned because it allowed her to forget her recent gaffe and repair a previous one.

'Oh, m'lord,' she exclaimed, startling Avory who was about to leave them. 'How delightful to see you again. But where are your companions? I trust that they have not deserted us.'

'Not at all,' said Charles gravely, including Avory in his bow to her and Marietta. 'Alan was summoned at short notice to a committee on the Hill and took Jack with him. Since my specialist knowledge was not wanted today, Jack suggested that I come along and assure you that he and his brother would join us before the afternoon is over.'

'We are being remiss,' said Marietta, trying not to sound as though she were reproaching Sophie, even though she would have liked to. 'I ought to introduce our new guest to our old one. Mr Stanton, may I pres-

ent Mr Avory Grant of Grantsville to you? He is one
of our most prominent landowners and a strong sup-
porter of the Union cause.'

'Oh, pooh, Marietta,' said Sophie when the cour-
tesies were over. 'You might as well explain to Avory
that Charles is really Viscount Stanton, or else he will
think that my calling him m'lord was a silly mistake.'

Marietta thought furiously that the only silly mistake was to insist on calling Charles Stanton m'lord
when he expressly did not wish to use his title in either
his public or private life! Her eyes met Charles's and
she signalled him a rueful apology for Sophie's *bêtise*.
He smiled and shrugged his shoulders.

What Avory made of this by-play was unknown,
especially since in order to impress Charles with her
image as a universal charmer, Sophie had re-engaged
Avory in animated conversation about his home and
was assuring him how much she was looking forward
to seeing it again.

Aunt Percival's arrival back from her errand, and a
sudden influx of would-be buyers, ended this ploy.
She took one brisk look at the situation, said hail and
farewell to Avory, and sent Marietta and Charles to
the tea-room, all while bidding an annoyed Sophie to
stay behind and do some work for a change.

Charles's perfect manners prevented him from making any comment on Sophie's less-than-perfect ones
to Marietta, other than by saying, 'One has to hope
that Jack will have Alan with him if they arrive at the
Bazaar while you are busy taking tea with me.'

This cryptic remark amused Marietta more than a
little. She said, as casually as she could, 'I gather from

Jack that you are something of a protégé of his brother.'

Charles picked up a large muffin and said before attacking it, 'Yes, indeed. He rescued me from being a backwoods country nobleman, or a soldier, when I wanted to be that odd creature a working engineer. I had a passion for all things mechanical and Alan's charm and power, working together, were such that he persuaded my father to allow me to indulge that passion.

'Alan Dilhorne is a most remarkable man. How re-markable I did not completely understand until I be-gan to work for him a few years ago. His brother Jack is very like him, but not, I suspect, so severe. Alan can be ruthless—should he so wish—which is not very often. I suspect Jack does not share that with him.'

Marietta could well believe that Alan was ruthless as well as severe. He had chosen to deceive Mr Lin-coln and the officials he had met by presenting them with a picture of an idle and somewhat stupid English gentleman and she was sure that that had been done with a purpose.

It was pleasant to forget her duty for once and delay returning to the stall in order to talk to a clever and attractive man who seemed to like her company. He was not Jack, but she had to admit that if she had met Charles first... But that was to flatter herself.

'How long do you propose to stay in Washington? I take it that you will be returning to London with Alan.'

Charles shook his head. 'No, indeed. I shall send

my report on our talks back with him when he leaves, and then I shall travel South to see what new inventions in the shipping line the Confederates are developing. I trust you will not take offence at my visiting your enemy. Great Britain is, I believe, unlikely to become an ally of either side in the coming war, so I shall have *carte blanche* to travel where I please.'

Marietta shivered. 'I have always hoped that civil war would never come, particularly since our family has relatives in the Deep South. It is dreadful to face the fact that friends, brothers and cousins might find themselves on opposite sides—perhaps to meet in battle.'

'Civil wars are the worst of wars,' said Charles. He pulled out his watch. 'My patron should be arriving any time now. Do you wish to remain here, or return to the stall?'

'If we all had our druthers—which is Deep South dialect for what we would rather do than what we ought to do—then I would prefer to stay here. But duty says that I ought to be helping Aunt Percival and Sophie to raise as much money as possible for poor children by selling baubles to rich women—an odd thought, that.'

'Ah, yes, duty,' murmured Charles. 'I can see why Alan likes you. He's great on duty.'

'So, I suspect, is Jack. Is it an Australian trait, I wonder?'

'Perhaps. Many Yankees seem to share it, too. I must do mine and return you to your worthy Aunt Percival.'

Marietta noticed that he did not mention Sophie although, once they were with her again, Charles's manners to her were those of the perfect gentleman—which he obviously was, even though Sophie greeted Marietta with, 'Whatever have you been doing to be away for so long? I have had a wretched time of it. Aunt Percival has left me to sell things and make change while she gossiped with all her old friends—and Jack still hasn't turned up. If he doesn't come, it will have been a totally wasted afternoon—I shouldn't have allowed you and Aunt to persuade me to attend.'

'Now, Sophie, that's no way to speak to Marietta—even if you are disappointed,' said Aunt Percival. 'Console yourself by knowing you have been doing your duty.'

'Oh, that!' exclaimed Sophie, shrugging her shoulders and rolling her eyes at Charles. 'Who cares about that? That's for servants.'

'And English viscounts apparently, by what he said to me in the tea-room,' Marietta was to tell Aunt Percival later that evening. 'It's a good thing that Sophie hasn't set her sights on Charles—he thoroughly approves of people who do their duty.'

Now she said nothing, other than, 'Well, we can all console ourselves with the thought of duty well done, and have our immediate reward for, if I do not mistake matters, Jack and Alan have just arrived.'

Sophie responded by jumping up and down again and beginning to semaphore in their direction—this time laughing and waving Aunt Percival's tolled-up sunshade to be sure of attracting them to her side immediately.

Both men responded by smiling at them before

making their careful way through the crowd of women—few men were present—to Marietta's now three-quarters-empty stall.

'I warned Alan,' remarked Jack when the formalities were over, 'that by the time we arrived we should find all the best bargains will have gone—and so they have. But that stern goddess Duty called us. Even if I might have frivolously declined to obey her on the grounds that I had a previous engagement, Alan, who is made of sterner stuff, would never have allowed such a consideration to move him.'

Duty again—and from Jack this time! Sophie pouted at him, and it was left to Marietta to say to him, 'I see that you think of duty as a woman, Jack. Do you have any authority for assuming any such thing?'

Jack put on a puzzled face, and it was left to Aunt Percival to inform them, 'Mr Jack, even if he does not know it, has the best authority for what he said—was it not Wordsworth who called duty, ''stern daughter of the voice of God''?'

'Bravo!' said the three men together, while Sophie stared at Aunt Percival. One might have guessed that *she* would remember such a useless piece of knowledge—and by boring old Wordsworth, too. She had unhappy memories of being asked to learn his Lucy poems by heart.

She was about to say something when Alan leaned forward, looked into her eyes, and half-whispered to her, 'I'm sure that Miss Sophie likes poetry which has a softer touch. For example…' And he began to quote

Byron to her in a voice which was so soulfully me-
lodious that even Jack stared at him.

> She walks in beauty like the night;
> Of cloudless climes and starry skies
> And all that's best of dark and light
> Meets in her aspect and her eyes…

The admiring look which he sent her on ending
gave Sophie the notion—totally unfounded—that,
smitten by her charms, he had been left with no al-
ternative but to celebrate them.

'Oh, Mr Dilhorne,' she simpered at him. 'You flatter me.'

'Oh, no,' he returned. 'Most apt, wouldn't you
agree, Charles?'

'Yes, indeed,' said that gentleman, trying to keep
his face straight.

Jack said nothing, but smiled a lot. Aunt Percival
looked bemused. She detected a false note somewhere
but, since no one said anything, she thought that she
must be mistaken. Unlike Charles Stanton, she was
not aware of how ruthless the handsome Mr Dilhorne
could be.

'When we have all finished showing off our learning,' Jack said, 'I should like to enjoy some bodily,
rather than mental, sustenance—it must be hours since
I last ate or drank. Miss Percival spoke a moment ago
of a tea-room. I wonder if you would like to accompany me there, Marietta?'

'Oh, no,' wailed Sophie. 'Why can't I take you?
Marietta has only just returned from it.'

'Splendid,' said Jack. 'Then she'll be sure to know how to find it, won't she?'

He had decided earlier on that day that he wanted to see more of Marietta Hope without having to share her with either Alan and Charles or with Sophie and Aunt Percival. This seemed an ideal occasion to discover whether she was quite as remarkable as he was beginning to suspect she was.

So far he had no sexual interest in her, or so he told himself. In the past his taste in women had always run in the direction of either pretty young blondes who looked adoringly at him and talked of nothing, or their more experienced sisters with whom he could have a jolly good time with no fear of any unwanted consequences.

His father, the Patriarch, as all his descendants called him, had despaired of Jack ever finding anyone sensible with whom he could settle down for life. 'Feather-headed and feather-brained, the lot of them,' he had once grumbled to Jack's mother, Hester, about the women Jack fancied. 'Will he never take up with anyone I might like to have for a daughter-in-law? Someone like Eleanor or Kirsteen?'

'You're not in a position to complain about him, Tom Dilhorne,' Hester had said. 'It took you long enough to sow your wild oats and settle down.'

Now what could a man say to that? Other than, resignedly, 'I might have hoped he'd be more sensible than his old father—although perhaps I ought to remember that if I'd settled down earlier we should never have married!'

On hearing Marietta's immediate offer to stand

down in Sophie's favour, Alan, who was well aware of his brother's wish to be alone with the plain Miss Hope rather than the pretty one, answered for him.

'Now, Miss Sophie,' he said. 'Later on you may have the honour of taking tea with me—but only after you have sold me that pretty brooch whose price seems to have been above most buyers' touch. I should like to take it home to give to my wife as a memory of a happy afternoon. I should be sure *not* to tell her of the charming young thing whose stall I bought it from.'

Since this came out in Alan's most seductive voice, Sophie tossed her head, saying, 'Very well,' although she jealously watched Marietta take Jack away, leaving her with a middle-aged married man and Charles Stanton, whose manner to her was cool in the extreme—and Aunt Percival, who didn't count.

'I should really have let Sophie take over,' Marietta told Jack in a worried voice. 'I've just had a cup of tea with Charles.'

'Ah, but did you have anything to eat?' asked Jack, who could be as cunning as his brother. 'I really can't be expected to partake of a solitary meal. Besides, after the waitress has taken our order, you can enlighten me on the current situation in the States *vis-à-vis* the proper conduct for a young unmarried gentleman who wishes to get to know an unmarried lady better.'

So all this gallant attention to her, Marietta thought glumly, was simply to discover how best to approach Sophie! How could she have expected that Jack might be any different from all the other young men who had fluttered around the beautiful Hope cousins while ignoring the plain one—or using her to get to know the prettier ones better?

'It's very much as I expect it is in England. You may not be alone with an eligible young woman— other than in the kind of situation we find ourselves in at the moment—in an acceptable semi-public place. You may go anywhere with her so long as a chaperon accompanies you—although I believe that we allow a freer life for our young gentlewomen than is allowed to yours.'

'As I thought,' said Jack. 'In a ballroom at home I am allowed to escort the favoured fair one to a table where refreshments are laid out—which I suppose equates to this. So, I suppose that if I asked you and Sophie to go riding with me—I ought, perhaps, to say us, for Alan and Charles would be sure to wish to accompany me—I might safely invite you?'

So that I can act as chaperon for Sophie, I suppose, and that was another dismal thought.

'Yes, or, on occasions where riding is not required, then Aunt Percival can act as chaperon.'

'And having got that out of the way,' said Jack, 'we can now talk of graver things. We in England think that Mrs Harriet Beecher Stowe's novel about slavery, *Uncle Tom's Cabin*, has been a great cause of friction between North and South. It has even been suggested that if there is a war it will have been a major cause of it. What, I wonder, is your opinion?'

One good thing, perhaps, thought Marietta, while giving him a reasoned answer, was that Jack would not have been likely to ask Sophie such a serious question. On the other hand, did she, Marietta, secretly wish him to talk to her in the same flighty way in which all the men who met her talked to Sophie? After all, wasn't he behaving with her in exactly the same way in which young men conducted themselves with the duennas of pretty young things, hoping to get them to favour their suit over everyone else's. Another dismal thought.

The only surprising thing was that Jack appeared to be genuinely interested in what she was saying to him. They went on to discuss Mr John Brown's failed insurrection at Harper's Ferry in 1859 and all the other incidents which had brought the United States to the verge of war. She couldn't believe he would have wished to discuss any of that with Sophie, either.

In return she asked him about his interests, and learned that he was shortly to visit New York with a letter from Ezra Butler to John Ericsson, who was busily engaged in trying to build an effective iron man-of-war.

Tea and cake over, Marietta pulled out her little fob watch and insisted that it was time that they returned to the stall.

'I am sure that your brother would wish to take tea with Sophie and Aunt Percival. You could assist me in selling whatever remains there—if anything does.'

'Surely,' said Jack enthusiastically. 'I should have informed you that my late father was a great man for selling things as well as buying them and we all seem to have inherited those talents—in varying degrees, of course.'

If Sophie resented losing Jack again by having to

do the pretty to Alan and Aunt Percival in the tea-room she did not let it show, but went off with them meekly enough. Charles had found a clerical gentleman with whom to converse about the coming war, so Marietta had Jack to herself again.

She was coming to know him so well: to know that a certain quirk of his mouth and a sparkle in his bright blue eyes always preceded some comic aside; that he possessed a good and shrewd mind, and that he had great respect for his parents and his elder brother. She had to be honest, though, and admit that merely to be with him was enough to set her all pulses throbbing.

His tall and muscular body and his face which, unlike his brother's, was not orthodoxly handsome, but a little irregular, though full of character, attracted her as no other man's physical attributes had ever done before. More than that, when with him she was full of a strange excitement even while they were discussing the most banal topics.

Did he feel the same about her? Marietta very much doubted it. He was plainly a man who attracted women and could have his pick of them, so why should he be drawn to her? Except that this afternoon he could easily have arranged matters so that he spent it with Sophie, but instead he had whisked her away and left Sophie behind.

That might simply mean, however, that for some reason he felt a need to discuss serious matters for once and so he had monopolised her. When it came to a ballroom or a rendezvous, it would most likely be Sophie whom he would choose for a companion— and perhaps for a wife.

Marietta shook herself. What in the world was she doing to be thinking of Jack marrying, and after a fashion that meant that she was thinking of him as a husband? She returned for a moment to being sensible Miss Hope again and, with Jack's help, sold most of the few remaining trinkets on the stall, after watching him charm and cajole passers-by into buying them. He had a nice line in patter and so she told him.

'You are wasted as an engineer, Jack. You should have been a barker at a fair. You would have made a fortune.'

He was not offended, but instead rolled his eyes and said solemnly, 'You flatter me, Marietta. My father was a master of the art, and Alan also. I am not of their calibre, believe me.'

He offered her a conspiratorial wink before hailing a passing matron with the words, 'Madam, I have to tell you that you are missing some of the greatest bargains in Washington today if you do not stay a moment at our stall.'

Marietta laughed up at him after he had successfully wheedled one of society's most miserly women into buying a vase which she didn't want.

'You are a rogue, Jack Dilhorne, a very rogue.'

He leaned forward to whisper conspiratorially to her, 'You should do that more often, Marietta, it becomes you.'

She was so unused to such compliments that she said abruptly, 'What…what did I do?'

'Laugh,' he told her, solemn now. 'You should laugh more often. I must think up some jokes.'

'Oh, Jack,' she riposted, 'you are a living joke.'

'In that case,' he shot back, 'you should be favouring me with a laugh all the time instead of rationing me so severely.'

Marietta did something which she had seen Sophie do quite often, but had never done herself. She slapped him gently on the wrist in playful reproof. 'Come, Jack, you must not tease me.' Which was another favourite phrase of Sophie's when she was flirting with an admirer.

Goodness, that's what I'm doing, flirting! How did he make me flirt? I ought to stop, I'm too old, too solemn, too plain, too serious… The litany unrolled itself in Marietta's head, but it didn't stop her from laughing again, or Jack from admiring her and trying to provoke her a little more.

He put out a gentle hand and loosened a strand of her glossy chestnut hair which had escaped its imprisoning bandeau. 'That's better,' he said. 'It goes with the laugh.'

Well, Jack Dilhorne knew how to flirt and no mistake! Which was perhaps why she was suddenly doing all those flighty things which she had never done as a young girl. It was all his fault, of course. How does it happen that he's making me think, behave and talk like a green girl of fourteen with her first beau?

Marietta tucked the errant lock of hair back. He promptly loosened it again.

'No,' she murmured at him. 'No, you will make a spectacle of me if you carry on like this. What will people think?'

'Nothing,' he told her. 'They're too busy with their own affairs to trouble about yours. Besides, why should you not be entertained by your gentleman companion? They think nothing when Sophie is.'

'Is that what you are, Mr Jack Dilhorne? My gentleman companion? How much of a gentleman are you?' But she was smiling when she teased him, and there was no sting in her words.

'As much as any other man whom you allow to help you at a charity bazaar.' He smiled at old Mrs Nuttall who had come up to the stall, her busy, curious eyes on Miss Marietta Hope, who was dallying with that handsome young stranger in a manner quite unlike her usual dignified restraint.

'Ah, madam,' he asked her cheerfully, 'what may I sell you this afternoon? I regret that Miss Hope has been so successful that there is little left for you to choose from.'

'Not Miss Hope,' cackled Mrs Nuttall. 'She's not been selling much this fine afternoon. You've been far too busy chaffering with each other for her to find time to sell anything to outsiders. Not that I blame you for showing an interest in her, young man—she's worth ten of that cousin of hers. She'd always have your dinner on the table when you came home after a hard day's work, which is more than I could say for Miss Flighty Hope if you were silly enough to settle for her—but then, you young men always go for show rather than quality!'

Marietta's face was one vast blush, but Jack, as befitted the true son of his father, was quite unruffled.

'Dear lady, I can see that, were I considering marriage, you would have much useful advice to offer me. But since, this afternoon, my life is dedicated to selling each last bibelot on Miss Hope's stall before the day is over, then I must beg you to turn your undoubted talents to inspecting what is left—and choosing the best.'

Mrs Nuttall's answering cackle was so loud it had every head in the room turning and staring at them, including those of Alan, Sophie and Miss Percival, who had just finished their tea and were returning.

'Land sakes, young man, with that silver tongue you should be a preacher, like Mrs Beecher Stowe's rascally brother. Why should I want any of this trumpery rubbish?'

Jack's smile was a masterpiece. 'The poor children, madam: it is for their sake that you should buy something and offer up a tribute to charity.'

'Don't madam me, young man. I'm Ida Nuttall, Mrs Ida Nuttall, and rather than take home something I don't want, I'll gladly give you a few dollars for the young 'uns.'

She pulled out a battered leather purse and extracted several dollars from it before pouring them into Jack's extended hand.

'Thank you, Mrs Nuttall,' he told her gravely. 'Great will be your reward in heaven.'

'Oh, pish,' she threw at him. 'I'd rather have my reward on earth by seeing Miss Marietta here married to a good man. Are you a good man, sir? By the look of you, I beg leave to doubt it.'

She gave another murderous cackle and strolled away.

Jack's answering laugh was rueful. He looked at Marietta and shook his head at her. Alan, who had arrived in time to hear Mrs Nuttall's last remark, said, with a grin, 'And that's you pinned down, little brother. How did she come to that conclusion so rapidly?'

'His silver tongue,' said Marietta, before Jack could speak. 'She compared it to that of Mrs Beecher Stowe's brother, whom she thinks to be a rogue.'

'Since I know nothing of the gentleman,' said Jack, as grave as a judge, or someone trying to solve a problem in logic, 'you might tell me something of him so that I may know how apt the comparison is.'

'That,' Marietta told him, 'is easy. He's a reverend gentleman who has made a name for himself as a great preacher, full of morality and pious advice. But, and I hate to report this, there have been suggestions that the good reverend is one of those who preach Do as I say, not do as I do.'

'Exactly like Jack, then,' offered Alan, at which the whole party burst out laughing, not least Jack himself.

'It's a good thing I'm not a conceited fellow,' he volunteered at last, 'or else I should be thoroughly downcast after all this criticism, but since I'm not—'

He was not allowed to finish. Even Sophie, who had found all this banter difficult to follow and was furious that Marietta was once again the subject of interest and not herself, joined in the laughter.

Marietta had not enjoyed herself so much in years—for that matter, neither had Jack. The States— or rather their lively women—were providing him with more entertainment than he could have expected.

So he told his brother and Charles on the way back to their various lodgings. Alan took this somewhat unexpected news gravely.

'In which of the two Hope cousins are you more interested, Jack?' he asked. 'Either, both or neither? I should like to think that you were aware that although Miss Sophie Hope does not possess a heart to break, her cousin is quite another case. She could most easily be hurt by someone who ignored how vulnerable she is behind her collected exterior.'

'Now, Alan,' said Jack, his easy smile moderating the sting of his reply. 'You are only my big brother, not my father confessor. I'm only trying to bring a little gaiety into what seems to me to be Miss Marietta's rather arduous life—and I am well aware of the different nature of the two cousins.'

'Excellent,' said Alan. 'I am glad to hear it—big brothers are traditionally allowed to act as advisers to little brothers, you know.'

'Agreed,' said Jack, 'so long as they don't overdo it. Now, let us tell Charles that he has a busy day ahead of him tomorrow. In the morning you are compelling us both to accompany you to the gymnasium you have discovered not too far from your lodgings, and in the afternoon we have all been invited to attend a Congressional committee which is meeting in the Capitol itself. That should make for an interesting day, should it not? Physical work in the morning and mental in the afternoon. It will be our duty to see that Her Majesty's unofficial envoy to the United States government doesn't arrive at the Capitol too heavily marked after his morning's exertions.'

Charles laughed. One of the pleasures of meeting

his patron's brother had been to discover that what Lord Knaresborough, who was Alan's mentor, had once said was true: that, judging by what Alan had told him, all the Dilhorne family were as remarkable as he was. Charles could not help wondering what the other members of it were like, particularly Thomas, who had become Fred. Was it because the Patriarch had been transported, and had spent his life away from England and its formal society, that they had turned out so strikingly original?

Like Alan, Charles was beginning to wonder which of the Hope cousins was engaging Jack's attention. He had thought at first that it was Sophie, which would have left the field open for him to pay court to Marietta, to whom he was becoming increasingly drawn. Lately, however, it seemed to be Marietta on whom Jack was fixed and that, sadly for his own wishes, she was attracted to Jack—indeed, had eyes for no one else.

Marietta herself, once the Dilhorne party had left, was confessing the same thing to herself. Her feelings for Jack had become such that in his presence every other man he was with seemed extinguished by him. Jealous Sophie, watching them, seethed inwardly.

It wasn't fair! She had met Jack first and she could have sworn that he had instantly been powerfully attracted to her; and then he had met Marietta on the afternoon she had been wasting her time on silly duty calls, and everything had changed.

How in the world could such a plain elderly stick as Marietta charm someone so lively and amusing as

Jack? Was it his nasty brother—for Sophie had begun to suspect that Alan was not as charmed by her as he appeared to be—who had turned him against her? Yes, that was it—and Charles Stanton was no better: he had eyes only for Marietta and treated her, Sophie, as though she were his troublesome little sister.

Well, just let her get an opportunity to dish Plain Jane's hopes with them all, and she wouldn't waste a minute before she took her revenge. She hadn't come to Washington to be outshone by her own elderly duenna—by no means.

Chapter Four

'I don't understand why you were so determined that Charles and I should accompany you,' Jack grumbled to Alan on the following morning when they entered Clanton's gymnasium. 'You know that I don't share your enthusiasm for the noble art, and nor, I gather, does Charles.'

'A good experience for you both,' Alan told him lightly. 'Wouldn't do for you to enjoy yourself all the time. Bad for you. To my certain knowledge Charles has never visited such a place before. No need for either of you to feel that you have to take any pleasure in visiting a gym. Just savour a new experience.'

'So noted,' said Charles sardonically, looking around the big room and making for some chairs which were strategically placed to have the best view of the ring set up in its centre.

Jack joined him, amused to see Alan stroll up and begin to try to charm a burly Yankee who had immediately made it plain that he hated all the English, and English aristocrats most of all. He gave a great guffaw when Alan informed him that he had come for a light workout in the ring.

'Nothing punishing,' Alan said. 'I'm too old for that, and I don't want my face marked. Wouldn't do. I'm merely trying to keep my weight down.'

Jack and Charles, amused, watched the way in which Clanton's face and manner changed when Alan stripped off and performed in the ring. Despite his size and his age there was little spare fat on him and, although he knew that time had robbed him of much of his speed and power, he was still as light on his feet and as tricky as ever.

Clanton had warned his bruiser not to damage the gentleman but, watching them, he had to admit, if grudgingly, that a few years ago the large Englishman must have been a formidable opponent.

After the session was over Alan sat on the stool in the corner of the ring, panting heavily as he towelled off: the sweat was running down his body.

'Enjoyed yourself?' queried Clanton with a grin.

Alan dropped the towel from his face and gasped an answer.

'Yes, but good God, I'm winded. I'm an old man these days.'

His trunk was scarlet where the boy who had been his opponent had caught him. He flexed his hand and sucked at his knuckles, aching though he had been using gloves in practice.

'I can't do this too often now, nor do it properly. I can't afford to spoil my gentlemanly looks.'

He offered Clanton his wolfish grin, having grasped that he had dispelled the man's original antagonism after he had revealed how remarkable a performer he had once been.

'Ruthless devil, aren't you?' said Clanton, who had known his man the moment he had seen him in action and, being a hard man himself, recognised another when he saw one.

'Yes,' said Alan. 'It runs in the family.' He jerked his thumb at the watching Jack who sat, a picture of easy amiability, beside the silent Charles.

'Does *he* want a go, a real go?' asked Clanton eagerly.

'Not I,' said Jack. 'I stick at riding and the foils. Soaking up that sort of punishment isn't my idea of fun.'

'And poking about with long-bladed table-knives isn't mine,' said Alan. He used one of his repertoire of comic faces after rising and saying, 'I shall be stiff for the rest of the day.'

'Come again,' invited Clanton before Alan strode off to dress. 'You were good once. Pity to go to seed too much.'

Alan shook his head. 'Thank you, but no. I'm too old and too busy—but you've a nice set-up here.'

Improbably that afternoon, since Jack had never expected to end up in such grand company, Alan took them both to the Hill. They walked through the Capitol for the first time, admiring the murals, even if they did represent the surrender of British troops under Burgoyne during the American Revolution.

Later Alan presented them to Gideon Welles, President Lincoln's Secretary to the Navy, whom Alan had already met, and a group of his associates who gazed suspiciously at the three Britishers—as they supposed them all to be.

Watching his brother, cold and inscrutable beneath his false veneer of an idle English gentleman who was drawling his incomprehension of the strange new world in which he found himself, Jack found it difficult to associate him with the grinning bruiser of the morning. He had not known Alan very well before he had settled in England, and now he found himself wondering which of the many masks his brother wore was that of the true man.

Senator Hope arrived in the middle of the discussion, his handsome old face alight with pleasure at the sight of the brothers and Charles. Like the others, though, he was putting pressure on Alan, trying to influence him in favour of the North. There was no doubt that Lincoln's government was suspicious of the British whom they thought, with some justification, favoured the South. They were trying to impress on Alan during these semi-formal conversations that they were worried that English ship-builders might give an advantage to the Southern rebels. The names of Lairds and Liverpool popped in and out of the conversation.

Alan's deceitful manner enabled him to give little away. He had introduced Jack as his brother who was knowledgeable about shipping and was by way of being a marine engineer and architect, too. He had been involved in the building of Sydney's first dry-dock at Balmain while still young, Alan said, and like Charles he was interested in the development of iron-clad ships, both for civilian use and for war.

'Thank you, Mr Dilhorne,' Welles said. 'We would now like to question your associate, Mr Charles Stanton—more properly Viscount Stanton, we understand—and your brother also.'

Someone had been doing their homework, thought Jack, preparing to be quizzed.

'Mr Stanton, please,' said Charles in reply to a question about his experience. 'I have been working with Cowper Coles, the British naval officer and designer, and one of my recent tasks was to assist him to design and build the first semi-iron-clad warship for the British Navy. Fortunately, or unfortunately,' he added, 'we have not had the opportunity to use it in action.'

This brought a few laughs, but one fierce-looking frontier type, who obviously held all Britishers in contempt, and was a little annoyed to find them let loose on the Hill, said contemptuously, 'We have as yet no iron-clads in these United States. I consider their possibilities in war to be greatly overrated.'

After that discussion grew brisk. A little clerk took notes and Jack was at pains to suggest that he was an amateur in such matters compared with Charles. He spoke of his wish to meet John Ericsson, the Swedish designer and ship-builder who lived in New York, and it was evident that many present had heard of him.

A naval officer, covered in gold braid, came in and joined in the discussion which grew rapidly into an argument. He, too, was contemptuous of Charles's quiet assertion that iron-clads would alter naval battle tactics. The talk grew so lively that Jack could not help thinking how much Marietta would have enjoyed it. The traditionalist naval officer grew verbally violent in pressing his belief that iron-clads would never be capable of fighting effective battles on the high seas.

'But it will come,' said Charles firmly, Jack nodding at his side, 'and soon. For if war breaks out here I am prepared to wager that iron ships will fight it out, somewhere, somehow.'

'So you say,' said the naval officer, tempting Jack to put his oar in to support Charles, but Charles did not need his support: beneath his quiet exterior he was a most determined young man. Hammer and tongs they went at it, and the frock-coated politicians stroked their chins and listened. Charles had the advantage of knowing at first hand what the European navies were doing and Jack listened carefully to him.

In the middle of all this a tall, dry-looking man came in and took Welles to one side, to speak to him at length. After his departure, Welles returned to the table, put up a hand for silence and said, 'Our discussion comes apropos, gentlemen. I have further news from Fort Sumter. The would-be rebels expect us to evacuate it—nay, they have demanded that we do so—but we are standing firm. It cannot hold for ever, and if they fire on us, the fort will fall—and the Union with it.'

The little group fell silent, and for the first time Jack felt the hand of war heavy on them all. Sumter had dominated conversations for days, and it was a matter of agreement that, if it were attacked, war was inevitable.

Welles turned to Alan, who had been listening to the discussion with great attention.

'You see our concern plain, suh.' He had a turn of speech common to many American politicians, oro-tund and formal. 'And when you return and report back to your masters, why, you will do so from the horse's mouth.'

'Always remembering that my role is an unofficial one,' said Alan. 'But I have heard what you have to say and will so note when I reach home.'

Jack saw Charles give a subtle smile when his brother said this. Shortly afterwards the meeting broke up, but it was agreed that all present would dine at Willard's that night. Jack knew that Alan would come under fire again, but this did not seem to trouble him.

Walking down Capitol Hill, Alan suddenly laughed out loud and said to Jack and Charles, 'Men are the same the world over; never forget that, and you cannot go wrong. Having dealt with Chartists and Rothschilds and now with these horse-trading Yankees, I find the same patterns hold good. They will try to get me to drink heavily tonight in the hope that I might commit myself—and they will try to ply the two of you with drink as well. I shall drink bumper for bumper, smile and smile, and give nothing away until it pays me to—and you must do the same. We shall all have thick heads in the morning.'

He stopped, and stretched himself, his arms held high, so that passers-by smiled indulgently at the big man. For his part, Jack grew ever more convinced that he shared with Alan and Thomas and their dead father a zest for life and conflict which added spice to their days and gave form and meaning to that which without it would be empty and void...

Jack called on the Hopes on his way home. He had much to tell them and, besides, he wanted to see Marietta again. Instead, he found Sophie installed in the parlour, drinking tea with Aunt Percival. They both welcomed him warmly.

Sophie said, 'What a pity, Marietta has just gone upstairs to copy some notes for the Senator. Never mind, I'm sure that we can entertain you. Will you be going to the Van Horns' Ball tomorrow evening? I shall be sure to look after you if you are.'

'Yes, we are all invited. It seems that we have become one of the curiosities of Washington—or perhaps it might be more truthful to say that Charles and Alan have. They are the ones who are the old English gentlemen, not me.'

'Oh, no,' said Sophie vigorously. 'I'm sure that you're wrong there. You are so much more like we Americans than Charles and Alan and are therefore more welcome.'

Jack made a suitably modest reply. Aunt Percival excused herself for a moment, and Sophie took the opportunity to lean forward and say, 'Now we may speak at ease. I never seem to say anything of which Aunt Percival approves when we are together. Of course, she thinks Marietta is the pink of perfection, but we cannot all be serious all the time, can we?'

'No, indeed,' said Jack, although he was thinking that one of Sophie's problems might be that she could never be serious at any time. One could forgive her, though. She was such a sweet young thing in her pretty pink-and-white toilette with a small posy of artificial rosebuds at her throat and a pale blue sash around her tiny waist. Age would perhaps mature her: after all, she was not yet twenty.

They were not to be left alone long, though. Aunt Percival reappeared with Marietta in her train. The look Sophie threw her would have slain a tiger at six paces. It was really too bad of the silly old woman to drag Marietta downstairs when she had had Jack to herself for once.

Inevitably the nature of the tea party took quite a different turn with Plain Jane there. Marietta wanted to know how Jack and the rest had fared on Capitol Hill, and insisted on hearing all the details. She tried to bring Sophie into the conversation, but to no avail.

'I am sick of hearing about the war,' she complained. 'It's all anyone wishes to talk about these days. Why can't they wait until it starts? If it does, that is. Nothing could be more horrid.'

What could her hearers say to her that would not distress her the more?

Jack said, 'Not everything takes second place to the coming war, Sophie, although it is not surprising that everyone is obsessed by it. You must allow me to escort you, Miss Marietta and Miss Percival to the theatre before we leave, and we can forget war and its pains while we are there. I hear that Edwin Booth's acting is so remarkable that he would put his London rivals to shame were he to visit England.'

He could see at once that this was not at all what Sophie wanted to hear. An evening at the theatre which included Marietta would be no fun at all. Why did he wish to drag her along?

'It is too bad,' she complained. 'Just when I came to Washington, too. None of my cousins had to compete with a war.'

'On the other hand,' Jack said with a smile, 'it's most likely that if it were not for the coming war then Alan, Charles and I would never have visited the States.'

'There is that,' she admitted. 'But you will not be staying in Washington long, I understand. Do you have to leave so soon?'

'Not so soon as Alan and Charles, but soon enough, I fear. All the more reason, then, for us to enjoy ourselves now.'

'You could come with us to the Wades' soirée this evening, perhaps,' she said eagerly. 'They would be sure to welcome you.'

'Alas, we are all invited tonight to a great official jamboree in my brother's honour at Willard's. It would be tactless if I were not to attend, seeing that they made such a point of inviting us all, so I fear that I must decline your kind offer.'

'Oh, your duty again,' said Sophie glumly. 'Do you always do it?'

'Not always, I must admit—but on this occasion I have to. One does not insult one's hosts—particularly when Mr Welles has promised to write me a letter of recommendation to Mr John Ericsson in New York.'

'Oh, how splendid,' exclaimed Marietta. 'We don't want to lose you, but you cannot snub Mr Welles after being given such a remarkable opportunity.'

'No, indeed,' agreed Jack. 'I shall be sure to return to Washington when my time with him is over—but you must understand, Miss Sophie, that I cannot give you a firm date for that.'

'The war, again, I suppose,' moaned Sophie. 'But we shall expect to see you before you leave the States.'

'That is one promise, above all others, which I shall keep,' he told them gravely. 'Meantime, I suggest that we all meet tomorrow morning to go for the ride which we have been promising ourselves since we first met.'

Excited agreement followed from Sophie, with the proviso that she be allowed to accompany them in the carriage.

'I do not like horses, nor do they like me,' she declared. Marietta's pleasure was muted but was none the less sincere.

Later, while changing into his evening togs before visiting Willard's, it was Marietta's smile of pleasure for him when he had bowed his farewells which he recalled, not Sophie's.

Alan had been correct in saying that they would all have thick heads in the morning. The dinner had been informal and had included not only most of the men on the afternoon's committee but also outsiders like the British newspaper reporter Russell. He was the war correspondent of *The Times*, already famous— some said infamous—for his frank and fearless reporting of the Crimean War, which had enraged the British Government of the time.

He joined them in the hard drinking at the bar after the dinner was over. He knew Alan, and his big, bearded face shone with pleasure when he shook hands with him. He smiled knowledgeably at the dead men littering the table.

He had one of the backwoods Congressmen with him: a big red-faced fellow who stared hard at Alan's urbane splendour and said nastily, 'Sparring at Clanton's gym this morning, were you—for so he told me—doing your diplomatic nonsense at the Hill this afternoon and drinking here tonight? What a busy old English gentleman you are! What other talents do old English gentlemen possess?'

He had been drinking hard and his tone was insulting.

Alan looked quizzically at him. 'As many as youngish Yankee gentlemen like yourself, I suppose.'

'If you weren't an old man, Dilhorne, I'd test your talents in the ring myself.'

'Not so old as all that, and if you wish to do so do not let my years deter you, Mr Whatever-your-name-is.'

'Macdonald, Dilhorne. My ancestors were kings in Scotland when yours were Saxon peasants.'

'Oh, do not dignify me, or yourself,' drawled Alan, who was beginning to feel the effects of heavy drinking, although no one would have guessed it. 'My father was a transported felon—your ancestors were doubtless Viking pirates, so there's not a pin to choose between us. Your ancestors narrowly missed the block and mine the noose.'

He leaned forward and grasped Macdonald by the wrist.

'Come, sir, what shall it be, arm-wrestling or the ring? I am ready for either. Not for honour, I dare swear, for if the truth were known, neither of us possesses any. When we are done, Mr Russell may well sell this story to *The Times*, and share the profits between us.'

Jack watched Alan and then caught Charles's eye on him. Charles had drunk little, and Jack not much more. Charles's expression was curious: it was one of gleeful anticipation. Jack thought that there was more to this than met the eye. He knew that it was Alan's last semi-official appointment before he left for home.

A frontiersman Senator who was barely conscious leaned forward and clapped Alan on the back. 'Beat him at the arm-wrestling, suh, and I'll take you on next. Lose, and you must guarantee to back the North when you reach home.'

'And if I win, what do I get?' grinned Alan. 'No, don't tell me, it might be an incentive for me to lose.'

'So noted,' Charles murmured under his breath so that Jack could scarcely hear him.

'Life was never like this in the House of Commons,' whispered Alan to Russell when Macdonald, his face eager, pulled out one of the tables and sat down on one side of it, waiting for Alan to join him on the other.

Frantic betting had already begun. The more sober and senior of the party, both so far as alcohol and status were concerned, looked disapprovingly on. One

man said to Alan, 'Do not humour him,' but Alan
shook his head.

'Dare I believe that you are actually agreeing to
take part in this frontiersman's contest?' queried Russell of Alan, more amused than amazed.

'Dare I not?' returned Alan. 'I must strive for the
honour of old England, or be shamed.'

He turned to Charles. 'You will so note, Mr Stanton.'

'So noted,' repeated Charles, adding, 'Return from
the contest like the old Spartan, waving your shield in
triumph or being carried home on it dead.'

Jack privately thought that Macdonald had no
chance of winning. He was soft and fat and Jack had
seen his brother's strength and power in the ring that
morning. If the man had been talking to Clanton, he
was a fool to challenge Alan.

He was right. Alan rapidly forced Macdonald's arm
down on to the table twice in succession, and no
sooner had he done so than others were clamouring to
have a go at him.

The frontiersman who had challenged him on the
Hill that afternoon, and who was now wearing a coon-
skin cap, pushed the defeated Macdonald away and
sat down opposite to Alan, grinning at him.

'If you win, Englishman,' he said, 'I promise you
a free ride at Bella Dahlgren's house with her best
girl.'

The more Puritan among the watchers closed their
eyes at this, but the rest were cheering, and Russell
knew that, despite what Alan had said earlier, this was
one despatch which he would never write or send

home, when Alan slowly defeated his new opponent after several straining minutes.

Well, it was plain that this was still a frontier society, for all its marble columns and stern Republican admonitions, thought Jack. It was not so long since Senator Charles Sumner had been brutally thrashed, without warning, in the sacred precincts of the Capitol itself, by a supposedly gentlemanly assailant.

'Enough,' proclaimed Alan as others strove to get at him. 'I have urgent duties to fulfil in the morning.'

A hand plucked at Jack's arm. 'Are you your brother's equal, me lad?' A bearded face grinned at him.

Jack shook his head and refused the offered challenge. He had never seen the man before, and the room was alive with shouts and cheers and the frontiersman was demanding that Bella Dahlgren's should be the destination of them all.

Alan picked up a bottle and began to pour spirits into his glass. 'Bourbon for me tonight,' he announced, drinking it down. His hearers were not to know that he rarely drank.

He saw Jack smiling at him. 'Little brother,' he told him, 'you may have my ticket to Bella Dahlgren's tonight. I'm too far gone.' He never patronised whorehouses, but that was another thing that he wasn't revealing.

By now the frontiersman, clutching his bottle, was on the floor, and cared little whether Alan was at Bella's or in bed at the Envoy's residence. The evening was not yet over, though, and before Jack and Charles manoeuvred Alan through the door he had treated them to his farewell oration, which brought the house down. Some of the spectators swore drunkenly that the cheering could be heard on the Hill.

Far gone though they both were, since even Charles had been compelled to drink to save the honour of England, Alan's two companions walked him home between them. Russell, staggering in their rear, was carrying Alan's stove-pipe hat and drunkenly declaiming that, 'The best despatches never get written—and he might have had the goodness to offer me his ride at Bella's!'

For the next few days the story of the night at Willard's and its ending ran round Washington. Those Yankees who had not been there were at first disbelieving, then amused and finally admiring, even though the joke was on them once all of the facts—some of them much embellished in the telling—came out.

'For it seemed,' said one witness to it, 'that this MP, this envoy, this fool of a Britisher, was as stiff and starched and pompous as only an aristocrat could be, with his Haw Haw speech and his formality, so that all that was left for a true Yankee was to despise him. He apparently had a friend and patron back home who was a cousin of the Queen, and by some means which baffled everyone who met him—for the man was such an effete ass for all his size—he had built up a business empire back home.

'His other patrons, the Rothschilds, must have lost their wits for once to have anything to do with this fellow who had made every politician and every committee he had encountered privately fume with rage and indignation as he danced them about so politely, asking idiotic questions and making heavy weather of their attempts to answer him.

'Oh, yes, he was *very* polite, and great on protocol, too…' and the speaker usually ran out of breath at this point and needed a few moments to recover himself before continuing with his remarkable tale.

'He spent his time expressing blank incomprehension when confronted by any form of good American speech which differed from his own and consequently needed to have everything carefully explained to him several times so that discussions with him went round and round…

'Well, on his last official day in these United States a number of Senators, Congressmen and their aides had banded together to take him to Willard's and get him royally, nay, Republicanly, drunk for his pains and in the doing gouge out of the fool what concessions to the Northern cause they could.

'While they were doing this and he was obliging them by saying yes to everything—even in those places where he ought rightly to have been saying no—that low-life ass, Macdonald, popped up and insulted him. Before you could say Haw Haw twice, my fine English gentleman accepted his foolish challenge and set about laying everyone low at arm-wrestling, no less—and offering to take them all on in the ring into the bargain. And that was no joke, either, as Clanton later testified, and a good thing no one took up his offer.

'To cap it all, at the end of the evening…' and the

speaker was usually near exhaustion by now, between amusement and indignation '…at the end of the evening, when he had drunk most of the party under the table, and he was sitting there, still conscious, but only just, Macdonald rose and proposed a toast to him. Everyone shouted "Speech! Speech!" so he got up—no one knew how—and gave them the sort of grin a Plains Indian gives you just before he takes your scalp.

'After that, he favoured them with a wickedly accurate impersonation of Mr Lincoln and half the politicians he had met, being particularly good when imitating the frontiersman, who by now was lying unconscious in the corner and who was bitter the next day about having missed this part of the fun.

'So much for his not being able to understand what everyone had been saying to him! At the end he had reverted to his normal voice—if he has one, that is—which was quite unlike that of the man whose plummy tones had bamboozled Washington for the past three weeks. "Finally, fellow legislators and honest Americans," he said, "This imitation of an aristocrat invites you all to a similar evening in London where I promise to wine and dine you as royally as you have feasted me tonight. I also promise to gouge as many concessions out of you as you have tried to wrench from me. What old English gentleman could say more? Mr Stanton, you will so note."

'Mad, drunken cheering followed. "Come back and settle here—you're wasted in the old country," Macdonald bawled at him. Half the company could have killed him for tricking them and the other half wanted to hire him so that he could do his tricks for them.'

This was what Russell did not send back to London and *The Times*. After Jack and Charles had struggled Alan into his bed, Jack asked, 'What did all that mean? What were you "so noting" all evening, for God's sake?'

'Oh, that's your brother's shorthand, a parody of a businessman ordering a clerk to take notes, only he means you to be aware that he's about to do something wicked and you're not to show surprise and give him away.'

'He's our father's worst,' said Jack, shaking his head, 'and I don't envy him his head tomorrow morning, and I don't much fancy mine, either. Did you see their faces at the end—particularly when he took off the coonskin-hatted gentleman?'

'Yes, and whatever will the British Envoy make of it?' Charles grinned. 'He's driven him and all his officials mad, too. The Envoy couldn't imagine why they'd sent out such an ass. Now he knows why. Alan has given nothing away and he's promised them nothing while learning as much as he could of what they didn't want him to know!

'What's more, he's signed off in such a fashion that they're aware that they've been fooled, and that we can be as hard as they are—and so he's ensured mutual respect. "It's a frontier society," he told me on the boat over, "and I'm giving a great deal of thought to how to deal with it. The diplomacy of the European monarchic states will be of no use in Washington, that's for sure."

'In the end he played them at their own game—and that they understand. I think that only Senator Hope had an inkling of what lay behind all the flim-flam. Beneath all the charm he's a hard man, and no mistake.'

Jack nodded. He'd seen little of his brother since he'd become a man himself, but he was shrewd enough to know that what Charles had told him was true. He wondered whether he possessed his share of the Dilhornes' cunning and decided ruefully that he did.

The three of them woke up the next morning with the thickest of thick heads—Alan's being the worst. None the less, they all honoured their promise to ride with Marietta after breakfast.

Alan groaned at the mere idea. 'I don't recover from these sessions so quickly as I used to. You young things—' and he gestured at Jack and Charles '—have the advantage of me now.'

Jack thought that Marietta looked superb in her bottle-green riding habit and her saucy little black hat with its high crown and silver buckle on its scarlet band. Its severity suited her and she controlled her mount as though she had been born in the saddle.

He and Charles galloped off with her, leaving Alan to trot gently beside Sophie's carriage. He was gallantry itself, talking nonsense to her to divert her attention from the other three, particularly when, later on, they dismounted and walked their horses along, talking animatedly. She was pleasant enough to him, but the sight of Jack, Charles and Marietta together served only to increase her dislike for Marietta.

'My father has asked me to invite you all to a dinner party on Saturday evening,' Marietta was telling them. 'He understands that Jack's brother will be leaving for England soon and that Charles will be journeying South. Unfortunately, Sophie will not be able to be present. She is off tomorrow to stay for a short time with another of our cousins who has a summer home on the outskirts of the city.'

Not unfortunate at all, was Charles's inward response, while Jack, who had once seen Sophie as a pretty girl well worth cultivating, was only too happy that it was she who would be absent, and not Marietta, who fascinated him more every time he met her. Both he and Charles expressed their pleasure at the invitation since they had come to respect the Senator, not only for the pleasure of his company, but for his shrewdness, both in the political and the social sense.

Alan, watching Sophie's expression while she was jealously staring after the other three, was thoughtful when the party was reunited and they all rode back together. Part of him was thinking of his journey home to Eleanor and his children by way of New York and 'the steep Atlantic stream', as an old poet had it, and the other part was preoccupied by Jack's relationship with the two Hope cousins and its possible consequences.

Chapter Five

Marietta dressed herself more carefully for the Senator's dinner party than she usually did, putting on a low-necked velvet evening gown whose rich chestnut colour echoed that of her hair. Instead of her hair being pulled sharply back from her face it was softly disposed to frame it: she had remembered Jack's determination to let it down. Emerald ear-rings, a matching bracelet, and a small gold band in her hair decorated with tiny emeralds and diamonds—all inherited from her mother—completed the ensemble.

Its effect, of which she was not fully aware, was stunning. It proved that, properly presented, she possessed an austere beauty far removed from the current conventions of fashion.

Seated opposite to her redoubtable father at table, with Aunt Percival and three handsome men to make up the company, she shone and glittered as much as her jewellery, and all four men wondered how anyone could ever have dubbed her plain.

It was Jack's doing, and Marietta knew that.

Whether he felt anything for her or not, was not the point. The point was that he was paying her all the attention which men usually paid to youthful beauties and at the same time was enjoying her informed conversation. It had been said of Lady Mary Wortley Montagu, another clever and not conventionally handsome woman in the eighteenth century, that 'to love her was a liberal education'. Whether or not Jack thought that of her, Marietta knew that to love him was a liberal education, and in the doing she had freed herself of the continuing disappointment of being 'the plain Hope cousin'.

She also thought that, if she had never met Jack, she might have fallen in love with his brother or with Charles Stanton. Alan, eating fruit at the end of the meal, was entertaining the Senator and Marietta who, by now, had heard of his performance at Willard's.

'You see, sir and madam,' he explained to them, 'like my brother Jack here, I am not truly an English gentleman, although back home I am accepted as one because of my marriage to the heiress of an old family in the north. Otherwise I am as big a buccaneer as Jack, or any of your self-made Yankees. My effete veneer deceived all whom I met because it was what was expected of me. Instead, I treated them to something of which my redoubtable father would have approved.'

He began to talk in a droll, languid manner, pointing a lazy finger at Charles. 'Now, haw, you see, haw, a dem'd fine specimen of an aristocrat, haw. Only he don't choose to behave or, haw, talk like one. Dem'it, Chawles, what possesses you to let the side down.

Hey? Hey? Do not laugh, Miss Marietta. If you ever come to England I assure you that you will find more in England like that, than like Chawles and me.'

He finished in his normal voice. 'Your hothouse peaches are excellent, sir,' he said to the Senator. 'Pray accept my compliments on them.'

'You should have gone on the stage,' Marietta told him. 'When did you acquire such a power to mimic? Did you learn it, or was it inborn?'

'Oh, inborn,' he told her. 'I inherited it from my father who was even more accomplished than I. Jack possesses it a little and our brother Thomas, I mean Fred, not at all. He's too serious, you see.'

'Oh, Mr Alan Dilhorne,' Marietta told him softly, 'do not deceive me. Beneath all the charm you, too, are serious—and Jack as well, I do believe.'

'Pray don't tell him so,' murmured Alan. 'You'll make him conceited.'

'Don't listen to him, Marietta,' Jack said, laughter in his voice. 'He's the world's biggest tease. I remember how he ran me round when I was a little fellow. I always knew where I was with Fred, but never with Alan. He's the original chameleon.'

'And very useful that is in politics,' said the Senator, who had been listening to all this, amusement written on his face. 'You, sir, managed to bamboozle everyone in Washington, and as a consequence go home full of information, I'll be bound, having given nothing away.'

'Now, that,' said Jack, before Alan could reply, 'is surely the first, last and best task of the diplomat—and the businessman—is it not?'

His hearers laughed together. Aunt Percival, watching Marietta blossom in the presence of so many handsome and clever men, thought that she had never looked to greater advantage than she did on Alan Dilhorne's last night in Washington. God send that Mr Jack is beginning to care for her, for by her manner she is attracted to him. Like the Senator, I would see her married—and to a good man. It's a blessing that Sophie has disappeared for the time being and can't spoil things by throwing her selfish tantrums.

Later, she watched Jack and Marietta settle themselves side by side on the sofa in the parlour. Alan was watching, too. More diplomatic work by the Senator, was his conclusion. And I do not blame him. Little brother is a good man, Miss Marietta is a prize worth winning—and the Senator means to have her won.

'So your brother is off to New York before you, Jack,' said Marietta.

'Yes. I once thought that I might go with him, but I have undertaken certain commitments for Ezra Butler and I must fulfil them before I leave. Had I known earlier that Alan would be in the States I might not have agreed to them.'

'Washington might not be the safest place in the USA if war is declared,' Marietta told him. 'Father thinks that the rebels will advance immediately on the capital in the hope that we are not prepared for them. They may think that a rapid attack would win the war for them in short order if, in the doing, they could capture the capital. He says that they must know that if the war becomes a long one they must surely lose.'

'I expect that that is what the Senator and my brother are looking so serious about. But what of you, Marietta? Will you stay here?'

'Of course,' she said simply. 'It is my duty to be with my father and he would not think of leaving while the North is in danger.'

They fell silent for a moment. Moved by a sudden impulse, Jack took Marietta by the hand which lay loosely in her lap with the idea of comforting and supporting her. It was the first time that they had ever touched—apart from lightly in the dance—and the effect on them both was remarkable.

Marietta had never experienced anything like it before. Her whole body began to vibrate, her eyes opened wide and she stared at Jack as though she had just seen him for the first time. She knew at once what her strange interior trembling meant. She both loved and desired him—a man she had only known for a few weeks but who, in some mysterious way, she had known for ever.

Jack was equally transported. He had known many women and made love to some of them, but never before had he felt so overwhelmed by the merest contact with one. The feeling was so strong and sudden that it was like a thunderclap in a clear blue sky. The words his father had used once ran through his mind. 'You will know the one woman when you meet her, Jack, and once you do you will be lost. Claim her, for you will never forgive yourself if you lose her.'

'Marietta,' he said hoarsely, gazing into her dazzled eyes and wishing that they were alone, so that he might…might what? He hardly knew what to say or do.

'Marietta,' he said again, 'I would like, of all things, to drive you to the Potomac one afternoon—as soon as it can be arranged. I am told that the views there are splendid. If it is not proper for us to go alone, then we must take Aunt Percival with us—although, if I am honest, I would prefer your sole company.'

Such a stilted thing for him to come out with when what he really wished to do was to tell her how much he loved and desired her.

Marietta was silent for a moment, scarcely capable of answering him sensibly: no man had ever looked at her as Jack was doing. At last she said, 'Of course I will go with you, but we must follow the forms, Jack, and take Aunt Percival with us.'

'Then that is settled,' he said softly. 'Though we might have to revise our plans if war is declared.'

Marietta shook her head. 'I think not. Father says that once it begins life will become more hectic, not less. There will not be less balls and gaiety, but more. In the face of death and destruction, he says, we always celebrate life by enjoying it come what may. A strange thought, is it not?'

'What I find strange,' Jack said, 'is that, so far as I can tell, one of the main causes of the war is the South's wish to retain slavery. It seems barbaric that they should insist on it so strongly.'

The Senator had overheard him, and said, sighing, 'There is more between North and South than that, but it is the question of slavery which divides us completely. Our family possessed slaves once, but they were all freed long ago. I fear that when the North wins the war—as I am sure it will—the hatred generated by it will create divisions in our country which may not disappear for generations. Man is a sinful creature; I will not say more than that.'

Aunt Percival spoke, her kind face troubled. 'Perhaps we can all pray that war will not come. God could not be so unkind as to allow such a dreadful thing to happen.'

In the silence which followed this heartfelt speech, noise could be heard in the distance. Shouts, pistol shots and cheering were followed by the sound of a tolling bell. The Senator, who was nearest to the window, drew back the curtains and looked out.

There was the noise of running feet as men fled by, howling indistinctly. The Senator threw open the window, all dignity gone, and called out, 'What is it? What is it?'

A large black man, his face alight, stopped in order to answer him.

'It's the day of Jubilo, sah,' he cried. 'Sumter has fallen, they say, and the war for freedom has begun.'

The Senator lowered the window, pulled back the curtain and turned into the room. His face was grave, his manner heavy.

'It is as I thought,' he said sombrely. 'Like Caesar of old, the South has crossed the Rubicon: the worst of all wars is upon us and brother will fight brother. Not even President Lincoln can hold it off much longer, however much he wishes to avoid the final conflict.'

The noise outside grew ever louder, and the sound of cheering grew and grew.

'They are cheering now,' said Alan. He was nearly as heavy as the Senator, and was showing his years and the gravitas which lay behind his normal, easy manner. 'I fear that they will weep before it ends. I wonder how many men will lie dead on the battle-ground between now and peace.'

There was silence in the room where a moment ago there had been pleasure: the earlier, happier mood of the evening had disappeared. Alan rose. 'I do not like to leave so early,' he said, 'but I must visit the Envoy immediately. Late though it is, I must be instructed by him on these developments before I leave Washington. You will excuse me, sir, I am sure.'

'Indeed,' said the Senator. 'You have your duty, sir, as I have mine. Do you also leave for England, Mr Stanton?'

'Not with my master, Alan,' said Charles. 'My way lies South. You understand, sir, that Britain will remain neutral and it is important that one of us goes there. Because of my interest and because Mr Dilhorne must report back home as soon as possible I shall remain behind. I will, with your permission, pay my respects to you again before I leave Washington.'

'You are always welcome here,' replied the Senator. He held out his hand to Alan. 'It has been a pleasure to meet you and Mr Stanton, sir. I shall think differently about English gentlemen now that I have met the pair of you.'

Before they left Jack found a moment to say a private goodbye to Marietta and to renew his invitation to her for a drive to the Potomac with him. War or no war, life would go on, and he intended to live it to the full.

War had been officially declared before Jack found time to drive Marietta and Aunt Percival to the Great American Falls on the Potomac. It was not quite the peaceful trip into a rural paradise which Marietta had imagined it would be. Driving along, they found that tents were already being pitched and preparations were being made all along the route in order to provide an improvised garrison for the troops who would shortly be arriving in Washington.

'The President has already asked for nearly half a million men to be recruited into the Army,' the Senator had told Ezra Butler and Jack when he arrived at Butler's office to invite him and Jack to meet yet another government committee in order to give it the benefit of their advice.

He sighed heavily. 'He does not think that it will be difficult to find them. The Army already has recruiting officers meeting the immigrant ships when they berth in Baltimore and the other East Coast ports. They are barely off the boat before they are persuaded into the Army. New Americans will fight old ones to the death, I fear.'

'True,' Jack said, 'the North will not be short of private soldiers, but Ezra has just been telling me that the majority of West Point officers who trained in the pre-war army have gone to join the South, which must be a great advantage for them.'

The Senator nodded. 'True, but however great their generals—and Robert E. Lee is a great general—or their officers, they cannot match our numbers or our industrial might. They have few railroads, and as fast as they build them we shall destroy them. No, Jack, they cannot win—particularly if the war is a long one.'

'Time will tell,' Ezra said soberly. 'It is worth re-membering, though, that victory does not always go to the most powerful.'

'The thing I most fear,' said the Senator, 'is that, whoever wins, war will inevitably change and harden us.'

Jack could not but agree with him. There was a ruthless determination beginning to show itself in the North and now that the war had begun it was becom-ing almost frightening in its intensity. The men pour-ing into Washington to make their fortunes in the war were hard-headed and single-minded in a way which his brother Alan understood but few others in Britain or Europe could or would.

Alan had spoken to him of it shortly before he had left for New York. They'd been in Willard's bar which had been more crowded and even rowdier than on the night in which Alan had shown his true colours.

'They are not aware back home of what lies ahead of us,' he had said. 'They don't understand that the USA is Rome and that we are turning into Athens. The future is here. If I had come to the States twenty years ago, instead of England, this is where I should have been most at home. They are not civilised yet, and neither am I.'

Jack had laughed at this, looking at his elegant brother, the very picture of an English aristocrat—but the picture lied.

'And I?' he'd asked, for he intended to settle in the States. 'Am I civilised?'

'More than I am,' Alan had said judiciously, 'but I have no doubt that you can make a good life here. Always provided, of course, that you choose the right wife. Avoid the little Sophie, Jack. She is for bedding, not wedding, and I would not even trust her in bed— unless she were tied down. Now the supposedly plain cousin—she is a different thing altogether. Sophie's looks won't last and once gone...' He'd shrugged. 'You are old enough to use your common sense.'

'You married a beauty, though,' Jack had said, re- membering the radiant Eleanor who had visited Syd- ney with Alan twenty years ago.

'But clever—' Alan had smiled '—the best of her family. I hope that it was not only for her looks that I married her.'

He'd embraced his brother fiercely. 'Little brother, you are a good man, better than I am, and deserve well of life, but I warn you, beware of Sophie. I don't like the way in which she looks at you and Marietta when you are together.'

Jack had watched him go. He loved Alan and his brother Thomas. He thought how sad it was that their passion for living had spread them across the globe so that they rarely met.

Well, he would be wary of Sophie, but he was sure that Alan was being a little too suspicious of her.

Much later he was to remember what his brother

had said, and to acknowledge that that master of deviousness had recognised another's possession of it, and that he would have done well to take more heed of his warning.

While he walked with Marietta beside the Potomac River, Sophie and Alan's harsh judgement of her were far from his mind. They stopped to admire the Falls and the beautiful scenery surrounding them.

'Truly are they called the Great American,' he said. 'For once the name is not a polite fiction.'

'Oh, everything is larger than life with us,' Marietta said, smiling. She was wearing a pale green cotton dress and a large straw hat and her hair was soft about her face because she knew that Jack liked it that way. 'European visitors often complain that we are great boasters—but once they see what we are supposedly boasting of and how truly magnificent it is…' and she left the sentence unfinished.

Jack did not argue with her: for one thing he was busy admiring the charm of her animated face.

'Everything is magnificent in America,' he said. 'The view I have at the moment is particularly fine.' And, knowing that they were out of sight of Aunt Percival, he leaned forward and, looking deep into Marietta's beautiful eyes, he kissed her on the lips, oh, so gently.

'You will forgive me, I am sure,' he murmured, 'but the temptation was too great for me.'

He was not lying, and kissing her had only made the temptation worse, particularly since she was looking at him with such great astonished eyes. Could it

really be that no man had ever done such a thing before? Was it possible that she had never been kissed?
And, if so, how could all the men she had met have
been so blind to her beautiful body and fundamental
charm? True, her beauty was not so obvious as Sophie's was, but it was there all the same.

Still silent, Marietta put her hand to her lips as
though to seal his kiss there. So entranced was she,
so wonder-struck, that Jack was tempted all over
again—and fell. This time he took her in his arms and
the kiss he gave her was deeper, more passionate and,
more to the point, she returned it, opening her lips a
little and putting her arms around his neck. She was
already learning the wordless grammar of love.

Jack said hoarsely, taking his mouth from hers and
stroking her soft cheek instead—something which,
strangely, excited Marietta nearly as much as his
kisses on the lips had done— 'I shouldn't be doing
this.'

Marietta, to her infinite shock, heard herself saying,
'There's no one about to inform on us.'

To which he replied, before kissing her again, 'I
know, and Aunt Percival can't see us, either.'

'Yes,' she returned, kissing him back with increased
ardour, 'but that doesn't make it right.'

'True, but I have the oddest feeling that, right or
not, you might be enjoying yourself—I know I am.'

Marietta gave a little gasping laugh. She was, as
Jack had correctly guessed, unkissed, a maiden lady
of mature years to whom no one had ever offered
anything but polite and distant admiration, and that
was only of her mind, never of her body. She could

not imagine doing…this…with anyone but Jack, and to her growing astonishment she didn't want him to stop. On the contrary, she wanted him to go on—for if she felt so overwhelmed by the outworks of love, what would arriving at its inner citadel be like? The mere idea made her feel faint.

So much so that it frightened her and she pulled away from him.

'Oh, Jack, we really shouldn't—and in the open, too.'

He almost forgot himself by telling her Oh, love in the open is always the best, but retained just enough self-restraint to say instead, 'We really should, you know, but this is neither the time nor the place for us to forget ourselves in…' He couldn't think of a polite word so came out with 'dalliance.' Where in the world had he ever heard *that*?

Marietta thought it amusing, too, for she had put on a prim face to replace the eager soft one which gentle lovemaking had created for her, and murmured sweetly, 'Dalliance? Jack? Is that what we were doing—and is that what they call it in New South Wales?'

'It's in some of the old novels,' he said, with— although he did not know it—his father's most knowing smile, the one with which he had won Jack's mother. 'I believe I came across it in one. We are a little earthier, I fear, in Sydney.'

'No doubt.'

They were apart now who had recently been so close. The afternoon, Marietta thought, had lost some of its brightness now that they were separate again.

Did he do this often, and to all the women he met?
It was obvious to her that he was as experienced as
she was inexperienced. Was she being especially favoured by him, or was she merely one in a procession?
When he went to New York, would he promptly forget her and go on to captivate another woman? More
to the point, why had he chosen her and not Sophie?
Surely she was a more obvious target than Marietta.

He took her hand while they walked slowly back to
Aunt Percival, who opened her eyes when she saw
them and said, 'Oh, you have returned sooner than I
expected. I hope that Jack was suitably impressed.'

'Oh, indeed, Miss Percival,' he told her naughtily,
giving her another of his father's smiles. 'I was most
impressed by everything I saw, as I am sure that Marietta will confirm.'

If Aunt Percival noticed the becoming blush which
overwhelmed Marietta when she seconded Jack's remark, she said nothing of that. She did, however, hope
that Mr Dilhorne might have spent his time with her
more usefully than in simply staring at the Falls, grand
though they were.

Instead, she confined herself to joining in the preparations for their picnic on the grass. They spread a
rug at the point where they had the best view of the
Falls and where Washington and the war could be
forgotten. There they unpacked the hamper which
Jack had brought with him. She and Marietta exclaimed over its contents. It was crammed to the brim
with ham and beef sandwiches, cheese, rolls and butter, cake, cookies and fruit.

'No muffins,' he told them, laughing, 'too dangerous.'

Yet another hamper contained china, glasses, sil-
verware, damask napkins and a bottle of wine. There
was even a damask tablecloth, and a small spray of
flowers in a tiny holder to act as a centrepiece. He
opened the wine with a flourish and passed the glasses
around as though he was entertaining them in one of
the finest dining-rooms in either London or Washington.

Marietta was amused and impressed by such cool
sophistication. Jack had the habit of transforming all
he touched, she thought. Wherever he went he cast a
glamour on life, whether he was organising a tea
party, a picnic, or even a simple walk—everything
was transcended, made interesting.

She told him so.

'Oh, it was the Patriarch, our father, who taught us
that life is what you make it,' Jack said, eating his
picnic meal with polite gusto. 'Penny-plain or tup-
pence-coloured, he told us, work for it—and then enjoy it. We must not be mean with ourselves; food and
drink were meant to be enjoyed and they are the lu-
bricants of life.'

Marietta was struck by the way in which Alan and
Jack spoke of their dead father. When she looked at
Jack, lazily stretched out on the grass, toasting the
Falls, charming herself and Aunt Percival as effort-
lessly as he charmed all those he met, she wondered
what his father could have been like, seeing that both
Jack and Alan regarded themselves as being inferior
to him.

Aunt Percival watched Marietta, not Jack. She was being responsive for the first time to a man and was offering herself freely to him with few reservations. She laughed with and at him, teased him, and, forgetting her supposed plainness, she became less plain.

Indeed, while the pair of them talked and joked together, admired the view and, lunch over, strolled by the river, she thought what a splendid pair they made. Beside Jack, Marietta was not too tall and his relaxed manner eased her. They had left Aunt Percival behind—at her tactful urging—to drowse in the early afternoon sun.

She saw them reach the bend in the path running to the Falls, saw Jack turn to Marietta, bend his head, take her hand and kiss it. They were too far away for her to hear, or guess, what they were saying, but his manner was unmistakable. Admiration and affection were plain in it—but was love there, too?

Oh, please God, thought Aunt Percival, seeing Marietta spark back at him, her manner also unmistakable, let him be serious. He is what she needs. She has so much to offer to any man who has the wit to see her as she truly is. She is worth twenty Sophies. Let it be more than friendship with him. He is too good for Sophie, even if he is not nearly good enough for Marietta! For Aunt Percival, no one was good enough for Marietta, but from what she had seen of Jack, she thought that, failing perfection, he might do.

She was not wrong to hope. Jack had originally been intrigued by Sophie's prettiness and her facile charm, but Marietta's good intellect and her strong sense of fun had gradually caused him to transfer his attentions from one cousin to the other. The more he saw of Marietta, the more his mere admiration had turned into love.

She carried her wit and learning with such ease, and she was so good to talk to. More than that, she also knew when to be quiet. She had allowed him to admire the Falls without overmuch chatter about delightful views, sublime scenes, poetic tropes and statements along the lines of Would that I had brought my crayons with me to fix the scene.

In short, it was like being with another man, with the advantage that she was very much a woman! When he had kissed her so suddenly she had not slapped daintily at him, or made a comic moue, or said something stupidly flirtatious and meaningless, but had accepted and returned his kisses without showing false shame or being brazen.

No, she was no longer plain Miss Hope, pretty Sophie's homely cousin: it was Marietta whom he thought of when he was not with her, and, when he saw or heard of something interesting, it was she whom he wished was with him so that he might share it with her.

It was Marietta who kept him from Bella Dahlgren's house, or from adventures with the pleasure-seeking ladies who made their desire for him plain, and with whom he might, at other times, have occupied himself.

I am becoming a monk, he thought with a grin, and I can imagine the Patriarch's knowing look if he knew of my unlikely goings-on. Would he be surprised at my equally unlikely choice of someone to love? I

think not, for he must have known that when the one
true woman comes along she often comes unan-
nounced—as he said Mother did.

So thinking, he tightened the hand which held Marietta's, for since they were in Aunt Percival's line of
sight they needed to be discreet. He felt her hand re-
sponding to his since that was all that was allowed to
them. Did she feel the same for him? Of course she
did, because her sense of honour would not have allowed her to return his kisses unless she truly cared
for him. Mere mindless flirtation was not a game Marietta would ever play—or had played.

Like Aunt Percival, Jack was right. From the moment she had walked into the parlour to find him waiting for Sophie, Marietta had known where her heart
lay—and it was at Jack's feet. He had only to enter a
room for its whole atmosphere to change for her.
Alan, who shared many traits with him, frightened her
a little because he was so formidable, but Jack scored
heavily because he was so approachable, so determinedly human.

I could not love Alan, only admire and fear him,
but Jack…and then self-analysis stopped because in
the end her body, as well as her mind, was informing
her of its needs, and this was a new thing for the cool
Miss Hope.

It was her hand now which tightened its grip on
Jack's. Her face which shone up at his and told him
what he needed to know: that what he felt for her was
reciprocated.

Aunt Percival, watching them come towards her,
knew that, at last, her beloved charge had found someone to love and treasure her as she deserved.

Chapter Six

'Uniforms! So many uniforms. There will shortly be no civilians left in Washington.'

'Come, Sophie,' said Marietta, 'that is surely an exaggeration. Even here, in the Van Horns' ballroom, there are still many men not in uniform.'

'But they're all so old,' moaned Sophie. 'There won't be any young men left when the Army marches out.'

'Unfortunately,' Aunt Percival said, 'it's the young men who fight the wars, and the old men who stay behind to organise matters.'

'Well, at least Jack won't be whisked away in uniform,' replied Sophie, looking about her. 'He said that he would be here tonight: Senator Van Horn had invited him, but I haven't seen him yet.'

'Not surprising,' said Marietta. 'I've never seen such a crowd—even at the Van Horns'.' The Senator and his wife were famous for the size and magnificence of their entertaining, but this surely beat everything. It simply bore out what her father had said earlier: that when the war began there would be more, not less, entertaining and excitement.

The small orchestra in the corner began to play a waltz and Sophie was soon whirled on to the floor by a succession of handsome young army officers. Marietta, as usual, sat herself down and prepared to be an interested spectator, not a participant in the gaiety.

She was not to remain a spectator for long. Avory Grant was crossing the floor to her. He was wearing the blue uniform of an officer in the Union Army, and he was smiling at her when he reached her.

'Will you do me the honour of dancing this waltz with me, Marietta? For old times' sake?'

She rose and offered him her hand, saying, 'Since you put it so prettily, then certainly, sir.'

He laughed at that, transforming his face so that he looked young again. 'I see that in my absence you have learned to flirt. You were a solemn young lady when last we met. What man has brought about this transformation?—one which I was unable to accomplish.'

Marietta blushed. It was Jack, of course, but she could hardly say so.

'Oh, one changes as one grows older.'

'True,' he said, twirling her round the floor, 'but you have changed very much for the better—which, you must confess, is rare.'

'Now *you* are flirting with *me*, Avory. We have both changed for the better, I think, since the old days—if you will allow me to say so.'

His face changed. His smile disappeared. He looked grave. 'Marietta,' he said, 'there is something which

I ought to tell you. I would prefer you to hear it from me rather than from some gossiping old crow.'

He spun her off the floor and into a double doorway which led to a corridor before he stopped, to look seriously at her.

'Has no one informed you of how my wife died?'

Marietta was for once at a loss. 'No, Avory. Only that she had. Why?'

'I thought that you might have heard,' he said. 'I forgot how long I have been living away from Washington, lost to the world I once knew. I have rarely corresponded with anyone. The occasion of her death was not a pretty one, and I must be the one to tell you of it.'

'Oh, I am so sorry, Avory. Do not speak of it if it distresses you.'

'No need to apologise, or be sorry. She died when the carriage in which she was eloping with her lover turned over. He was so crippled that he could not walk again: she was killed instantly. Sin is rarely punished so rapidly.'

His voice when he said this was unemotional, as though he were speaking of someone else's tragedy. 'Fortunately she did not take our daughter, Susanna, with her. My only grief in joining the Union Army is that I have had to leave her behind.'

Marietta had been imagining him happily married while she vegetated in spinsterhood. She wondered what their lives would have been like if she had married him.

'I thought it best not to tell you on a ballroom floor, but I had to forestall others who might gossip unkindly to you,' he added. 'What's past is past and regret is a useless emotion.'

He held out his hand to her. 'Let us hope that the music has not stopped but, if it has, then I claim the next dance with you.'

The music had not stopped, and he swung her around as though their waltz had not been interrupted. Marietta thought that his story explained the change in his manner and appearance. He had been a light-hearted cheerful boy when she had known him. Now he was a serious man.

They ended their dance near to where Aunt Percival sat. She had been joined by Jack, who was obviously entertaining her since she was laughing—something which she did not often do.

Jack rose and offered Marietta his chair. His manner to her was faintly proprietorial in order to let this handsome young officer know of his interest in her.

If Avory noticed it, he made no sign. Marietta said easily, 'Avory, I must present you to a new friend whom you just missed meeting at the Bazaar. May I introduce to you Mr Jack Dilhorne, who hails from New South Wales and is by way of being an expert in naval architecture? Mr Avory Grant,' she explained to Jack who was busy, like Avory, in following society's prescribed rules for a first meeting, 'is an old friend of my youth who moved to the Carolinas on marriage.'

'Not so much old, perhaps…' Avory smiled '…as no longer young. Only in Washington, I suppose, could one meet someone from the Antipodes at one's first social engagement.'

'Oh, all the world makes for the States these days,' Jack said, wondering exactly what Marietta meant by 'old friend' in this context. 'You mentioned the Carolinas: a friend of mine from England is thinking of travelling there. He is interested in naval architecture, too. We heard today that their experimental iron-clad, the *Merrimac*, which was scuttled when the Norfolk Navy yard was attacked, has been raised from the sea bottom and is going to be rebuilt.'

'True,' said Avory, 'but although I have lived in the South for the last ten years, my family home is near Washington and my heart is with the Union. My aunt has come back with me and will be settling at Grantstown with my little daughter for the duration of the war. I have left a factor behind to manage my Carolina estate.'

'You must visit us before you leave for the war,' Marietta told him. 'My father will be pleased to see you again.'

'And we must meet at Willard's to celebrate another new friendship for me,' Jack said. He wanted to know more about the handsome stranger who was looking at Marietta so admiringly.

'Indeed,' replied Avory, 'although I fear that my stay in Washington may not be long.' He bowed to them again. 'You will excuse me, I trust; there are a number of my old friends present tonight and this may be the last occasion when I shall have the chance to meet them.'

'He is greatly improved,' said Aunt Percival thoughtfully, after Avory had left them. 'He was, I remember, a callow young man, whose only notion was pleasure.'

'Yes,' said Marietta, 'but tragedy has touched him.' How to put it tactfully? 'His wife died eighteen months ago, and I gather that the marriage was not a success.'

A widower, thought Jack: intuition told him that Avory Grant and Marietta had once been close.

Sophie's return brought this line of conversation to an end. She had been giggling in the corner with some old friends of her own age, but had rushed back to be with dull Marietta and even duller Aunt Percival when she saw that not only were they entertaining Jack, but also another handsome man in uniform.

'Was that Avory Grant with you?' she exclaimed eagerly, rudely interrupting Aunt Percival who had begun to answer Marietta, for once ignoring Jack who had risen again on her arrival.

'Really, Sophie,' said Aunt Percival, 'you are old enough to remember your manners. You are no longer a child. Pray do your duty to your cousin Marietta and Mr Dilhorne.'

'Oh, pooh to that,' said Sophie scornfully. 'They can see perfectly well that I am here—and you haven't answered my question.'

'Yes, it was Mr Grant,' said Marietta mildly, anxious to avoid yet another scene, and a public one, at that, with Sophie.

'He looks divine in his blue uniform,' breathed Sophie, rapt. 'You might have kept him with you until I returned.'

Aunt Percival, less inclined to avoid a scene than

Marietta, said severely, 'Had you remained with us instead of running off and amusing yourself with heaven knows who, then you would have been here and would have been able to talk to him. As it is, you must remain content until he returns—or when he visits us, which he hopes will be soon.'

'The sooner the better,' announced Sophie gaily, not at all put down by this rebuke. 'Aren't you going to ask me to dance, Jack? I detest balls where I do nothing but sit around and watch others, don't you?'

'And what,' asked Aunt Percival belligerently, when she had dragged Jack away, 'could the poor man do after that but ask her to take the floor with him? I shan't be happy until the time comes for her parents to reclaim her and take her home again.'

'Nor I,' sighed Marietta. 'But I fear that we are saddled with her until the autumn. I never thought that she would be so unlike the rest of my cousins. It was a pleasure to look after them, but Sophie…' She shrugged, not wishing to speak the unpalatable truth about her.

Jack had not heard this exchange but he, too, felt that he was saddled with Sophie. The more he had to do with her the less he liked her. He had meant to ask Marietta to dance the next dance with him, and here he was, being bored by Sophie's constant and frivolous chatter, while Marietta sat alone.

But not, he saw, for long. Avory Grant had returned and she was on the floor with him—again. He would have a quiet word with Aunt Percival and try to discover whether Grant could be considered a rival. He was well aware that Aunt Percival approved of him—

but would she approve of Marietta's old friend even more?

Sophie had been talking rapidly to him and was obviously expecting a reply. He really ought to pay attention to her. As usual she was complaining about something.

'I thought that at least the war would be exciting once it had begun,' she was saying petulantly, 'but it is nearly as boring now it has come as it was when we endlessly talked about it coming. You must consider yourself lucky that you are not an American since, if you were, you would soon be in uniform and disappearing, hopefully not for good.'

'On the other hand,' Jack told her quietly, 'it makes me feel guilty to know that I am safe when others are going to put themselves at risk for what they believe in.'

'Goodness,' said Sophie. 'It's not your war, is it? You ought to be glad you're out of it.'

'No,' said Jack, still quiet, 'it's not, but I might yet play some part in it. The President has invited me to a meeting at the Capitol tomorrow which is to discuss what he calls ''The Naval Question''. After that, who knows what I may be doing.'

All this was too much for Sophie. She hadn't asked Jack to dance with her in order to discuss dull questions—even if it were President Lincoln asking them!

She yawned. 'Goodness,' she exclaimed again. 'How serious we are getting! I hope that all balls aren't going to be like this one. Perhaps when the war's been going for a few months we shall forget it and find other things to talk about.'

'Perhaps,' said Jack, wondering how he could ever have been attracted to her. A few moments later, the dance over, she dragged him to where Avory Grant and Marietta were talking.

Jack took the opportunity to whisper to Marietta, 'You will dance the next one with me, I hope.'

She looked at him, genuine disappointment written on her face. 'Oh, dear, I shall have to refuse you. Charles Stanton is here and has already asked me. He leaves for the South in the morning, he says.'

Well, Charles could scarcely be described as a rival, particularly as he was on his way out of Marietta's life, so Jack swallowed his disappointment with a smile.

'The one after that, then.'

'Agreed,' said Marietta, who would rather have danced with Jack than with Charles, who was already approaching her to claim her as his partner.

They were halfway through their dance when he said to her, 'If I asked you if I might speak privately to you for a few minutes, would you refuse me?'

It was an odd way, Marietta thought, to ask such a question. On the other hand, it was typical of Charles's pleasantly reserved manner. He never took anything for granted and she had already noticed with what careful consideration he always behaved towards others.

'No,' she told him. 'I would not refuse you because I know you well enough now to understand that your request is a serious one.'

'Excellent,' he said in his calm way. 'Perhaps when this dance is over we could find somewhere quiet

where we could talk for a moment and not be interrupted.'

Marietta could not but be surprised at the interesting
fact that this was the second occasion this evening on
which a gentleman had made such a request of her,
and she wondered what the gist of it would be this
time. The dance over, she led him to the ante-room
where she had spoken with Avory. He beckoned her
to a chair but refused to seat himself, standing before
her, his grave face even graver than usual.

'First of all,' he began, 'I must inform you that were
it not apparent that your affections are engaged else-
where I would have attempted to woo and win you
for myself. It is rare to find in one person all the traits
which I most admire in women. Had I met you before
Jack did, then I would not have hesitated to press my
suit but, knowing you both, and admiring him as well
as his brother, I decided to stand back. Having said
that, and wishing you both well, I feel compelled to
tell you of something which is troubling me.'

He paused before continuing. 'It grieves me to have
to do so, for two reasons. The first is that it concerns
a relative of yours, and the second is that I may be
wrong, but I fear that I am not. It is this. I have noted
the manner in which your cousin Sophie looks at you
and Jack when she thinks that no one is watching her.
I would ask you to be on your guard where she is
concerned. Having come to know her, I believe that
she would not hesitate to injure in some manner either
or both of you.

'Take care, Miss Marietta. If you were a man I
would say, Watch your back. I regret to say that I

believe that there is a strain of viciousness in her such that she would stop at nothing if she thought that she could injure you. You may dismiss what I have to say as moon madness, but I beg that you will not. I shall not speak of this again, nor shall I mention it to Jack. I have only spoken to you of it on this, my last night in Washington, and that with the greatest reluctance.'

Marietta hardly knew what to say to him. 'I think, perhaps,' she ventured hesitantly, 'that her bark is worse than her bite. Oh, she is rude to me, I know, but I cannot believe that she would do anything actually wicked—which is what you are suggesting.'

He bowed to her. 'Your goodness does you credit, Marietta. I can only pray that you are right.' He leaned forward and took her hand which, unconsciously, she was twisting in her lap.

'You will allow,' he said softly, and kissed the back of it before relinquishing it. 'I wish you well, and Jack, too, and trust that I am wrong. Honour demands that I leave you once I have returned you to Miss Percival. I may not speak more with you.'

Marietta watched him go, straight-backed and tall, and wondered whether she would ever meet him again. He had hardly left her before Sophie rounded on her.

'That was Charles Stanton with you, wasn't it?' she exclaimed. 'Thank goodness he's off to the South. I shall be spared his frozen face and his boring conversation.'

She could scarcely have said anything more calculated to make Marietta wonder whether Charles's doom-laden warnings about her should be given any credence. The arrival of Jack, ready to claim his dance with her, drove Charles and Sophie out of her head. Long afterwards she was to ask herself whether her introduction to passion had made her unwary, had given her the illusion that happy endings, particularly for herself and Jack, were easy, and that Charles was exaggerating what he thought that he had seen.

Held lightly in Jack's arms, enjoying the dance and its music, Marietta surrendered to life's pleasures— something which she had rarely ever done before, and had never thought that she would.

Sophie's moanings about the war were reinforced when Washington became even more a city under siege. After the Southern sympathisers had flocked out of it, profiteers and entrepreneurs flocked in. Behind them came a large train of women, there to serve the needs of the vast body of unattached men who filled the city and found themselves idle before the fighting began.

Expensive and stately, poor and cringing, their advertisements in the daily papers made their presence known to the virtuous women of Washington. For her part Marietta found it difficult to pretend that they did not exist, nor that they were not necessary—opinions which, of course, she could not voice.

Jack privately commented to the Senator one day that only in the United States would such services be openly acknowledged, to be met with the Senator's wry answer, 'At least, sir, we do not pretend that these women have no existence, which I believe is the attitude taken in Britain and its colonies.'

The coonskin-hatted gentleman, Brutus M. Clay, of

Kaintuck, or Kentucky, whom Alan had imitated on that famous night at Willard's, went so far as to set up a Strangers' Guard, a group of vigilantes led by himself, all handsomely equipped with Bowie knives as well as hats like his. They were dedicated to maintaining law and order, as well as being ready to save Washington from subversive attack.

'An attack from what?' joked Jack when he heard the news. 'One might rather think that Washington might need a guard to protect it from *him*!'

'Oh, but,' said Senator Hope quietly, 'little though I like the man, there are many here who privately sympathise with the South, and who knows what might happen if the South suddenly seemed to be winning the war? If Clay discourages them, all to the good.'

Not for the first time Jack was compelled to face the difference between Transatlantic and European manners. There was an initiative, a sense of doing what one had to do without overmuch deference to normal forms. The frontier was never far away. Behaviour in New South Wales, he felt, lay somewhere between the two extremes.

He said so to Marietta one morning. He had driven her, the Senator and Sophie to Pennsylvania Avenue, there to cheer the entry into the capital of the 7th New York Regiment.

'They look like the Praetorian guard of ancient Rome come to life again,' said the Senator when watching them march past. Like many of America's rulers, he was fond of a classic turn of phrase and not afraid to use it in private as well as in public.

There, on that bright morning, in the first fever of the war, when few had seen action and scarcely any lives had been lost, the soldiers were received hysterically. Even Marietta forgot that she was a lady and cheered them, there in the street, forgetting all etiquette. Only Jack, not so emotionally committed to the war, was left to wonder how many of the smiling boys, received with such ecstatic delight, would survive the months of fighting to come.

For the moment, however, no one was fighting and dying near Washington. Not only were the soldiers' uniforms bright and unspotted, but their presence had the charm of novelty—a novelty which would be lost when the war became bloody and brutal and dragged on and on.

For the present, though, all was new and exciting, and even when President Lincoln took on the powers of a dictator no one complained: it was the necessities of war which had compelled him, after all. Normal democratic procedures took too long, and when Lincoln realised that iron-clad warships would never be built if their orderly but slow democratic procession through various committees was adhered to, he promptly side-tracked everyone and everything by setting up a final committee and telling them to get on with the business at once.

'Instanter,' Jack said, laughing, when he told Senator Hope the news on his return from the Capitol. He and Butler had been summoned there to give expert advice. 'That was the word the President used to urge the legislators on. Several senior Civil Servants nearly dropped dead on the spot from shock. It appears that he thinks that it would be a good thing if they did. Once dead, they couldn't thwart him. After it was over he gave immediate orders for the building of an iron-clad to go ahead once a special panel has decided which submitted design to use. Ezra and I think that the order is sure to go to John Ericsson and the New York yards because only they have the ability to build something so innovatory.'

'You will be leaving us, then,' said the Senator.

Jack nodded. 'Not immediately. The Secretary of State has asked me to be the only civilian member of the largely Naval special panel. After that I shall leave to work with whoever wins the order. I hope that it will be Ericsson. I also have to gain permission from Ezra to go to New York. He's a bit of a traditionalist, wedded to wooden ships, but even he can see where the future lies, so I'm sure he'll give it.'

Sophie, who was present, yawned her boredom while the others talked enthusiastically about the war and its ramifications. Jack's enthusiasm particularly made her want to scream. What made everything worse was that she had patently lost him—to Marietta of all people; there could be no doubt of that. All that he wanted to do these days was talk to her about the most boring things under the sun.

How could someone as attractive as Jack *want* to talk for hours on end to that plain stick? He hardly knew that Sophie existed any more. He had eyes, ears and tongue only for her—and the war, the dratted war, of course.

Marietta, on the other hand, was delighted for him. The only fly in her ointment was that he would shortly be leaving Washington.

* * *

Ezra Butler made no bones about Jack leaving him to work with Ericsson in New York. 'All the better for the peace when it comes,' he said. 'We shall be up to date, our know-how will equal anyone's.'

'True,' replied Jack. 'It wouldn't do for Butler and Rutherfurd's to be left behind when the world turns and iron ships rule the seas. I am quite determined to work with you when that happens. I am applying for American citizenship.'

Ezra looked at him and thought of Jack's father, and thought, too, of how much he resembled him, although he would never be quite as cunning: Jack was too good-natured.

'I'm willing to offer you a full partnership,' he said, thinking of Jack's wealth as well as his know-how. 'If you've half your pa's savvy you'll be a real acquisition—and God help our rivals.'

'Oh, I'm not the Patriarch,' said Jack gaily. 'There'll never be another like him.'

It was a judgement which he was to remember years later, in very different circumstances, when he was compelled to acknowledge ruefully that foretelling the future is a tricky business—particularly when the Patriarch's unlikely re-incarnation had not even been born!

'We are, of course,' he added, 'assuming that the North will win the war.'

'Not a doubt of it,' asserted Ezra robustly. 'It will take some time, though. There are fools who think that one big battle will end it soon. Besides, we're not as ready as they are. I heard today that General Beauregard and his Secessionist army are only thirty miles away, and our troops are even greener and more raw than his are, and that is saying something! I fear that there will be a battle soon and that the North will not win it. On the other hand, the longer the war lasts the more certain we are to win it, and the less the South's chances are.'

Jack nodded agreement. He, too, had been listening to the generals and politicians talking.

'There is one point which is worth considering. If the Southern army is so near to Washington and it does win a major battle, what is to prevent Beauregard from advancing on the capital and taking it—and so ending the war in their favour before it has even begun?'

'There is that,' said Ezra, nodding. 'But my bones say otherwise.'

'Mine, too. Let us hope that they are speaking the truth—even if that means that we shall have a long and difficult road to travel before peace is restored.'

Neither Jack nor Ezra shared in the foolish optimism with which the majority of Washington's citizens faced the coming war. Jack wondered how long it would be before he saw Marietta again once he had left for New York. Never before had the prospect of leaving a woman behind touched his heart.

How was it that I was once able to love 'em and leave 'em so easily? And that is not a difficult question to answer: I hadn't met Marietta Hope then!

Chapter Seven

'Really, Mama, it is more than time that we had the battle which will end this war,' announced Sophie. 'All the eligible men have left to fight it and only the dull and the crippled remain behind. Thank God Jack hasn't gone to New York yet. At least I have one healthy partner left to dance with.'

July had arrived and Jack was still in Washington. Despite the President's cutting of constitutional corners, it had taken quite a long time for designs for a new iron-clad warship to be submitted and examined. Neither had the war progressed in any material fashion. General Beauregard still sat and faced Washington, maintaining an ever-present threat. He was waiting for General Joe Johnston to bring up enough troops from the South by using the nearby railroad to make an assault on the capital possible.

Mrs Hamilton Hope said indulgently, 'Well, count your blessings then, my dear. Your papa tells me that the committee are near to reaching a conclusion and it may not be long before Mr Dilhorne leaves Washington.'

'What a bore,' wailed Sophie angrily. Marietta, sitting in a corner, engaged in canvas work, was grateful that she was no longer responsible for her. Sophie's parents, Mr and Mrs Hamilton Hope, had retreated to the capital from their Maryland estate whose safety they thought was threatened by the nearness of raiding Southern troops. Senator Hope had left for Boston on business while Aunt Percival had been called upon to act as midwife for yet another Percival relation, so that she, too, was absent from Washington.

Consequently Marietta had moved in to the Hamilton Hopes' residence at their request. 'You cannot be left on your own in that great house, child,' Mrs Hope had exclaimed, as though Marietta was no older, nor more responsible, than Sophie herself. 'You must come and stay with us.'

It would have been impolite to refuse, little though Marietta wished to leave her own well-run, comfortable home. She also missed Aunt Percival's earthy common sense, which had little patience with Sophie's whim whams, as she called them.

Aunt Percival, indeed, would have had little truck with Sophie's latest proposal with which she was now bombarding her parents. She had been visiting Senator Eakins's daughter Charlotte and was big with news.

'The Senator says that at last something exciting is going to happen. It is nothing less than a great battle near Centerville which will end this horrid war. General McDowell is on the march and the Senator is going to take Charlotte and her mama to watch the battle, and he has suggested that Papa might like to take us all along with them. Do say yes, Papa, we may never get the chance again if we whip the Rebs straight away, for the Senator says that if we do—and we're sure to—the war will end immediately.'

Neither Sophie's father nor her mother ever opposed her wishes in anything, not even when it concerned such a dubious scheme as Marietta thought this to be. Like most of their friends, they had no notion of what war, or a battle, was really like, and when it became apparent that the majority of their circle was preparing to ride out to watch one they, too, decided to have a ringside seat. This was a frequent expression which Hamilton Hope used when he was talking to his friends in what he thought was a manly fashion.

Marietta's protests were in vain. She had no wish to see the battle herself, and thought that it was neither safe nor proper for the Hopes to indulge themselves in undertaking such a dangerous expedition.

'People will be killed,' she said earnestly. 'We might even get caught up in the battle itself. I am sure that when we have arrived there—if we arrive there safely—we shall not like what we are sure to see.'

'Oh, you are always a spoilsport,' exclaimed Sophie crossly. 'The first time anything interesting happens you wish to put a damper on it. You really are a wet blanket, Marietta.'

Her annoyance with Marietta since Jack had defected to her could not be contained: it burst out all the time.

It was useless for Marietta to argue, to talk of blood, broken limbs and death.

'We shall not really be very near,' said Hamilton Hope comfortably, 'and if it looks as though it may be growing dangerous we shall leave instanter, you may be sure of that.'

'But it is not an entertainment,' said Marietta desperately. 'Young men will be dying, real young men shedding real blood. It will not be a play.'

'Pooh, then,' said Sophie rudely. 'You need not come. I would never have thought that you would be a coward, Marietta, but then, you have never done anything exciting in your whole life, have you? Life, in fact, has passed you by.' The look which she then gave Marietta was both patronising and scornful.

This stung. 'I am not a coward,' said Marietta stiffly. 'But I find the whole thing unseemly and immoral.'

'Immoral!' said Sophie, raising her eyes to heaven. 'We are fighting a war to end slavery and Marietta finds it immoral!'

The urge to slap Sophie had never been so strong, and only the presence of Sophie's doting parents restrained Marietta.

'I am sure,' said Hamilton Hope, 'that you will wish to accompany us, Marietta. It will be something for you to tell your grandchildren.' Privately, though, he thought that his ramrod-straight niece was highly unlikely to have any. What man would want such a cold piece?

It was useless, thought Marietta wearily, quite useless to continue to protest. The Hamilton Hopes were plainly going to consider it an insult to Sophie and themselves if she did not accompany them.

'Very well,' she said at last. 'I will go with you, but under protest, mind. I think that the whole expedition is quite mistaken.'

'Whoever would have thought that my brother Jacobus would have such a self-righteous and plain old maid for a daughter,' said Hamilton Hope to his wife later. 'Really, the woman is impossible. She is so sure of herself that she will be prating about Womens' Rights next!'

'I must own that I, too, am a little worried about going on such an expedition. It could be dangerous,' said his wife hesitantly, but she was not allowed to continue: Mr Hope was not to be deprived of his pleasure.

'Nonsense,' he returned robustly. 'Sophie has more spirit than both of you put together. I don't wonder that Marietta has never married. Who would want such a rigid opinionated stick? Sophie is right. And when I think of her lovely mother!' He sighed and shook his head.

Marietta wished that she could have had Jack's advice, but he had been out of Washington on business with Ezra and so had not visited the Hamilton Hopes in the week since she had been their guest. She was not to know that Jack, on his return that day, had decided to make the journey to watch the battle, not as an entertainment but because he wished to see artillery in action.

He had asked Ezra to accompany him, but Ezra had drily replied that it was enough for him to make weapons of war without wishing to watch them in action, but if Jack thought it useful to go then he wished him well.

'You are not worried about being caught up in the battle?' he asked.

'Do you think that there's much chance of that?' said Jack, who possessed a cheerful optimism which his father and older brothers had sometimes deplored.

'Depends,' said Ezra. 'Battles aren't chess games, you know. They're not orderly things. They stray about, I'm told, and are liable to start in one place and finish in another.'

'I'll take my chances,' said Jack. 'I shan't be fighting myself, and I would like to see how what we make is used. It may give me ideas for further developments.'

Later in the war he was to look back at his foolish self in some wonder: he had learned to take as few risks as possible. He would, however, have been horrified to learn that the Hamilton Hopes were going and intended to take Sophie and Marietta with them.

Fortunately for his peace of mind he remained unaware of their plans. He packed a meal of sandwiches and fruit in a canvas bag, together with a sketch book, pencils and coloured chalks. When he made his way to the livery stables to hire a carriage, he discovered that half Washington, or so it appeared, was determined to see the battle, and consequently the price of hire had risen to great heights.

Russell of *The Times* was there, trying to make his way to the battle. He was arguing vigorously with the keeper of the stables, and finally had to settle for a sum far higher than he had originally hoped for.

The keeper, however, knew Jack, and let him have something more reasonable, whispering behind his hand after Russell had gone that 'damned insolent Britishers who write unpleasant stories about our great and free nation deserve to pay over the odds for anything they want'.

Jack counted himself fortunate to end up with a buggy, a coloured boy for a driver, and a frayed-looking animal which proved to be more reliable than it looked at first sight.

The boy was a cheerful young chap who remained optimistic throughout the ups and downs of the rest of the day. He assured Jack that 'our side' would whip the Rebels so thoroughly that the war would be over before it had started, and that he wanted to be there to see this famous victory.

Jack was a little troubled by all the careless optimism flowing so freely around Washington. He thought of what Russell had privately told him and would publicly write: that the North still had no real idea of how harsh and bitter the war would inevitably be.

He was astonished by the number of carts, carriages, buggies and wagons, both privately owned and hired, which set out from Washington in the early morning sun in the wake of McDowell's troops.

He had taken the opportunity to have a private word with Russell before *The Times* man left. Russell had told him of his reservations about the civilians who were setting out so cheerfully to enjoy what they thought was going to be a day's fun.

'They should have been in the Crimea,' he said morosely, 'and have seen what happened there to civilians silly enough to want to watch a battle. War's not a picnic or a spectacle to be enjoyed, whatever ignorant fools who have never experienced it may think.'

He had already said something similar to his Washington acquaintances who had arranged to go, and they had jeered at him for being an over-cautious Brit. After that he had held his tongue. Time would show them who was right, he thought.

Riding in the middle of the concourse which was setting out so gaily were Hamilton Hope, his wife, his daughter and his niece. It was pleasant in the clear early-morning air before the day grew hot. They had had to make a prompt start to ensure that their long journey would be safely completed, leaving time for both horses and passengers to rest before returning home.

Marietta had decided that, if she were compelled to join what she thought of as an ill-advised expedition, she would at least try to savour the experience even if she thought it regrettable. Sophie had dressed herself impressively for the trip, as though she were going to a ball. She was wearing an elaborate white dress over a crinoline cage so large that she took up most of the carriage. Her shoes were of light kid, almost slippers.

She jeered openly at Marietta who was wearing a plain dark dress with few skirts and no crinoline cage, as well as sturdy, sensible walking shoes. Marietta said quietly in reply to her cousin's criticisms that it was possible that she might need to be able to walk unhampered.

'We are riding in a carriage,' said Sophie severely. 'I do not intend to walk.'

'Who knows what we might need to do before the day is over?' countered Marietta.

The Hopes had taken an enormous amount of food with them, enough for a banquet, and Marietta privately thought that the whole thing was most improper, never mind the fact that many others, including Senators and Congressmen as well as their wives and children, had come along on the outing similarly laden.

The day grew hotter as they rolled along the dusty roads, and she tried not to think of all the vibrant young men who would be dead by nightfall. They were still some distance from the supposed site of the battle when they first heard the distant thunder of cannon. Although low and muted, it was insistent and non-stop.

Nothing deterred the sensation-seekers from Washington. They pressed on towards Centerville, finding when at last they reached it that it was a small sleepy hamlet, barely a town, which had been elevated into history by the chance of the main Confederate attack being near it.

Like many of the small towns in the district it had been looted by the very Union troops supposedly sent to protect it, but this didn't stop its inhabitants from cheering everyone and everything which passed through, including the many civilians who had been arriving since early morning.

Sophie looked around her. Her face, which had been one smile when they set out, had grown increasingly worried when the noise of the cannon grew louder and louder. She was relieved to discover that beyond Centerville was a hill, the only high ground in the area, and it was here that the Hope party found that the spectators' carriages were already drawn up. Below the hill the battle was already raging, and a mob of men stood around the carriages trying to make out exactly what was happening through the trees, the scrub and the several miles which stood between them and the armies of the North and the South.

'Time to get out and stretch our legs,' said Hamilton Hope cheerfully, 'and have a bite to eat.'

'Oh, need I get down, Papa?' wailed Sophie. 'I would much prefer to stay where I am. They are saying that there is little to see as yet. I do so hope that we've not come all this way for nothing.'

Marietta, despite her reservations, was curious enough to be helped down to walk to the point where most of the spectators were gathered, talking, eating and drinking as though they were at a ball or a reception. She had expected to see blood and destruction everywhere, but Sophie was right: little was visible from where they stood.

An observation balloon, tethered to a cart, was the subject of much interest and comment, much of it ribald—but its occupants could probably see more than the representatives of Washington society who had made this long and tiring journey apparently only to admire the scenery.

Suddenly puffs of smoke, both black and white, rose above the trees and the cannons' roar grew louder and louder. Lines of soldiers, clad in blue and grey, appeared out of the murk below them, only to disappear again.

'How very disappointing,' drawled one middle-aged Senator. 'It's almost impossible to tell what, if anything, is happening.'

Sophie and Aunt Serena Hope had joined them from the carriage. Aunt Serena had brought her opera glasses with her, and occasionally passed them to Marietta and her daughter, but little more could be seen with them than without them. After a time some of the men offered learned—and patronising—explanations of the course of the battle to the women, although how accurate they were, since little could be seen, Marietta found it hard to tell.

Sophie was no happier out of the carriage than in it. She could hardly have said herself what it was that she had expected to see, but, as was common with her, she soon became bored.

Marietta, on the other hand, was trying to understand everything about her. Among the growing crowd of spectators were foreign diplomats, as well as many of her Washington friends, who had made this hazardous trip. Unlike Sophie, they were determined to enjoy themselves even though, in their ignorance of the unseen death and mutilation below them, they found the whole experience anti-climactic.

Sophie, indeed, complained bitterly that so far she

had seen nothing but puffs of smoke and trees, as well as a few men vanishing into the distance. 'If it were not for the trees,' she sighed, 'we might have had a better notion of what was happening.'

Marietta, however, was grateful at not having to witness the gory details of the actual fighting, and could only wonder how Sophie, who screamed at a bleeding finger, would react if the battle drew near enough for her to make out the shattered limbs and the broken bodies which must surely lie below them.

What none of them understood when they opened their hampers and picnicked on the grass was that the battle was beginning to move towards them while the Northern troops fell slowly back.

Jack and Russell were now on the edge of the battle area itself, which was being fought around Bull Run stream, or Manassas as it was sometimes called. Russell had led a horse with him and was determined to get into the thick of things, particularly since various senior officers had confidently informed him that 'our side is whipping Johnny Reb' when his experiences in the recent Crimean War led him to believe that quite the opposite was happening!

Jack, being an innocent in these matters, had no idea who was in the right, but he was worried that the noise of battle was growing nearer and nearer when, if the North was winning, it ought to be diminishing. What surprised him, as it surprised the watchers on the hill, was how aimless it seemed to be. He had, quite wrongly, visualised something neat and tidy taking place. Instead, all was haphazard: parties of men ran across his line of sight; occasionally a troop of horsemen emerged from the grey and black smoke—only to disappear again.

A little time later Russell disappeared, too. He mounted his horse and rode off into the thick of things in order to have something tangible to put in his despatch. When, in the early afternoon, it became quite plain that the battle was drawing nearer and nearer, Jack ordered his horse and buggy to be ready for a rapid departure. He was beginning to suspect that Russell had been right and that the rebels were winning.

Above him the spectators were still in a state of innocent optimism, believing that the battle was almost won. They were joined by a group of senior officers who assured Hamilton Hope that all was well.

'We shall shortly have them on the run,' one of them said importantly, 'and after that, the way to Virginia and victory will lie clear before us. It won't be long before we can all go home.'

Everyone around him began to cheer, quite unaware that at that very moment the Southern troops had broken Northern resistance, and that the home army was retreating across the turnpike road which they had crossed to get at the Rebels' batteries. Instead, it was the Northern batteries which had been captured and consequently a massive general retreat had begun; a retreat which neither General McDowell nor his officers could control.

Once started, the retreat took on a life of its own. Shell-shocked officers and men began to make for the rear, carrying all before them: caissons, supply wagons, the commissariat, medical carts and orderlies, everything streaming madly back towards Centerville and the hope of safety.

The spectators from Washington lay directly in their path and were quite unaware that a massive retreat, involving the whole Union Army, had begun. At first they merely saw small groups of men walking listlessly away from the action, heads hanging. An odd wagon careered by. So far the battle had seemed so inconsequential that no one realised exactly what was happening.

Suddenly a group of men, mixed up with every different kind of conveyance, came towards them at the run, shouting, 'Git, darn yer, git. We're whipped, we're whipped.'

Men were throwing their weapons away in order to make their flight from certain death the more rapid. Some of them, hampered by the spectators who still did not fully understand what was happening, shook their fists at them as they passed, cursing them for their presence, for being in the way of their retreat from the intolerable which lay behind them.

The spectators, realising at last that the supposed victory had turned into a rout, ran towards their carriages, shouting to the drivers to point them towards home and prepare to leave at once.

Marietta's party had been sitting at some distance from the Hopes' carriage when the unthinkable began to happen. They dashed towards it; Hamilton Hope was the first to reach it. He climbed in and, taking the reins from the driver, began to wheel it rapidly in the direction of Washington, shouting to the others to hurry up and jump aboard.

Marietta, already prepared, pushed her Aunt Serena into the carriage, before turning back for Sophie— only to discover that she had mislaid her bonnet, taken off when the sun had moved away from them, and was hunting about for it.

'Leave it,' exclaimed Marietta impatiently. 'We've no time to lose,' and when Sophie wailed 'No' and ran away from her, she seized her hand and began to drag her towards the carriage and safety. She was hampered in this not only by Sophie's crinoline cage, which restrained her movements, but also by Sophie's determination to take her time since she was more annoyed by Marietta's urgency than by the approaching danger.

So much so that, although Hamilton Hope was shouting to them to hurry, they were still outside the carriage when a wagon, out of control, careered by with soldiers hanging out of it. Its driver was purple in the face and desperate, and on seeing that the Hopes' carriage was directly in its path he shouted, 'Out of my way, damn you,' and brought his whip down, hard, on the flank of the nearest Hope horse.

With a shrill neigh the horse bolted, taking the carriage with it, instantly to be carried away in the midst of the struggling mass of men and wagons. Within seconds it was lost to Sophie's and Marietta's sight, its driver unable to return to help or to collect them.

Sophie began to scream, only for the sound to be lost in the thunder of the retreat gathering pace around them. Marietta, terrified that the pair of them would be trampled underfoot, tried to push Sophie off the road. Behind them the bellowing guns had moved up, and were now firing directly at them. Sophie screamed again when a shell landed among the crowd of men and conveyances in their rear, leaving the dead and dying sprawling on the road.

Marietta, indeed, tried to keep her head while Sophie progressively lost hers. There was no question of regaining the Hopes' carriage, and chivalry had died in the *sauve qui peut* of the general retreat. Holding Sophie firmly by the hand, she pushed and shoved her way through the cursing mob, trying to avoid being run down by men on horseback, and by men driving carts and carriages of all description.

In the general panic no one made any attempt to assist the two helpless women: it was doubtful, indeed, whether anyone actually registered their presence. In the end Marietta forced the pair of them off the road in an attempt to reach the open fields beyond, where they might not be trampled in the rush.

Sophie's screaming, alternated with sobbing, was now continuous but somehow Marietta managed to drag her to the edge of a cornfield through which parties of frantic soldiers were running in an attempt to escape from the dreadful battle which had been raging since dawn.

As soon as they stopped Sophie sat down, shouting at Marietta, 'Whatever you say, I can't run any more. I can't, I can't. I shall wait here until Papa comes for me.'

'You must carry on walking,' said Marietta, still panting from the effort of trying to save them both.

'If you want to escape death or dishonour—or perhaps both, since your father is, by now, far ahead of us and unable to turn back. You will find it easier to run if you take off your crinoline cage and gather up your skirts.'

Far from calming Sophie, this useful advice set her screaming again. The tears running down her face, she demanded her father, her mother, anyone and anything which would deliver her from this nightmare.

Exasperated, Marietta said, as reasonably as she could, 'Since there is no one here to save us, Sophie, we must try to save ourselves and we shan't do that by crying and lamenting. We must try to be practical.'

This didn't answer, either. The bravado which Sophie had assumed since dawn, and before the rout began, had quite disappeared. It had been lost at the moment when she was confronted with the stark realities of war. Left to herself, she would have stayed on the ground and refused to rise. Someone else must save her, preferably a man, and certainly not Marietta, whom she resented more bitterly than ever for her brave attempts to save them both from a terrible fate.

She underestimated her cousin's determination to survive. Marietta pulled Sophie to her feet, slapped her hard on the cheek and began to lift her skirts in order to rip the crinoline cage from her.

Sophie's screams stopped. She shrieked at her cousin, 'You beast, you beast, you hit me,' but she consented at last to help Marietta to untie her crinoline cage. She stepped out of it and, complaining bitterly, allowed Marietta to use her sash to tie up her skirts so that she could walk more freely.

They set off again. Marietta gripped Sophie's hand as firmly as she could, while Sophie howled at her, 'I shall never forgive you for hitting me, never. No, never,' before wrenching her hand away and sitting down again.

'Oh, damn that,' said Marietta, forgetting everything ladylike by which she had always lived. 'Think rather how we are to get home again—and we shan't do that by cursing each other.'

She took Sophie's hand again, pulled her to her feet, and began to drag her along in the direction in which she thought Centerville lay. If they could reach there they might yet survive—but it would have to be by their own efforts: the retreating troops were ignoring their plight, concerned only with trying to save themselves.

They walked and stumbled for about a mile with Marietta taking progressively more and more of Sophie's weight, occasionally half-carrying her. The further Marietta led them away from the road where they might be trapped, the rougher the ground grew until they came to one of the many shallow streams for which the district was famous.

Sophie collapsed on to the bank. Exhaustion was preventing her from screaming. She whispered in a dull, defeated voice, 'I really can't go any further. You can't ask me to. Someone will have to carry me across the water.'

Marietta's patience snapped again. Dragging Sophie along was tiring her to the point of collapse, but somehow she had, so far, managed to find a reserve of strength which she had not known she possessed. Despite her dislike for her cousin, she had no wish to save herself and return to Washington on her own, leaving Sophie behind to suffer whatever doom awaited her.

She hauled Sophie to her feet, and shook her violently, shouting into her face, 'If you won't try to save your own life, at least think a little of mine. I didn't even want to come on this stupid expedition, and if you won't help yourself I shall leave you here to be a plaything for the Rebel soldiers when they capture you.'

Sophie was so astonished by Marietta's ferocity that she allowed herself to be dragged into the water. Both of them slipped and stumbled on the stones, their skirts growing progressively heavier as they worked their way across the stream. Sophie's light shoes were useless for this sort of work and Marietta's own strong pair fared little better: they were not intended for a forced march across open country.

Their dreadful walk now began to take its toll on Marietta. Her strength was gradually being drained by the efforts of supporting her cousin, who was still making so little effort to help herself. Both women were bathed in sweat; their wet hair clung to their heads and faces, their clothing to their bodies; their feet were blistered and their breathing had turned into a desperate loud panting.

Marietta dared not allow them to rest, for she was fearful that if they stopped Sophie would not be able to start again; only the knowledge that the Confederate Army was hard on their heels kept her going. Once they had left the stream behind she saw that the traffic on the road had slackened a little.

There had been a break in the retreat, caused later, she was to find, by the road bridge, further downstream from where they had crossed, being hit by a shell, thus splitting the retreat into two. It also meant that gun and private carriages were stranded on the wrong side from Washington. At the time, seeing that the retreating crowd had thinned, Marietta steered Sophie back towards the road where walking would be easier for them.

And then the unbelievable happened.

Marietta heard her name being called.

She turned in the direction of the sound to see, of all people in the world, Jack Dilhorne.

Jack, who had left the field when it became apparent that the Union Army had lost the battle, had been caught up in the mêlée, but had fortunately managed to cross the bridge just before it was hit. He had stopped for a moment in order to allow both his horse and driver to rest when he had seen two women walking in the cornfield adjacent to the road.

To his horror he recognised Marietta and Sophie. He stood up and waved and shouted to them, calling Marietta's name in desperation. How, in God's name, and by what means, had they come to be here, caught in the general rout—and alone?

The feeling of relief which swept over him when he finally caught Marietta's attention was almost overwhelming in its strength. Sophie he barely recognised, so bedraggled and filthy was her appearance.

Jack's face was white with shock. It was bad

enough to find himself caught up in the retreat, being fired at by the enemy, but to discover that Marietta was lost in it, too, almost overwhelmed him.

'What in the world are you doing here, Marietta?' he exclaimed when the two women reached the buggy. 'And Sophie, also,' he added the last almost as an afterthought as he jumped from the buggy to help the two exhausted women into it.

'Too long a story to tell you now,' panted Marietta, helping him to lift Sophie into the vehicle, using her last reserves of strength to do so. Sophie could not speak at all. The sight of Jack had set her crying, from relief this time, for here at last was the saviour for whom she had been waiting: a man to see her safely home—and save her from Marietta.

All three of them were light-headed from relief and exhaustion after the terrible events of the long day. Marietta clung to Jack's hand when he helped her into the carriage: seeing him was manna in the desert for her. She now had someone who would help her to reach home safely—God willing.

She explained briefly that Hamilton Hope had brought them to see the battle and how they had come to be lost and abandoned in the thick of the rout.

'You are not hurt, Marietta?' he said when she had finished, again adding as an afterthought, 'And Sophie, too.'

Sophie who was beginning to recover a little, was enraged that he had taken so little notice of her—he seemed to have eyes only for Marietta. She said in an angry voice, 'Oh, do let us get away. This is no time for billing and cooing. We are not safe; the enemy is almost upon us.'

Jack ignored her until he saw Marietta comfortably seated before ordering the boy to drive on. His evident concern for her cousin started Sophie sobbing again. He turned to her, saying, 'Are you hurt, Sophie? I wouldn't like to stop the carriage, but if its motion troubles you—'

She interrupted him, muttering, 'Only my face. It's only my face which hurts me. She hit me. Marietta hit me—here,' and put her hand on to her cheek.

'Oh, goodness,' exclaimed Marietta. 'I only did so to make you take off your crinoline cage so that you would be able to walk more easily. If I hadn't, we should both have been captured by the rebels by now, and what do you think would have happened to us then?'

Sophie ignored this, putting out her hand to show it to Jack. 'And she hurt my wrist when she pulled me along—look, she bruised it.'

It was true that her hand and wrist were scarlet, but that was because of the strength which Marietta had needed to use to drag her to safety since she had refused to help herself.

Jack, who had seen Marietta pulling her along when he had first caught sight of them, said to her as gently as he could, 'I'm sure that Marietta was doing all she could to get you safely home.'

Sophie's sniffles grew louder and she began to shiver dramatically. 'And I'm so cold and wet because she dragged me through the stream as well.'

Nothing would silence her. Jack took off his coat

and put it around her shoulders in order to quieten her
as much as to warm her. He ordered the boy to take
off his jacket and give it to Marietta so that she could
be protected as well. He was quite aware that only
Marietta's courage and determination had brought the
two women to a place where they could be rescued,
and that she had succeeded in doing so without Sophie's co-operation.

More and more he was coming to admire her as
well as love her: it was difficult to tell where one
feeling ended and the other began. How could the
Hopes have been so foolish as to take her to watch a
battle—and then lose her? She was sitting quietly
now, still composed, her face white except for the
mauve smudges of exhaustion about her eyes and
mouth.

After a time Sophie fell into a dazed sleep, worn
out by the long day and its horrors. Jack took Marietta's hand into his own, and when she, too, slept, it
was on his shoulder, his arm now around hers, until
they reached the outskirts of Washington where he
gently roused her, leaving Sophie to sleep until they
reached the Hamilton Hopes' doorway.

When, carried along by the rout, they arrived back
in Washington, the Hopes had been almost beside
themselves. Hamilton Hope had tried to turn back
when they had reached Centerville, only to be prevented by the military. Belatedly they had now recognised that the presence of civilians on the battlefield
had been a mistake, and were busily engaged in mov-

ing them on without consideration for wealth, position or senatorial rank.

To Hamilton's plea that his daughter and niece were lost, he was told that even more dead and wounded had been left behind on the battlefield and in the general rout, and that to try to find two females in the general disorder would be a hopeless task.

'Doubtless someone will rescue them, if they are seen,' said the harassed staff officer whom Sophie's distracted father had approached, waving his rank as a State Senator and his brother Jacobus's as a senior member of Lincoln's government. Neither brought him any assistance. Instead, he was told, roughly, to be on his way at once; he was merely holding up the Army's intention to regroup before the rebels marched on Washington—for such was the immediate fear.

They had reached home shortly before nine o'clock at night to find the town buzzing with rumours of the hideous defeat which the arrival of the demoralised remnants of the Union Army and the civilian refugees merely confirmed. The notion that the Unionists had simply to show themselves to defeat the damned rebels lay in ruins. No one now doubted that the enemy was formidable, and that the war would be long and hard.

So complete had the South's victory been, so utter the rout, that if, in those last days of July, the Southern Armies had advanced on the panic-stricken capital the possibility of victory was theirs. They were never to be so near to it again.

Hamilton and Serena Hope sat, numb with despair in their drawing-room, denied the possibility of return

to search for Sophie and Marietta—fearful that they
were dead or dying.

'Or worse,' said Hamilton, who was beginning to
think the unthinkable—that he might never see his
daughter again.

'What shall I say to Jacobus if his daughter is lost?'
he said. 'Who could have thought that such a disaster
would be possible? They should all be shot, all of
them, generals and private soldiers alike. Shameful,
their behaviour was shameful. It is only God's mercy
that they have not taken the capital itself.'

He had forgotten the euphoric mood of the morning
when they had set out so gaily to see the battle.

The journey back to Washington was long and hard,
not only for Jack and his companions but for all the
struggling crowds who walked and rode towards sal-
vation. Somewhere among them Russell sat on his
horse, mentally composing his dismal tale of rout and
panic for his *Times* despatch. It was an account which
was to enrage the entire North since it told of incom-
petence, cowardice and failure. The greater the truth
the more it hurt. The infant Republic writhed beneath
the scorn of Europe. The sheer ferocity with which
the North later fought the war owed a great deal to
the derision which it had earned at Bull Run or First
Manassas, as the battle was also known.

During the long drive home, Jack wondered how
long the North would hold out after such an unfore-
seen and stunning defeat. He remembered, though,
that Alan had told him that the war would be a long

one and that the North's victory would not be easily achieved, but that they would certainly win in the end.

His main consideration was to see the cousins safely home. Later, when they reached harbour, as it were, at one in the morning, beneath a splendid moon, and he handed them over to the Hopes, they could not say or do enough to thank him for rescuing them.

'No,' he said to Hamilton Hope, drinking the brandy and eating the food which the Hopes had forced on him, '*I* didn't rescue them. Marietta had done that long before I arrived on the scene. They were clear of the enemy then, thanks to the bridge being blown up behind them. One way or another, Marietta would have made sure they reached home again: her courage was exemplary.'

He said nothing of Sophie for there was nothing to say. He had watched the two women being taken up to bed to be bathed and cosseted, but not before, unseen, while they waited for the Hopes' butler to answer the door, he had kissed Marietta on the cheek in return for her gallantry, and had whispered to her that he hoped that it would be the first of many more yet to come.

Chapter Eight

'A ball! The Van Horns are going to give a ball tonight, only two days after the battle—what can they be *thinking* of?'

Ezra Butler, who had not experienced the realities of war as Jack had, shrugged his shoulders. 'Van Horn's words to me were, "The damned secessionists shan't stop me from ordering my life as I may, defeat or not." Since I agree with him I intend to go. Nothing is gained by putting on mourning: a brave face is much better.'

'I suppose there's something in that,' agreed Jack thoughtfully. 'I have had an invitation so I'll accompany you.'

He wondered if Marietta had sufficiently recovered from her ordeal to attend.

Ezra smiled. He knew why Jack was so eager to visit the Van Horns. 'It's Marietta Hope you want to see again, isn't it?' he asked. 'You should know that she's with the Hamilton Hopes at present—after all, you took her there the other night.'

'I don't particularly wish to visit the Hamilton Hopes,' said Jack, who had no desire to see Sophie, who had been so hateful to Marietta who had saved her. He was unaware that Marietta had already returned home, unwilling to be in Sophie's company after her conduct during the retreat. She was fearful that she might lose her temper and say something unforgivable.

She had hugged the memory of the drive home from Manassas to her heart. She and Jack had barely spoken. They had both been tired and exhausted, but speech had not been needed. She had fallen asleep because she trusted him and was happy in his presence, whatever the external danger.

The following morning he had sent a messenger round to the Hopes' residence with a note in which he trusted that she was feeling recovered after her ordeal and in which he praised her bravery. It was after that that she had made her decision to leave the Hopes, even if it meant living alone until Aunt Percival or her father returned. Fortunately, Aunt Percival, her midwifery duties over, had arrived back in Washington on the afternoon of the battle, although the Senator was still absent.

Ignorant of all this, Jack found himself at the Van Horns' place where, despite everything, those in Washington who had spent Sunday watching and fleeing from the battle, now spent Tuesday evening enlivening others' dull lives with their tales of it. He looked eagerly around for Marietta, but he could not see her.

Bored, and about to leave, fearing that he might yet have to risk a visit to the Hamilton Hopes, he looked in the conservatory where he could hear voices and a woman's low laughter. It was Sophie. She was surrounded by her cavaliers and was entertaining them with her adventures in the rout.

To hear her talk it was she who had saved Marietta, and looking at her as she sat there, enchanting in forget-me-not blue, it was difficult to reconcile her appearance with that of the bedraggled, complaining doll whom Marietta and he had hauled into the buggy. He could have borne her lying and deceitful account except that someone asked after Marietta, and Sophie said, with a laugh, 'Oh, she is here, but what a pother and to-do she made in the rout.'

She pulled a comically deprecating face, and altogether made it sound as though Marietta had been the one who had needed to be shouted at and coaxed and cajoled to behave properly.

Disgusted, Jack walked into the conservatory. She saw him come in and her face closed. She had the grace to look a little embarrassed.

'Jack,' she said, raising her little bouquet to her lips, 'the very man. I was just telling my friends of our adventures after the battle and of your gallantry.'

It was unwise, if not to say ungentlemanly, but Jack could not prevent himself. 'And were you telling your friends, Sophie, of how you shrieked and screamed and needed to be half-carried home by Marietta—and of your lack of gratitude for her saving you?'

Her pretty face suddenly grew ugly. 'One has to suppose,' she said, unable to resist a savage thrust at him, 'that an ugly bean-pole has to be of some use for something—Marietta would have made a useful drill sergeant, don't you think?' and her eyes glared at him.

Jack had immediately regretted his own outburst, but to hear her malign and belittle the woman who had saved her had been too much for him to endure without reproaching Sophie for her blatant untruths.

Sophie, too, was beginning to regret the spite which had filled her voice and had caused some of her hearers to have second thoughts about her which were not quite so flattering as their first. She added, with a toss of her pretty head, 'I suppose that you wish to report to her. She and Aunt Percival are doing their *devoirs* with all the old Senators from Capitol Hill. Such a bore.' Her light laughter followed him out of the conservatory.

He discovered Aunt Percival and Marietta in the main salon. Marietta's face bore the stigmata of tiredness far more than Sophie's did, but then, she had been the one who had displayed the spirit and the energy to get them to the place where he had found them. It lit up when she saw him, and his own pleasure was such that he thought that he might as well be carrying a banner saying 'I love Marietta Hope,' so plainly was his affection for her written on his face.

'Jack!' she greeted him. 'I'm so pleased to find you here.' She turned to Avory Grant, who was standing beside her, having made his way back to Washington after his regiment had broken and fled the field. 'I was just telling Avory how gallantly you rescued Sophie and me.'

'No gallantry,' said Jack. 'You were rescuing yourself when I found you. I was merely the master of the

chariot on which you travelled the last part of the journey home.'

Avory nodded his approval. 'I'm sure,' he said,
'that one might trust Marietta to do the right thing;
she makes a habit of it. She should have been leading
the Army.'

Jack was not sure that he felt happy at hearing another man, who was a possible rival, praising her. The
admiring attention of both men had brought a lovely
flush to her face which hid her tiredness and improved
her looks.

How could anyone call her plain? thought Jack. She
makes Sophie look like a characterless and importunate kitten. Avory was thinking the same thing. He
was also, somewhat ruefully, registering that Marietta
only had eyes for Jack, and that his own hopes of
winning her were vain.

Marietta was aching for Jack. She wished them all
away: Avory, Aunt Percival and the crowd around
them. She wanted to be in a place where they only
knew each other. In some way the journey from Manassas had sealed whatever had already lain between
them and had made it deeper and stronger. They had
both learned how transient and fleeting life was, and
that the opportunities for fulfilment in it must be
grasped, not lost.

As though he were aware of what lay between the
lovers, Avory said, relinquishing his last claim on
Marietta, 'You will wish to be alone to talk over what
passed after the battle. I am sure that Aunt Percival
and I will be only too happy to excuse you.'

Etiquette or no etiquette, Jack and Marietta needed

no second invitation. With a grateful 'Thank you,' Jack led Marietta away. Aunt Percival—she had known Avory since he and Marietta had been children together, and was also Avory's distant relative— turned to him and said, as kindly as she could, 'It has been like that with them since they first met.'

Avory nodded. 'I was too late. I can only say how pleased I am that she has found happiness at last—I can only wish that she had accepted me all those years ago.'

'You were both too young then,' said Aunt Percival, still kind. 'You had to grow up, and unfortunately, when you did, Jack had found her first. He is a good man from what appears to be a remarkable family.'

'Her father told me the other day,' Avory said, 'that his brother is a member of the British government and has a title. Better than that, they are, I understand, both clever men. On the other hand, if he does not treat her properly, be sure I shall always be there for her.'

'Oh, I don't think that you need have any fears for her future happiness,' were Aunt Percival's last words to him: brave words which she was to remember later.

'Supper,' said Jack, when they had left the others. 'Let me take you into supper.' He told himself that he was the true son of his father, to whom food had always been important.

'Supper,' agreed Marietta, laughing up at him. 'I do believe that the only time that we did not talk about food was on the way home from Manassas.'

'Too busy eating humble pie,' said Jack obligingly.

'We had gone there for a victory and it turned into a rout.'

The smile left Marietta's face. She looked around the supper room at the gaily dressed crowd eating and drinking. 'Yes,' she said quietly. 'I feel guilty about being here and enjoying myself—junketing, as the British say. On the other hand I also feel that it is important that we show the flag and are not down-hearted. There will be other battles and we shall not lose them all, I hope.'

They were neither of them hungry so they soon moved out of the supper-room and on to the terrace where they were, for a time, alone. The moon was already high, and Jack found that her nearness, as well as the scent of lily-of-the-valley perfume and Marietta mingled, was heady enough for him to take her into his arms. He began to kiss her.

He had meant to be gentle at first, but her response to him was so immediate that all caution, all holding back because he knew that in the lists of love she was untried, flew away at the first touch of her tender lips. She was warm and comfortable in his arms as though that was where she was always meant to be.

He kissed the cleft between her beautiful breasts before slipping her dress down the more to reveal them. She made no demur at all, clinging to him the harder, finding from she knew not where exactly what a woman should do when being embraced by her lover. His desire for her and hers for him was so powerful that they could have fulfilled their passion there, on the terrace, all decorum, all rules of conduct, ignored.

What saved them from committing themselves completely was the sound of other guests coming through the glass doors. They sprang apart and began to re-order their clothing, pretending that they were admiring the garden and the beauty of the warm summer night.

'You will visit me tomorrow?' she asked him while they strolled back into the ballroom. 'I am home again: you will not have to run the gauntlet of Sophie and the Hopes.'

He took her hand in his to kiss her farewell. 'Be very sure that I shall. My time in Washington is nearly at an end and I intend to make the most of it.'

If there was a double meaning in his words, then so be it. Having tasted for a moment of the sweets of mutual passion, neither of them could wait to enjoy them again. Both of them were unaware of the eyes trained on them: Sophie's were jealous and vengeful ones, Avory's sad and regretful, while Aunt Percival and her friends agreed that it was time that such a sterling treasure as Marietta Hope should find happiness at last.

Marietta was alone when Jack arrived the next day—or rather Aunt Percival tactfully removed herself when he was announced. 'You don't want an old woman making a fifth wheel,' being her trenchant comment to Marietta. 'I'll go and arrange for tea to be served.'

It was pleasant to be with Marietta again without either Sophie or her aunt to be considered, Jack thought. He had sternly told himself to behave properly when he was in her own home, but the sight of her did dreadful things to his composure. By her expression Marietta was suffering from the same affliction.

Nevertheless, as the servants came and went with the tea, they behaved themselves. 'We're just like an old married couple,' was Jack's remark when they had gone, which set Marietta choking over her tea cup.

'I don't feel like an old married couple,' she said when she could speak again.

'Nor I,' said Jack. He looked naughtily at her over the rim of his cup. 'Dare I suggest that we meet somewhere where we are not likely to be interrupted at any moment? I learned this morning that I shall be leaving for New York tomorrow—with the Presidential Committee's blessing. I am to work with Ericsson on his newly designed iron-clad, the *Monitor*, in both an official and an unofficial capacity. I have the feeling that the Patriarch would approve of my double duties. More to the point, I feel that we have much to say to one another privately before I leave.'

Marietta put down her tea cup and said in a prim voice, 'I suppose that you might have some suggestions as to where this important conference should take place?'

'Only one,' said Jack. 'I fear that I must ask you to visit my rooms—tomorrow.'

'Fear,' said Marietta, raising her eyebrows. 'Are you sure that fear is the right word here?' She was discovering in herself a previously unknown ability to flirt with a gentleman in a manner which could only be described as suggestive. Now, wherever had she learned to behave like that?

'Hope,' returned Jack. 'I hope that you will agree to visit me there. Is that better? After all, hope is your name.'

'Much better,' said Marietta. 'We are agreed, then?'

'As ever,' said Jack. He wished that the Patriarch had lived long enough to meet her—his one woman; there was no doubt of that.

'We must behave ourselves,' she added.

'Of course,' Jack said, giving her a wistful smile. 'I would not wish to do anything that you would not wish me to do.'

There was a double meaning in this, too, but Marietta ignored it. Where Jack was concerned, all the rules which had governed her quiet and orderly life seemed to have disappeared. She could hardly wait for tomorrow afternoon to come so that she could do that dreadfully wrong thing, be alone with a gentleman in his lodgings, but she did not tell him so.

The thought of their private meeting on the morrow enabled them to behave as decorously as even the most severe book of etiquette could wish. Aunt Percival came in shortly before Jack left, and he told her of his coming visit to New York.

'We shall miss you,' she said, and sincerity rang in her voice. Here was the one man to whom she would give her charge without compunction, for she still thought of herself as Marietta's guardian. She might not have been so happy had she known of their coming secret tryst, for neither of them mentioned it, and when Marietta left the house on the next day Aunt

Percival assumed that she was making one of her regular visits to an old friend and relative.

'Comfortable, but not luxurious,' was Marietta's verdict on Jack's rooms. He had taken her bonnet and placed it on the dresser which occupied one wall. He had a spirit lamp with a kettle boiling on it, a tea-pot and cups and saucers ready for her. There was even a plate of small sweet biscuits on the table before the sofa. Everything, indeed, seemed orderly and proper—except the inward emotions of the two principals in this impromptu tea party.

Actually drinking the tea compelled them to behave themselves as though they were in the Senator's best parlour. If Jack had thought at all of what might happen when Marietta visited him, he might have imagined them engaging in some light and amusing conversation after which he would ask her to marry him. Once he had done so, they might perhaps indulge themselves in some light and juvenile lovemaking guaranteed not to frighten an untried maiden lady in her late twenties.

At first everything went as he might have imagined it would, for Jack had absolutely no intention of seducing Marietta and she was equally determined not to be seduced. Even their brief bout of passionate lovemaking on the Van Horns' terrace had not warned them of how strong their feelings were for one another.

Matters began to go wrong—or was it right?—shortly after the tea was drunk and the biscuits eaten. Jack moved the table away from the sofa and sat down beside Marietta, who was glowing as though she were in her late teens. First the strong wind through which she had walked to Jack's lodgings, and then the combination of tea, biscuits, Jack's exciting presence, and the knowledge that she was doing something daring, had all combined to excite her. Her eyes shone and her voice trembled.

She looked so enchanting and inviting that as soon as Jack had sat down beside her he could not stop himself from turning towards her and taking her in his arms and kissing her. The kiss began as an innocent, friendly one, but as a result of Marietta's enthusiastic response to him it rapidly turned into something more passionate.

In an instant they were lost.

She was so warm and welcoming in his arms that Jack could not restrain himself from stroking her intimately, only to discover that beneath her prim dress she was not wearing stays or any of the usual carapaces which ladies saw fit to put on beneath their dresses. This knowledge excited him so much that he went on to become even more bold and definite.

First he unbuttoned the high neck of her walking dress and pulled it down so that he could get more easily at the treasures which it hid. Far from preventing him from unveiling her most private self, Marietta assisted him—not only by undressing herself but by undressing *him*.

She removed his stock: next his shirt took on an abandoned air when Marietta briskly unbuttoned it so that she might return his caresses with interest. All of this was accomplished without the necessity for speech, unless broken and breathless endearments, freely offered to one another, could be counted as such.

Given that Marietta's previous lovemaking had been confined to a few chaste kisses offered by Avory, it was surprising how quickly she mastered the basics of it, and at times took the lead herself. It could have been a matter for debate which unbuttoned the other the more readily, their clothing seeming superfluous to the matter in hand.

There was no doubt, indeed, where their ultimate destination lay. They saw and felt only each other as they struggled, mouth to mouth, across the room and through the door into Jack's bedchamber.

Marietta, whose body vibrated as though it had been invaded by a thousand butterflies, suddenly felt the bed behind her knees through the thick fabric of her dress, and then she was on her back on it, Jack above her, his hands busily removing her remaining clothes. What shook her most in memory afterwards was that she could not wait to be free of them, she wanted him so.

She remembered how, long ago, one of the women servants at the old Percival plantation had told her what men and women did in the act of love, and how it had horrified her. The servant had given a fat laugh. 'Oh, you'll want it, right enough,' she'd said. 'When it happens to you, you'll see.'

And now she did want it. Oh, let him not be a gentleman and stop, I could not bear it. He is all I want—and this—for her body was suddenly free of clothing, and was his for the taking.

Jack was beyond being a gentleman. The long weeks of continence, of seeing her, of suddenly wanting her, and not being able to do anything but hold her hand, had brought him to this. Her face, called plain by others, was never plain to him: he saw her bright intelligence, her wit and her gallant spirit shining through it. He loved her so much that he could almost have killed Sophie for her mockery of her cousin at the Van Horns and before that, when she had tried to demean her after Marietta had saved her at Manassas.

Her body, divested of its clothing, was as beautiful as he had thought that it would be. All of the rules which he had made for himself, of respecting untried, unmarried women, were cast to the winds when her passionate responses fuelled his, until, linked together in mind and body, they climbed the mountain to where joy and fulfilment waited for them both.

They had celebrated their first happy meeting over their mutual delight in food and drink, and now it was their bodies' deeper demands which they obeyed on their last meeting before Jack left for New York.

Afterwards they dozed off, with Marietta's head on Jack's chest. She woke up to find that Jack now had his head on her stomach and was kissing it gently, doing improbable things with his tongue. The butterflies which had undone her earlier when she had first arrived at his lodgings were undoing her again.

Jack suddenly raised his head and looked up at her.

'I shouldn't be doing this,' he told her earnestly, 'any of it. It is all quite wrong. I never intended to seduce you, things just got out of hand. You must believe that, Marietta.' Having said that, he started to seduce her again, so that even her toes curled up as a consequence of the sensations he was creating in her errant body!

She felt a wild desire to laugh immoderately, to do a delighted jig around the bedroom; instead, she said to him, equally earnestly, 'Pray do not stop now, on my account. The deed is done.'

Such odd feelings were coursing through her that she found speaking difficult. 'We may as well continue to enjoy ourselves,' she gasped out at last, 'since we seem to deal so well together…oh…oh…oh…' Speaking suddenly became impossible: gentle groaning seemed to be in order.

After a few moments of bliss Jack lifted his head again to say wickedly, 'It is all your fault; you should not be so beautiful. It leaves a poor man no defence.'

'There is no need to resort to empty flattery to excuse your behaviour,' replied Marietta severely. 'I am well aware of my own lack of looks. I can only be surprised at finding myself where I am, doing such impossible and improper things. Oh, please, don't stop,' she begged him when he looked up again. 'It is far too late for repentance. I am well and truly ruined!'

'I was not referring to your face, although you have a very nice face,' said Jack, before addressing himself to her nether regions again, 'whatever that cat Sophie says of it. No, I mean your body, Marietta. How fortunate I am that I am the only man to see it—you would be knocked down in the rush to get at it if it ever received as much exposure as your face. Your legs, my darling, are superb,' and he proceeded to favour them with his attentions, too.

Marietta thought hazily that this was all quite different from what she had occasionally pictured might happen to her. She had expected a decorous wedding night—if she ever married, that was. How was a decorous wedding night ever possible? Could this... this...experience...ever be decorous? This wild and irresponsible lovemaking without benefit of clergy, after matters had got out of hand so quickly once they had drunk their tea, came as a considerable shock to her.

Was tea taken alone with one's lover an aphrodisiac? She had, by accident, come across the word once and had read about it with some disbelief. With savages, powdered rhinoceros horn seem to be involved, but she could hardly believe that Jack had fed her *that*. Really, though, all that aside, the biggest shock of all was her own willing and gleeful co-operation in her downfall.

Fortunately for her reasoning mind, Jack's ministrations produced such a delightfully hazy sensation that the ability to reason disappeared altogether. Sensation took over again, and really, she thought, when for a moment everyday Marietta Hope surfaced again, since I have been well and truly seduced, and I am now transformed into a wanton, I might as well enjoy myself to the full. For who would have thought that I would ever be here, in bed with Jack, doing this...?

This was so exquisitely pleasant that thought flew away again. It had no place on the wilder shores of love. Neither had guilt, nor shame, nor remorse—although they might reappear later.

The gods looked kindly down on the lovers entwined on the bed. On the experienced Mr Jack Dilhorne, who thought that he had found his life's love at last, and on the novice Miss Marietta Hope, the earnest bluestocking, who had just discovered that she was as good at lovemaking as at everything else she did. Better still, she had also discovered that an athletic body and an enquiring mind had their uses in bed, particularly when she was in it with someone as dear to her as Mr Jack Dilhorne was proving to be.

All delights come to an end, some harshly, some gently. Marietta, resuming her clothes, those thick encumbrances which hid the true woman from the world, was tenderly aided by her lover whose care and consideration removed any embarrassment which she might have felt in the aftermath of passion.

In turn she fastened his shirt for him and tied his stock, hiding away his own good body which had pleasured her so, and would again, she hoped, when he returned to Washington.

Jack was suddenly shy, and was a little, but only a little, ashamed at what he had done. It was a strange condition for such a usually self-confident man.

'You must forgive me, my darling,' he said when, fully respectable, they sat side by side on the bed. 'I was wrong, Marietta, to do what I did, to seduce you—for seduction it was. But, oh, it has been torment for me to be near you these last few weeks.'

'And for me, too,' she said gently. 'If there is blame

for what we have done, then I must share it. For it was I who willingly came to you, who encouraged you, who made no effort to stop you, and would have been distressed had you done so.'

He shook his head. 'But I am the man, and the experienced one. I knew what I was doing, and where we were going. It was my part to hold back—'

She put her hand over his mouth. 'No, Jack, I am no young girl. I am in my late twenties. I knew perfectly well what we were doing and where it would end. I came here intending to be your lover in every sense of the word; you must know that. I even left off my stays, and if that makes me wanton, then that is what I am. I could not bear the thought of you going away without ever having known you in love.'

'Yes, Marietta, my darling,' he said eagerly. 'We must be married, as soon as possible, you know, because, because...'

'Because of the possible consequences,' she said. 'I knowingly took that risk.'

He took her hand and kissed it. 'No risk, because I love you, and I am only sorry that I may not stay in Washington with you. I will write to your father, asking for your hand as soon as I reach New York, and I know my address there. If there are... consequences...then we must be married at once.' Jack laughed at his own eagerness. 'Oh, Marietta, I am so determined that you shall be my wife that I have not even proposed to you properly! I have taken your consent for granted.'

He stood up, put his hand on his heart and bowed

to her. 'You will marry me, I trust, Miss Hope, and make me a respectable man at last.'

'Only if you intend to make me respectable, too, Mr Dilhorne!'

Marietta's face was rosy and relaxed. Her body felt more supple than she had ever known it; she was so exquisitely aware of every part of it, from the soles of the feet which he had kissed so passionately, to the crown of the head which had been equally favoured.

'We may write to one another,' she said, smiling, 'and I promise you I shall live for the postman's knock.'

'And I, too,' he said. 'Oh, we must be married soon. I want you with me, not only to make love to you, but also to be my companion, my other self. I must stop, Marietta, or I shall begin to make love to you again, and you must be home soon, or be ruined. Oh, how stupid I am! I have already ruined you.'

'If this is being ruined, then we must do it more often,' she said, smiling at him, and nearly depriving him of common sense again as she did so.

'Please be serious, my darling, if only for a moment. You have been away from home so long that I grow fearful that you might cause some suspicion.'

'Do not worry, my own heart. I am a born intriguer. I have spent the afternoon with an old friend. I walked there, and shall walk back—my passion for exercise is well known.'

'Then let me come with you for a little way,' he said ardently. 'There is still time before my train leaves tonight. I am sorry that the Senator is away from Washington so that I may not speak to him of our marriage before I leave. Still, I must remember that it will not be long before we are together for good.'

Chapter Nine

Jack wrote his first love letter to Marietta as soon as he arrived in New York, even before he had used the letter of introduction to John Ericsson, which he had been given by the Secretary of the Navy. It asked that Mr Jack Dilhorne should be allowed access to the building of the iron-clad, now known as the *Monitor*, so that he might report back to Washington as an unofficial, but skilled, observer, giving his assessment of the efficiency of the craft.

He had spent several days in Baltimore on the way, since he needed to speak to some of the engineers at Butler and Rutherfurd's, which had a ship-building factory on the quay there.

Marietta, my darling,
I will not tell you of New York and its wonders for, strange though it seems to me, it must be commonplace to you. I am staying for the moment at the Brevoort House, and you may write to me here until I find rooms of my own—which

I will do as soon as possible. When I leave I will ask the desk clerk to forward your letters to me.

I am enclosing one to the Senator in which I formally ask him for your hand in marriage. I have reason to believe that he will look upon my request with favour. I fear that he might not approve of our afternoon in heaven, but he will surely be pleased that we are to marry.

Jack paused before he went on to write of his longing to see her again soon, and of his hopes that the Senator would agree to as early a wedding ceremony as could be arranged. His one regret had been that the Senator had been absent on business when he had been called to New York so that he had been unable to ask for Marietta's hand in person.

'My letter will serve to reassure you of my love,' he ended, and the one which he wrote to the Senator was done so from a full heart, with his love for Marietta plain in every word of it.

Before he retired for his first night in the United States' financial capital he took the letter, and its enclosure, down to the desk, and saw that the clerk put it with the other mail due for collection.

As it happened, the mail was not picked up the next day, and it was to be a week before his love letter arrived in Washington.

By chance, as she at first thought, Marietta had fallen ill with a sickness of the stomach shortly after her afternoon with Jack. She awoke one morning feeling dizzy and disorientated, and, on trying to rise, was overcome with faintness and a dreadful desire to vomit. She rang for Aunt Percival, who took one look at her drawn yellow face and sharply ordered her to stay in bed for the day.

On her way downstairs Aunt Percival met Sophie on the first landing. She was looking sullen and annoyed. Her parents had left her in Washington again with Marietta, whom she now hated beyond reason. Not only did she loathe her for making off with Jack, but Marietta's stern treatment of her during the retreat from Manassas had given Sophie an almost manic determination to hurt Marietta in any way she could—and as soon as she could.

'You have no occupation, I see,' said Aunt Percival reprovingly to her. 'Marietta is unwell this morning. You may make yourself useful by sorting and opening the Senator's mail for her.'

'Must I?' pouted Sophie. 'I know she does it for him, but why should I? He's my uncle, not my father.'

'He's your host and your senior and you owe him a duty on both counts,' said Aunt Percival so severely that Sophie shrugged her shoulders and unwillingly made her way to the Senator's study where a fire was always kept burning, even in summer, so that unwanted papers and correspondence might be immediately destroyed.

A neat pile of letters and parcels had been stacked on the Senator's desk. Sorting through it, Sophie came upon a thick envelope with a New York postmark which was addressed to Marietta. Sophie knew at once that it came from Jack Dilhorne. She had seen his un-American writing often enough on her dance programmes, and as she held the letter in her hand a wave of hatred for Marietta passed over her.

It was, without doubt, a love letter from Jack, who had had the audacity and the bad taste to prefer Plain Jane to beautiful Sophie. Well, here was one letter which Marietta would never receive. Almost without thinking, Sophie walked over to the fire and pitched the letter into its heart before holding it down with the poker to help Jack's loving message burn more quickly and more efficiently.

Only when the deed was irretrievably done did a worm of fear gnaw briefly at Sophie's heart. Jack would surely write again, or Marietta would write to Jack and its loss would be discovered.

Goodness, she told herself, it's wartime and letters are likely to go astray so the US mail will take the blame. She had barely had time to comfort herself with this thought than an even better one occurred to her. Might she not take over the ingoing and outgoing mail from Marietta? She would be killing two birds with one stone. She would gain praise from Plain Jane and Aunt Percival for taking a more serious view of her life and duty, and at the same time she could destroy all Jack and Marietta's correspondence without anyone being aware of what she was doing.

The whole idea gave her a sense of power quite apart from the destruction of the correspondence itself. It might be very revealing to discover what the Senator's mail consisted of.

She began to sing quietly while she opened the letters and arranged them in neat piles, and when Aunt Percival arrived to find her so busily engaged, she said approvingly, 'There, child, even a small occupation brings its own rewards.'

Sophie smiled up at her sweetly, before saying, 'Oh, yes, dear Aunt, it does, it certainly does,' hugging to herself the knowledge that she was striking a major blow at her detested cousin while gaining the reputation for being a reformed character.

Despite her physical distress, for her wretched weakness did not leave her, but grew daily worse, Marietta looked eagerly through her mail each morning. She knew that Jack intended to visit Baltimore on his way North, so she did not expect a letter for at least a week.

So at first she did not worry when none arrived, but when the week became a fortnight, and then three weeks, she began to fret a little. After a month she became quietly frantic.

Something which should have happened, had not happened; this was rare. Her courses were usually as regular as clockwork. She pushed the slight fear occasioned by their first non-appearance to the back of her mind, but when the second month passed without them, she faced the unpalatable truth. Even then her real misery lay in Jack's continuing silence.

She remembered the delights of their last afternoon together, and the tenderness on his face when he had spoken to her of marriage, and had told her that he would write to both her and her father when he reached New York.

But the Senator had now returned from Boston and had not received a letter from him, either.

It could not, it must not, be that he had merely taken his pleasure with her and, having done so, had deserted her: that he had changed his mind once he had left Washington. Could it be that, despite all the loving compliments which he had paid her, he did not want a plain woman for his wife?

She had a slight remission from her sickness, but she still felt, and looked, extremely ill. Aunt Percival, watching her, said one morning, 'Marietta, I think that we ought to ask the doctor to take a look at you. You have been ill quite long enough.'

'No,' she said quickly, too quickly. 'It is nothing. Merely the sickness which occasionally afflicts Washington. I am over the worst.'

Her aunt said, 'Let us trust that you are, but if this persists much longer I shall insist that you do as I ask.'

The last thing Marietta wanted was a doctor examining her. She still hoped that Jack would write, and that they might be married quickly so that the child which she was now sure that she was carrying could be given a name. She made up her mind that she would sink her pride and write to Butler and Rutherfurd's in Baltimore, asking them to forward a letter to Jack in New York, seeing that she had no knowledge of where he might now be living.

Sophie saw the letter, Marietta's first to him, in the outgoing mail. She had been conscientiously destroying Jack's letters to her which had been arriving at the rate of two a week. She was by now quite hardened and thought no more of burning Jack's letters than of destroying the Senator's unwanted papers for him—it was simply one of Marietta's duties which she had taken over during her cousin's illness, part of her day's work.

After another week of silence Marietta wrote again. She was astonished at her own fortitude, her strength of mind. No one watching her could have guessed either her secret, or the dreadful misery which Jack's seeming desertion, now quite plain, was causing her.

She was so composed, indeed, that Sophie was almost angry. She would have liked to see Marietta show distress or some emotion. But as Marietta recovered a little from her illness and began to escort Sophie around Washington again, she almost seemed to vindicate Sophie's actions. If she cared so little for Jack, then burning their letters was no sin.

Inside, however, Marietta was shrieking, and she did not know which pain was the worst, that of desertion, or the awful knowledge that she was undoubtedly pregnant. When she arrived at her third month and there was still no letter from him she became increasingly desperate.

At first Jack was not worried that no letter had arrived from Marietta. He was well aware that the post, owing to the War, had become erratic. But as time passed and still there was no word from her, loving or otherwise, he began to worry.

His days were so busy that he had little time to concentrate in anything other than the building of the *Monitor*, particularly once the keel had been laid down, but at night it was a different thing.

He seemed doomed to relive, again and again, the flight from the battlefield of Manassas and their last passionate afternoon. As the weeks passed, which then turned into months and still no letter came for him, he began to ask himself bitterly whether that afternoon had meant so little to her, however much it had meant to him. He could scarcely believe that the woman he had come to know and to love could betray him so easily.

Perhaps their lovemaking had disgusted her after all. Perhaps she was ashamed of it, but he had asked her to marry him, and had written to the Senator asking for her hand. The only conclusion he could draw was that she had changed her mind and had destroyed the Senator's letter so as not to trouble him.

One evening he met a pretty woman journalist— one of a new breed—at a reception given by Ericsson. She reminded him a little of his lost love. She made what he could only describe as a determined set at him. Three months had passed since he had written his first letter to Marietta and still he had received nothing from her. He was beginning to accept that he had lost her.

On the way home he decided that if no letter came in the morning he would write to her for one last time, and then, if she still didn't write to him, he would put her behind him. He had to face the fact that their afternoon of love had been but an interlude for her, unbelievable though that might once have seemed to him. She could have no notion of the grief he felt, of the passions which tore at him whenever he thought of her.

Yes, he would cut loose from the happy past and try to rescue himself from the slough of despond into which he had fallen, he would forget her, and everything between them.

On the next afternoon he wrote his last letter to her, and posted it with a heavy heart before setting out to begin his new life without her.

My darling Marietta,
If you have changed your mind, or regretted our last afternoon together, or if you have found another love, at least I beg of you, write to tell me so, and I will try to understand.

But, please, whatever you do, do not abandon me like this, without a word. I thought that I knew you, that between us we had found something precious to share, and I cannot believe that it will end, like this, in nothing.

If you do not answer this I shall not write again, for writing to you has become a torment for me, since I fear that you find me importunate. Because I love you I would not distress you by reminding you of my unwanted affection. And yet, I cannot forget you, and, indeed, will never do so. Even if you write to tell me that I am unwanted, I cannot reproach you, for you were always your own woman, and that is why I love you.

But, oh, my lost darling, my regrets at losing you are as deep as my love, and that is deep, indeed. Can it really be true that what we shared meant nothing to you?

And then he added one last despairing plea— 'Oh, write, please write, if only to release me from the pain of not knowing. Jack.'

She was the one woman and he had lost her: it had, perhaps, simply been an illusion that she might have been his to call wife. Their brief interlude had merely been that for her, but it would be with him for ever, even if he met another woman. For he could never love anyone else as much as he had loved Marietta.

He, who had always been ebullient, always cheerful, was thought to be a silent, sombre man by his new colleagues, a man who attacked his work frantically and seemed to live for little else.

'Have you any notion why Marietta should not have heard from young Dilhorne once he arrived in New York? I was sorry to be away from home before he was called to New York. Is it possible that they quarrelled before he left?'

Senator Hope might be old and ailing, but he was still astute: the keen mind which had helped him to accumulate his millions and then build a major political career was still as sharp as ever, able to note the changes in those around him.

He loved his daughter dearly, had always lamented that she had never married, and the arrival of John Dilhorne had seemed to him to be a belated blessing. He liked the clever young man, had made discreet enquiries about him and was satisfied that he was in every way a suitable husband for Marietta.

It seemed sensible for him to question Aunt Percival, who he was sure was well aware of everything which passed in his household, however trivial it might be. Her reply puzzled him a little.

'My dear Jacobus,' she said gravely, 'I was of the impression, before he left, that he was about to propose to her, and that makes it all the more strange that he never replies to any of the letters which I know that she has been writing. I did not think of him as a Don Juan or a trifler, but I am beginning to fear that he was.'

She was beginning to fear something else, but she did not tell the Senator that. Time would soon tell her if her suspicion about Marietta's strange illness was correct, and then not only she but the whole world would know the unhappy truth.

'Hmm,' said the Senator. 'I agree with you. I thought him a most worthy young man. I suppose it only goes to show how easily we may be deceived.'

This statement did not truly represent what he was beginning to think. That there was something wrong, something odd, about the whole business, particularly since Marietta's agony at Jack's continuing silence was becoming hard for her to conceal.

The Senator did not like his niece Sophie. She was the only one of the pretty cousins whom he did not care for, and this was because of her cruel treatment of Marietta. It was obvious to him that young Dilhorne's defection was pleasing the girl. More than once he had caught an expression on her face when she was looking at Marietta which could only be described as gloating. This happened whenever she thought that she was unobserved.

Among the wrongnesses which seemed to have afflicted his household was the fact that idle Sophie had suddenly become enamoured of being at his side. He had always thought that she disliked him, too, and now here she was cheerfully carrying out all those duties which she had previously jeered at Marietta for performing.

He was sure that she was up to something. It gave him an odd feeling. It was feelings like these which had helped the Senator to make a fortune whenever he had paid heed to them. Something lay behind Sophie's transformed behaviour—but what? He did not deceive himself that she had suddenly begun to care for him, so that he was daily confronted with a puzzle, and a puzzle which he did not like.

'I shall write to the man myself,' he told Aunt Percival abruptly. 'In the meantime, I shall go down to the study and collect my mail at once, instead of having Sophie bring it up to the library.'

A conversation with her might enlighten him as to her motives. He had always avoided talking to her because he sensed that she saw him as an uninteresting old man. Well, that uninteresting old man would try to solve the puzzle she presented by drawing her out.

He opened the door to the little downstairs study where the mail was usually placed before it was sorted out for the different members of his household to collect. It was a pleasant room, and there was already, at this early hour, a small fire burning in the grate. Over the mantelpiece was a portrait of the Senator's beau-

tiful wife. She was looking down at Sophie who, as
the Senator quietly opened the door, was busily sorting the mail.

She had not heard him, and for a moment he stood
there watching her. She was in an uncharacteristic
pose, her pretty face serious, intent on the letters before her. He was grudgingly acknowledging the con-
scientious nature of her labours when she suddenly
abstracted a letter from the pile before her, read the
superscription on its envelope, and then held it as-
sessingly in her hand for a moment.

The Senator concluded that it must be one for her,
and was about to make his presence known when she
waved it before her, almost in derision, making no
attempt to open it, or to read it.

Curious again, he paused when she suddenly leaned
forward and tossed the letter deep into the heart of the
fire.

The wrongness about her, which had plagued him
for weeks, suddenly shrieked at him that something
here was going badly awry. To investigate the matter
further he moved briskly into the room and spoke to
her sharply.

'Why are you burning that letter, Sophie? Is it yours
to burn?'

He still had no suspicion of what she was really
doing, but when her face flamed first bright red and
then ashy white, and she flung at him, 'Oh, it's nothing. It's one of mine from an unwanted suitor,' he
went over to the grate and bent down to see if he
might find out to whom the letter was addressed.

By some freak of the fire as the envelope flared up

Marietta's name was plain upon it, and then, before he could read anything further, the poker in Sophie's hand pushed the letter deep into the flames and it was lost.

The Senator suddenly knew why his beloved daughter had never received a letter from Jack Dilhorne. He straightened up to meet Sophie's enraged and defiant gaze, before saying thickly, 'Why are you burning Marietta's letter?'

His words came out with great difficulty because the world had gone strangely dark as his violent anger seized and consumed him. In an effort to control his failing senses he put out a hand to take the poker from Sophie's grasp, before demanding, 'How many have you burned? And did you burn her letters to him as well?'

'It was my letter,' she exclaimed defiantly. 'My letter, not Marietta's. You are growing too old to see properly. I may burn my own correspondence if I wish. It is no business of yours what I do with it.'

Her insolence, the patent lies which she was telling him, and the injury to Marietta, fuelled his anger even more. He tried to speak again, to confront her with her wickedness, but even as he stared into her pretty, vicious face, the rage finally overwhelmed—and destroyed—him.

Sophie's face disappeared, to be replaced by Marietta's, alight with the joy which had filled it on the night when Jack had told her of his love for her, and then everything disappeared into the dark. He fell forward on to the hearthrug, prone at Sophie's feet, quite

still, the hand with the poker in it flung in the direction
of the fire…

Sophie, dazed, picked up the poker and stared down
at him with something approaching horror. The Senator never moved, and she suddenly realised that she
was saved. She flung the poker into the hearth, and
fell on her knees beside him, screaming in a terror
which was not all assumed. Somehow she had killed
her uncle, and, whatever else, she had not meant to
do that at all.

The door suddenly opened and Marietta appeared.
She took one look at her father lying still and quiet
before her, and then another at Sophie, who with great
presence of mind had risen to her feet, still screaming.
She carefully placed herself before the fire lest any
evidence remain there of what she had done.

Marietta's first act was to pull the bell for the servants, and then, saying, 'Stop that immediately,' to
slap the still-screaming Sophie sharply on the cheek,
thus adding one more to the catalogue of wrongs
which Sophie felt that she had suffered at her hands.

Still careful to keep herself before the fire, Sophie
began to sob quietly. Marietta, who was now down
on her knees, trying to discover how ill her father was,
said sternly, 'Enough of that noise. Be of use for once.
Go and tell Aunt Percival to send a servant for the
doctor.'

She began to lift her father's lolling head, in order
to place a cushion beneath it, although her common
sense had already told her that this was quite useless,
as would be the services of any doctor whom Aunt

Percival might summon. Her father had died before she had entered the room.

Before her, unheeded and unrecognisable, Jack's last despairing letter to her crumbled into its final ashes. No earthly evidence remained of Sophie's treachery and its dreadful consequences. Sophie hugged this thought to her all the way upstairs, and although she might have wished that what had just happened could have been in some way avoided, she knew that she was safe and Marietta finally thwarted.

In the turmoil which followed the Senator's sudden and unexpected death Sophie was not only as unhelpful as might have been expected, but, to both Aunt Percival and Marietta's surprise, spent her days having fit after fit of screaming hysterics.

'Really, Aunt Percival,' said Marietta one afternoon after the doctor had been sent for and Sophie had been dosed with laudanum to make her sleep, 'her behaviour is astonishingly excessive, considering how little she either loved, or liked, my father.'

'Attention drawing, as usual,' said Aunt Percival nastily, not knowing anything of Sophie's mixed feelings of guilt and relief. She had stopped Sophie screaming on that dreadful day before the doctor had arrived by slapping her so severely that her cheek was bruised. She was thus promptly added to Sophie's list of people to be dealt with one day.

While Marietta and Aunt Percival maintained a stoic calm at the funeral, Sophie distinguished herself by having her worst fit yet. She was promptly sent home with her parents by Aunt Percival, who told them that her consideration must now be Marietta, whose calm was as distressing to her as Sophie's excesses had been.

'I want her out of the house today,' she had announced, 'her proper place is with her parents.'

To Marietta she had said, just after the funeral when they were alone together again, once tea had been brought in and the curtains had been drawn, 'Now all this is over and everyone has gone, you and I must have a serious talk, my girl.'

Marietta said with feigned innocence, 'What about, Aunt?'

'You know perfectly well of what I speak,' said Aunt Percival. 'You are expecting a child, are you not? A child who has no father, for he has abandoned you. A child who will ruin you, for all your fortune. Have you thought once of what you intend to do to save yourself? Or do you intend to carry on and bear it before all Washington, to be a show and mock for Sophie and every other mean-minded gossip?'

Marietta stared at her aunt sitting there, placid, after she had uttered these scarifying words.

'I intend to go away—' she began, but her aunt interrupted her as though she were a child again.

'On your own, one supposes, without telling me.'

'And how did you find out that I was pregnant?' counter-attacked Marietta, the tears she had so far refused to shed falling down at last.

Her aunt looked sadly at her. 'Do you take me for a fool? I've not spent thirty years of my life watching over errant servant girls without recognising the symptoms of their folly—which you are showing so plainly.

'Going off with that man on his last afternoon. Oh, don't tell me you were at Katy Hoyt's, I know better. Coming home that night with the sort of face on you that you had as a child when Cook gave you a plum bun instead of a plain one. Keeping your underclothing from the wash that week, missing your courses, enduring morning sickness. And a pregnant woman has a special look which I got to know well.

'And here you are, so good and sensible and clever, and you've behaved no better than a poor servant girl when the first sweet-talking man comes along to seduce her and to leave her saddled with a bastard.'

'Oh, it's worse than that,' sniffled Marietta defiantly. 'For it was I who seduced him. I knew what I was doing and I'd do it again tomorrow. I can't say that I regret that afternoon, even if I didn't think I'd end up abandoned with a baby on the way.'

'Didn't think you'd end up with a baby?' echoed Aunt Percival incredulously. 'Why in the world you never thought of such a possibility beforehand beats me.'

'Oh, I suppose it was because it's a bad joke that the Hope women are slow to conceive, and Father and Mother were married for so many years before I was born. I must have thought that I was the same, and it was only one afternoon, and I thought that he loved me,' she ended breathlessly.

'You didn't think at all,' said Aunt Percival severely. 'You just jumped into bed with him with your head on fire—and now look at you!'

'Oh, don't,' wailed Marietta. 'I know that I'm wicked and a fool, and all that you say. I know that

I'm a fallen woman and that I've lost my lover. What's more, I want him back again almost more than I want respectability. I know that when the news is out that I'm ruined. Sophie will dance on me all over Washington.

'But I don't care. I want Jack, and I want my baby, oh, I do, I do…'

Grief over her father's death, added to the pain of her sad situation, overwhelmed her so much that Aunt Percival took her into her arms and rocked her as though she were the baby she had once been.

'There, there, my pretty,' she crooned. 'I can't get him back for you, and I don't want to after he's deserted you like this. But we'll save your good name for you. Trust me. I know exactly how to go about it.'

Marietta lifted her wet face to look wonderingly at her aunt. 'You do?'

'Yes, my darling. We'll go deep into the country to a farm where I have a distant female relative, and where no one else but her knows us. You shall be my poor niece whose husband was killed in that skirmish at Blagg's Crossing and who was left a widow to bear her baby alone. You had a breakdown, my dear, went mad with grief, and the doctor said that you needed country air to restore you before it was born.

'Oh, I can be an inventive liar when I want, and I have helped so many poor girls before you that it would be a sad thing if I can't help you.'

'But how shall we explain my disappearance from Washington?' asked Marietta anxiously.

'My dear, you were so distressed that you could not

bear to stay in the capital and went to visit relatives in Maryland. No one, knowing how close you were to your father, will query that.'

'And afterwards,' Marietta said. 'What about afterwards? And what about my baby? I don't want to lose him, too. I'm sure that it will be a him.'

'We'll think about that while we're in the country,' said Aunt Percival. 'Now dry your eyes and drink your tea. Thank God that because you were so close to your father no one will think it strange that you have fits of crying and are poorly as a consequence of grief over his death and will need to keep to your room before we leave. I shall tell everyone that you collapsed when everything was over. No one will question that—you were bound to do so in the end, they will say, looking wise.'

Marietta looked at her admiringly through her tears. 'Oh, you're right, you *are* an inventive liar.'

'Good, now put your feet up and I will bring you some sherry wine. Better for you than tea. You must take care of yourself now, and do as you're told for the baby's sake.'

Marietta lay back and let her aunt look after her. All her will-power, all her determination, had drained out of her since her father had died. She was content to be idle, to let Aunt Percival do the planning. The baby would come, will they, nil they, and afterwards…why, afterwards would take care of itself.

The weeks went by and Jack never received an answer to his letter. Morrison, the man with whom he was working, said to him one day when they were drinking in the bar at the Brevoort House, 'What's wrong with you, Dilhorne? Butler told me that you were a jolly fellow, but since you came here you've been anything but that. You look ill, too. Is it your health generally, or is it woman trouble?'

Jack nodded a 'yes' to the last question, but offered nothing in the way of an explanation.

'You'll be no good until you've cleared it up,' said Morrison bluntly. 'Back in Washington, is she? Did things go wrong there?'

'No,' said Jack. 'They went very right, and that's what worries me. I've never heard a word from her since I left, although she promised me most faithfully that she would write to me as often as she could. I would not have thought her to be a woman who would break her word.'

'Why not take a week off? God knows you've been working all hours. Go back and clear it up one way or another. You'll drive yourself into brain fever and break down completely otherwise.'

It seemed good advice, Jack thought. 'You'd give me a week off, then?'

'It would pay me in the end,' said Morrison bluntly.

'I'll think about it,' Jack said. 'Why not?'

He was still thinking about it that night when he went to a reception where he met a Senator who was a friend of the Hopes. On impulse he asked after them.

The senator looked grave. 'Haven't you heard?' he asked.

'No,' said Jack, 'I haven't heard anything about them since I left Washington.'

'Senator Hope died suddenly of a heart attack,' said his informant soberly.

'Oh,' said Jack, greatly shocked on hearing this sad news. 'And Miss Marietta,' he added, 'what of her?'

'Very sad, that,' said the Senator. 'She had a nervous breakdown, has left Washington and is travelling to recover from it.'

Jack's heart descended to where? Certainly lower than his boots.

'Left Washington,' he echoed, his voice hollow.

'Yes, indeed. Pity that, but it's understandable—she worked for her father for so many years that his death must have been a great blow.'

'I'm sure,' said Jack. Anything further he could say other than 'I am most sorry to hear it' sounded inadequate

He was numb. It would be pointless to travel to Washington. He wondered where Marietta was and what she was doing. And that was pointless, too. Whatever she was doing, and whomever she was with, she did not want him. She had not even answered his last letter, not even to tell him of her father's death, and she must have known how much he had liked and respected the old man.

No, it was plain that Miss Marietta Hope had finished with Mr Jack Dilhorne.

He must try to forget her—if he could.

Chapter Ten

⤜⤛⤜⤛⤜

Alan Dilhorne to Jack, September 1st, 1861

I cannot tell you how pleased I was to read in your latest despatch—you really do rival Russell of *The Times*—of your intention to settle yourself with the charming and clever Miss Marietta, and of the successful outcome of your adventures on the battlefields of the United States. I'm delighted to learn that you resisted the lures and wiles of Miss Sophie—a proper little scorpion, that one—avoid her, Jack, avoid her. Her behaviour at the battle, and that of Marietta, was exactly what I would have expected of both of them. The South's victory was also exactly what I would have expected at this stage of a war which I am sure the North will win—although whether we over here ought to want it to is quite another matter.

The rest of the letter dealt with family affairs, until the Postscript at the end.

Little brother, I have opened this before sending it, originally to tell you that they are making me a knight—Sir Alan, if you please—now that the male Hatton line has come to an end with Beverley's untimely death. Eleanor says that it is only fitting that the owner of Temple Hatton should have a title, and then my own joyful news was darkened by the sad tidings in your last letter.

So you have lost Marietta. I count that as a tragedy, as you must do. Her desertion of you surprises me. I had not thought that she would be so fickle, since she and her father both struck me as good and true. I can only commiserate with you and wish you better luck in the future. I live in some hope that you may yet hear from her.

Marietta Hope's Journal, Hentys' Farm, Maryland, October 3rd, 1861

I can only think that I feel the need to confide in a Journal because I have never had the time to keep one before, and I now have so much time to spare, and nothing to do in it, that my journal is almost my best friend—after Aunt Percival, of course. Besides, when I am writing about the day's non-events I have no time to think of Jack, only about the gift he has left me—for whose birth I wait with an impatience which surprises me. It certainly surprises Aunt Percival! 'Goodness, child,' she told me yesterday, 'I scarcely know you.' The only reply I could have made would have been, I scarcely know myself. Which is nothing less than the truth. I think that Mrs Henty thinks that I am a little simple—or have been left simple by grief for my poor dead hero of a husband!

Today I milked a goat. I think I like being mindless.

Jack Dilhorne to Alan, November 4th, 1861

Dear Sir Alan—what would the Patriarch have said to *that*?

Despite your last kind wish I have still heard nothing further from Marietta, and I am trying to forget her, which is difficult. I am also trying to persuade the Navy Department and Ericsson to allow me to accompany the *Monitor* on her sea trials, and form part of her crew when she goes on her maiden voyage. I think it is important that there should be a marine engineer on her who can report at first hand to her inventor on her performance in battle.

Wish me luck. Perhaps, if I have been unlucky in love, I might be lucky—or luckier—in war.

Sophie Hope to Avory Grant, November 17th, 1861

Will you be at the Norrises' Reception on Saturday evening? I am hoping to be allowed to go. It seems to me that mourning for Uncle Jacobus's death has gone on far too long. It isn't as though he was a young man. No, in answer to your letter, I have no notion where Marietta has gone to, or any address to which you may write, either to her or to Aunt Percival. I hear that all the Percivals are in mourning for some backwoods cousin who was killed at Blagg's Crossing. Really, this war is becoming too dreary for words. I shall be only too happy when it is over. I shall be sure to save a few dances for you if you are at the Norrises'.

Jack Dilhorne to Alan, late February, 1862

You see in me a survivor from the first sea trials of the *Monitor*, but only just! She really ought to be called a submersible, or a submarine, she rides so low in the water. Her most amazing feature is a gun turret which revolves so that she may fire at enemy warships from any direction without changing course—*if* we ever manage to sail her safely to any place where an enemy is to be found, that is. People over here are annoyed at the British for trying to break the blockade which Lincoln has ordered against the Southern ports. They feel that a war against slavery ought to be supported by a free people, not opposed.

I have still heard nothing, nor do I now expect to, from Marietta. I have met a pretty young woman journalist, Peggy Shipton, who believes in all the things which advanced young women in the States are taught to believe. I suppose that I really ought to try to console myself for Marietta's loss by becoming interested in her. She has already told me that if we wish to enjoy ourselves we can go to bed together, whenever I am willing to oblige her, because she believes in free love, and that marriage is an institution designed to make slaves of women. Before I met Marietta I might have taken advantage of such a splendid offer, but I am foolish enough to entertain a vague hope that we might yet meet again, a hope that grows fainter with each passing day.

Marietta's Journal, January 21st, 1862

The war—and Jack—seem so far away. I dreamed about him last night. It was an odd dream and I had an even odder conversation with him. We were on a ship—or what passed for a ship—it wasn't like any I had ever seen before. He said, 'What do you think of it?' I said, 'I don't think about much these days—only about the birth of our son.' I'm sure that he's a boy. Why, I don't know. Jack said, 'It could be a girl.' I said, 'What a strange thing for you to say. You don't even know that I'm expecting your child.' He waved a hand around the strange ship, and said, 'I don't understand *you*. This is my child.'

And then I woke up.

Jack Dilhorne to Alan, March 10th, 1862

Forgive me if my writing is barely legible, but I spent yesterday taking part in my first sea battle. We set off from New York in the *Monitor* on March 3rd, making for Chesapeake Bay where the *Merrimac*, the South's iron-clad, had been sinking our wooden ships which had no defence against it. We didn't discover this until we arrived in the Bay, to be asked to defend those ships still afloat, to keep the *Merrimac* away from them and, if possible, sink her.

We finally engaged her on Sunday, March 9th—the crew later named it Bloody Sunday. We had barely slept for the two days before the battle—keeping the *Monitor* afloat took all our time and strength. One day I will tell you all about it. The most surprising thing was how noisy it was. I am half-deaf today. As a civilian I was supposed to stand about and observe, but that proved impossible when I saw my friends being maimed and killed. Suffice it to say that I did what I could.

In the middle of the battle I had the strangest experience. I have been having odd dreams about Marietta ever since Christmas. I remember that in one I was trying to show her the *Monitor* and she kept babbling nonsense at me which I could make nothing of. This time, when the gun turret was hit and Captain Worden was badly injured, I knelt down to comfort him, and said something encouraging, I can't remember what. Instead of Worden, I saw Marietta. She was lying on a bed, her face distorted. Someone, I think that it was Aunt Percival, was holding her hand. She seemed to be in pain. For one mad moment I thought that it was she whom I was comforting, not Worden. I put out my hand to her—and then she was gone, and I was holding on to Worden's instead. He had been blinded by the shot which had hit the turret. My vision of Marietta was brief, but was intensely real while it lasted.

I write this to you in order to hold on to my sanity. I was told that strange things happen in battle, but I had not expected anything so strange as that. Suffice it that we finally drove the *Merrimac* off. We did not destroy her, but she was so badly wounded that she will not prey on our ships again. War is even more dreadful than I had thought. When I was helping to design the *Monitor* it was simply lines on paper. I never thought that what I was doing would kill and destroy— but necessity makes savages of us all. Hold on to your peace over there—we do not value it properly until we lose it.

Marietta's Journal, March 10th, 1862

Aunt Percival is scolding me for writing my Journal so soon after I have given birth, but I most desperately want to record everything which happened on the day I was blessed with my beautiful baby boy, who came into the world nearly a month early. All the pain and agony, and the long dreary months of waiting, were rendered worthwhile when I first saw his dear little face and his beautiful blue eyes, so like Jack's.

I haven't told Aunt Percival. She already fears for my reason, and would fear even more if I were to tell her that at the worst moment of my agony I suddenly saw Jack holding out his hand to me. 'Hold on,' he was saying. 'Hold on, help is at hand.' And then he was gone. I was only able to recognise him by his beautiful blue eyes. His face was black and his forehead was bleeding. Before I had time to wonder what in the world was happening to me, I gave one last push—and there was my baby. We are going to call him Jacobus, after my father, but he is so small I can only think of him as Cobie. Aunt Percival agrees. Jacobus is far too pompous for such a little mite. I never dreamed that I could be so happy.

The Naval Attaché at the British Embassy in Washington reporting to Sir Alan Dilhorne, Cabinet Minister, March 12th, 1862

I have to report that the latest news from Chesapeake Bay, detailing the battle of the iron-clads at Hampton Roads, is of the utmost importance to all the navies of the world, as Captain Cowper Coles prophesied that it would be. Wooden ships are obsolete and the task of rebuilding our navies to replace them must begin at once now that the *Monitor* and *Merrimac* have proved their use in battle. A little bird whispered to me that your brother Jack was present at the action, which he survived…

Aunt Percival to her friend, Allegra Van Horn, March 15th, 1862

I still have sad news of my dear niece Marietta. The shock of her father's death continues to affect her. She is quite overwrought, and hardly seems to know what to do these days, but is content to ply her needle and spend her time reading novels, by which you will judge how greatly changed she is. To add to our woes, my cousin Henty's girl has died having a baby boy. You may remember that she married another cousin of mine, Lieutenant Philip Percival, who was killed in that wretched skirmish at Blagg's Crossing. I am trying to persuade Marietta that it is our duty to adopt him, particularly since his mother's last wish was that he should be named Jacobus after the Senator. The Hentys cannot afford to bring up yet another child, having so many of their own. His christening produced the first smile on my darling's face since her father's death.

Marietta's Journal, May 5th, 1862

Aunt Percival bullies me unmercifully these days. She says that it is time we left our Arcadian fastness and went home. I am so happy here, looking after my darling Cobie, that I have no wish to return to Washington where I must pretend that he is not mine. In my heart I know that she is right. I have agreed to leave in early June so that I may continue to feed him myself for a little longer. My uncle Hope has written me an urgent letter saying that I am needed to agree to some changes which the war has forced on us in the disposition of my father's estate. I worry that everyone who meets me will guess that I am now

a mother. Aunt Percival tells me not to talk nonsense, but I know that having Cobie has changed
me very much.

Avory Grant to Marietta Hope, June 20th, 1862

I cannot tell you how delighted I was to meet
you again last night and discover that, despite
your illness after your father's death, you have
not only recovered completely but have acquired
a rare beauty which leaves me more regretful
than ever that you refused me all those years ago.
I shall be at the Van Horns' ball tomorrow, and
I hear that you will also be present. Save me a
dance, no, make that dances, my dear. We must
not waste any more time.

Marietta's Journal, August 1st, 1862

Today Avory Grant proposed to me and I accepted him. I have finally to admit that Jack has
gone for ever and that Avory is a good man and
will make Cobie an excellent father. When he
arrived this afternoon and begged me to agree to
marry him this time, I did not immediately reply,
but told him the truth about Cobie, for I could
not deceive him by pretending that he is not
mine. Everyone here knows him as Jacobus Percival, Aunt Percival's ward. To my surprise he
looked at me in the grave way he has these days
and said, 'My darling, I knew that he was yours
that first time I visited you on your return, when

he began to cry. You rushed into the other room to pick him up and the look on your face told me everything. It explained your long absence and the glory which motherhood has given you. Forget the wretch who fathered him, and betrayed you, and let me take his place in every way. He shall be Cobie Grant, a brother for my dear Susanna who already loves him.'

Well, that is true enough, and although I do not feel for Avory what I felt for Jack, this new feeling may be a better one. We are to be married soon, for, as he says, we are neither of us getting any younger and the war may take him away now that he has recovered from his wounds. He makes me feel young again and his kindness and love for my little son is all that I could wish for. May God bless our union. Last night I dreamed of Jack for the first time since Cobie's birth. How strange that I should have seen him that morning, on the day of the Battle of Hampton Roads in which, Ezra Butler told me yesterday, Jack took part. I must try to forget him: my future is with Avory.

Ezra Butler to Jack Dilhorne, August 1st, 1862

By the by, your old flame, Marietta Hope, is back in Washington, having recovered from her father's sudden and tragic death. She is in fine form and the talk is that she may marry an old flame of hers from the distant past, Avory Grant. I believe that you met him once when you first came to the States.

The Washington Post, *August 10th, 1862*

The marriage between Captain Avory Grant, the war hero, and Miss Marietta Hope, the daughter of the late Senator Hope, was celebrated at her home yesterday. At the wishes of both of them it was attended only by the families of the pair.

Sophie Hope to her friend, Isabelle Tranter of the Boston Tranters, August 12th, 1862

Would you believe that, after all the high hopes I had of him, Avory Grant deserted me for that poor stick, Marietta, when she returned to Washington with Aunt Percival and a squalling child who was sick all over me the first time I visited them. To cap it all, he married her two days ago. Of course, I had to go to the wedding and pretend how happy I was for them. What is it that she has that neither of us possess? First she took Jack Dilhorne from me, and now Avory. Why should we, who are nearly half her age and possess twice her looks, be left on the shelf? Having written that, I have high hopes of Hunter Van Horn. He's not bad-looking and will inherit the Van Horn fortune, which I understand is considerable. Wish me luck!

Jack Dilhorne to Sir Alan, August 15th, 1862

I have recently heard that Marietta has married Avory Grant. I am not sure whether you met him when you were over here. He was a good fellow and something of a hero from his conduct in one of the War's earlier skirmishes. She should be happy with him. I shall be leaving New York and going into the field myself to help with the Naval River War in the South. Remember the woman journalist I told you of recently? She and I finally had the affair she wanted. I proposed marriage, but she would have none of it. Unless she changes her mind it is over. My departure seems a suitable time to end it. I am growing old and wish to settle down…if I can ever find anyone to replace Marietta, that is.

I think of her constantly. Perhaps, in the crucible of war, I shall forget her.

Hunter Van Horn to Sophie Hope, September 2nd, 1862

I wish to make it quite plain to you in writing that I have withdrawn my offer of marriage to you after your recent disgraceful conduct at the Winthrops' ball. I could not ally my family and myself to a person who spoke of, and to, Avory Grant's wife with such churlish rudeness in a public place for all to hear. Pray do not attempt to visit me: I shall not change my mind. To spare you I am prepared to put it about that we parted by mutual agreement. Should you continue to pester me, I should not hesitate to publish the true reason for the breakdown of our engagement.

Marietta's Journal, November 20th, 1862

The day we have been dreading has finally arrived. Avory has been posted as Colonel and is to accompany General Ambrose Burnside, who is the new Commander of the Army of the Potomac, with orders to drive General Robert E. Lee from Fredericksburg, on the Rappahannock River. We have been so happy together, and I had to summon up all my courage when the time came for him to leave so as not to disgrace myself breaking down. I could not help but remember that when I last saw Jack we hoped for a happy reunion in the future—and look what happened to that! Aunt Percival was her usual tower of strength, but Susanna, who is now old enough to understand that Papa may not return, was inconsolable when he had gone.

Avory was his usual quiet and stoical self: the self I have come to admire and love. 'I must do my duty,' he said. 'I am not the only man to leave a loving wife and family behind.' Among the many things which he said to me on the night before he left was that I must distrust Sophie, for he felt that she would do me a mischief if she could. I told him that I would be careful. How odd to think that if I had accepted him all those years ago Susanna would have been my child and Cobie would not have existed. Aunt Percival was quite cross with me when I mentioned this to her. 'Land sakes, child,' she roared at me. 'You have enough to trouble you without letting your imagination run riot and making yourself more!' As usual she was right.

The Washington Post, *December 14th, 1862*

General Burnside has been relieved of the command of the Army of the Potomac following the disaster at Fredericksburg, where it appears that he has lost much of his Army and failed to dislodge Lee. No details are yet in.

The Washington Post, *December 18th, 1862*

Listed among the dead is Colonel Avory Grant, the hero of the skirmish at Compton's Landing in 1861.

Aunt Percival to her cousin Ginny in Boston, December 20th, 1862

What a poor Christmas we shall have of it this year! I grieve for Marietta. She has had much to endure and I can only hope that this latest blow will not destroy her will to live altogether. What can God mean by treating my good and brave darling so harshly?

Marietta's Journal December 20th, 1862

This is the last entry I shall make. In future I shall try to live for the day and forget the past...

Jack to Sir Alan, April 27th, 1863

I have not written to you for some months
since I have been travelling on the Southern
front, inspecting everything which moves on water and seeing war in all its horror. I think that,
at last, I have finally grown up. The Patriarch
always said that suffering and privation made a
man out of a boy and, as usual, he was right. So
many of the soldiers, living, dead and dying, are
little more than boys. They called me Grandad!
I never thought that thirty-one was old, but they
have brought the passing of the years home to
me—and I regret the loss of Marietta more than
ever.

I contracted a light fever which would not
leave me, and the Navy doctor who examined me
told me bluntly that since I am still, technically,
a civilian, I ought to go home to rest since he
diagnosed me as suffering from overwork and exhaustion, so I shall be obeying him. There is sure
to be work waiting for me in New York, but it
will not entail me wondering whether I shall be
alive at the end of the next five minutes!

Sophie Hope to Isabelle Tranter, July, 1863

Would you believe it? Hunter Van Horn has
proposed to Marietta! What's more, she turned
him down! She's still in mourning for Avery. I
think that she must have a preference for black.
I thought that James Whitmore was about to pro-

pose to me—and then the next thing that I hear is that he is to marry that snub-nosed little Judy Griffin.

I hear that you are to marry Walker Cabot. Congratulations and all that. I suppose there are more eligible men in Boston than Washington, what with the war and all. I shall try to persuade Pa to allow me to visit you this summer. If you can manage to catch a man, then I certainly ought to be able to.

Aunt Percival to Mrs Leila Henty, July, 1863

We are all well here in Washington, despite everything. Marietta is being very brave. I sometimes think that the only thing which is stopping her from succumbing to all her losses is young Cobie. He really is the most precocious child. He's not yet eighteen months old, but he walks and talks like a child years older. He's such a good little thing, and he always behaves himself in company—except when his cousin Sophie visits. She's always sure to bring on a tantrum. It must be his good taste.

I shall be glad when this war is over.

In her Journal she wrote, for no one to see: 'I think that Marietta still grieves for that wretch who deserted her. I could wring his neck—until I look at Cobie.'

Chapter Eleven

August, 1863

Go home, the Navy doctor had said to Jack. What was home? It was merely a cold, half-empty mansion on Long Island where no one was waiting for him.

Travelling North was a tedious business, except on the one occasion when, by some odd chance, he met Charles Stanton who was also on his way home.

'If I didn't have my grand house, my useless title, and all the responsibilities that go with them,' he told Jack, 'I would stay in the States. I agree with Alan—who, as usual, is always right—the future is here, not in Europe.'

Jack had nodded agreement. After that he told Charles, who had asked him for his news, of his loss of Marietta, and of her marriage. Charles gave him an odd look, before saying slowly, 'I find it difficult to believe that she abandoned you. If it were not that she has married Avory Grant—I remember him, a decent enough chap—I would tell you to return to Washing-

ton and try to discover what went wrong. I'm a little
surprised that you never thought of doing so.'

'I did,' said Jack sadly, 'and then I had news of her
father's sudden death, and that she had retreated into
the country—no one knew where.'

'Um,' said Charles, who was never long-winded, 'a
pity, that,' and tactfully abandoned the topic. Later he
was to wonder briefly whether Sophie had taken a
hand in the game, but concluded that, all things considered, the notion was somewhat fanciful.

Jack finally arrived home on a dark rainy day, a day
which matched his current state of mind. Letters were
piled high in the hall. One was from Peggy Shipton.
To his surprise, it told him of her marriage. She added
at the end, 'I refused you because you still had that
other woman on your mind. Why don't you go back
and find out what happened?'

She was the second person to tell him that, but how
could he? Marietta was married to a good man and
that was that.

The last letter was from Ezra Butler, delivered all
of eight months ago, just after he had left for the
South, asking him to visit Washington as soon as he
was free to do so. 'I grow old,' he wrote, 'and need
a successor for the business. You are like enough to
your late pa to make a good one.'

There was a postscript to this letter which contained
a surprise for him.

Thought that you might like to know that news
has just come in that Marietta Hope's husband

was killed at Fredericksburg. She seems dogged
by ill luck, poor thing. First the Senator's tragic
death, and now this.

Jack put the letter down thoughtfully. He had not
fully understood that the Senator's death had been
tragic, and he wondered a little at Butler's motives in
sending him the news.

So, her husband was dead, poor devil. They had not
been married long. He wondered why she had married
Grant—perhaps that was why she had cast him off.
On second thoughts, that seemed a little improbable.
She had not married Grant until nearly a year had
passed since he had last seen her. Perhaps he, Jack,
had seemed second-rate when Avory had come back
into her life. It was still an agony not to know why
she had abandoned him.

Jack had once said that, like his late and formidable
father, he never looked back. Perhaps it was time to
do so. There were several reasons why he ought to
visit Washington. Not only did he need to accept Ezra
Butler's invitation to go there, but he had half-
promised to visit the Secretary of State for the Navy
in order to report to him the details of his journey to
the river war in the South.

And when—and if—he saw Marietta again, what
then? Would he at last discover what had gone wrong,
and why she had left him after their last golden afternoon together? And if he did find out, it might either
destroy or ease the ache in his heart which plagued
him whenever he thought of her.

Perhaps simply to see her without explanations or

recriminations would relieve his pain. All in all, she was unfinished business and, one way or another, he would finish it.

Washington was dingier than he remembered it. It was crammed with people: soldiers were everywhere, and whores stood on each corner. Every building in the capital looked seedy, and war had transformed Willard's into something less than it had been. He was staying with Butler and was grateful for his hospitality.

Ezra had aged in the two years since Jack had last seen him. Ezra thought that Jack had changed, too. He was more serious, less light-hearted. At dinner that first day, he looked speculatively at his guest and asked, 'What did you think of my PS?'

'About Mrs Grant?' replied Jack, as though there had been another. 'I was sorry for her, of course.'

'Only sorry?' queried Butler. 'Forgive me for being an old gossip, but I had thought that there was more to your relationship with her than that implies.'

'There was,' said Jack. 'But something went wrong. I may try to find out what it was.'

'I'm not sure that she's in town,' said Butler. 'She's seen occasionally in public, but she lives a restricted life compared to the one she enjoyed with the Senator and later with Grant.'

'Yes,' said Jack. His behaviour confirmed Butler's belief that he had changed. He was a harder, more mature man than he had been before he had left for New York. Ezra dropped the subject. Jack was obviously a big enough man now to look after himself. They talked business.

'You're going to be one of those whom this war will make rich,' commented Butler. 'The USA is going to be the number one world power when this war is over. Just let those Europeans watch out!'

'Yes,' said Jack, 'and that makes me feel a little guilty because I shan't have fought in the war.'

'You shouldn't,' said Butler robustly. 'You'll only be getting rich because of all you've done for the Union and from what I hear you've certainly done your bit. You went to war with the *Monitor* when you needn't have done. And your behaviour in the South was certainly beyond the mere call of duty.'

Jack said nothing to this. He looked tired, Butler thought, and he ordered him to bed. Tomorrow was another day and young Dilhorne ought to be ready for it. Besides, he was now sure that the Jack Dilhorne who had returned from the war would be the ideal young man to take over Butler and Rutherfurd's when the time came for an old man finally to admit his age.

In the meantime he would hope that somehow Jack would be reunited with his Marietta again.

If Jack harboured any such hopes he did not say so. He thought that he would let a few days pass before he called on Marietta. Once he would have called on her the moment he had arrived in Washington and stormed the doors, but something that was almost superstition made him delay.

Perhaps he had been too forward in the past, taken things for granted. This time he would be more cautious. So it was with mingled hope and fear that he approached what was now Marietta Grant's home. The blinds were drawn, he noted with some dismay, and the house had a deserted look about it. Nevertheless he rapped the knocker smartly.

No one answered for some time and then the door opened to reveal Asia, who had let him in on his first visit to the mansion. She stared at him for a moment before her face broke into a broad smile.

'Oh, it's Mister Jack. Fancy seeing you again.'

A woman's voice from within, not Marietta's, called, 'Who is it, Asia?'

'It's Mr Jack, Miz Percival, come a-calling.'

Aunt Percival called back peremptorily, 'Tell Mr Jack Dilhorne to go away at once. He's not welcome in this house.'

'I've come to see Marietta—Mrs Grant, that is,' Jack said, astonished at the dislike and contempt he could hear in Miss Percival's voice. He wondered what could have provoked it.

'Indeed, you may not see her. Nor does she wish to see you. Asia, bid the man good afternoon, and close the door.'

All of this was conducted by Marietta's aunt, with whom he had been something of a favourite, from inside the house and without even doing him the courtesy of showing herself.

Asia offered him a wistful smile and murmured, 'Best go, Mr Jack. I know from what I have overheard that Miss Percival means what she says.'

Jack nodded. What else could he do? He watched Asia secure the door against him, and then began to walk away, wondering what he could have done to have inspired such hatred. Strangely enough, the very venom with which Aunt Percival had spoken inspired him, not to give up the battle to regain Marietta, but to pursue it with increased vigour.

Although how he would be able to do any such thing remained, for the moment, a mystery. The only things which might help him were those which his father had always relied upon: time and chance.

'You would not, could not, guess who came to see you today, my love, and if I could conceal his arrival from you, I would, but I must tell you, lest others do, for it was Asia who answered the door and wanted to admit him.'

Marietta had just seated herself with a weary sigh, the result of a difficult afternoon. She had just returned from a visit to the Hamilton Hopes. She had had no wish to make it, but the man was her late father's brother and she owed him the duty of kinship. They had particularly asked that she bring Cobie, and Avory's daughter, Susanna, with her. She had done so, praying that Sophie would not be present.

Alas, Sophie, on being informed of the invitation, had turned down another engagement for the afternoon, even at the risk of offending her hosts. She felt a terrible need to see Marietta at close quarters. They had barely met since Marietta and Avory's marriage.

She had been sitting in the parlour, magnificently dressed, when Marietta had arrived. She had treated pretty little Susanna to a cold stare, and glared at Cobie, who had been trotting along, holding his foster-sister's hand. He loved Susanna dearly; indeed, at this stage of his life he loved everybody dearly, but Susanna most of all.

Sophie had little time for children, and had said to her mother on hearing that she had invited Susanna and Cobie as well as Marietta, 'I can only hope that you are arranging for their nursemaid to take them to the kitchen for tea. Children do so spoil conversation.'

'Certainly not!' Mrs Hope had exclaimed. She was growing tired of Sophie's many large and small self-ishnesses. 'That would be most uncivil. Susanna is a war hero's child, and Cobie is the best behaved little boy I have ever come across. He conducted himself like an angel on my last visit to dear Marietta. Besides, it would do you good to entertain them: you will have children of your own one day and will need to know how to look after them.'

If 'God forbid' was Sophie's secret reaction to that unwelcome statement it did not show. Unfortunately, her mother, determined to encourage her to amuse Marietta's charges, picked Cobie up and began to cuddle and pet him—something which he always enjoyed.

'Come,' said Mrs Hope, handing him to her daughter, 'let cousin Sophie look after you.'

'He is not my cousin,' said Sophie sullenly, perching him on her knees and offering him nothing of the loving warmth to which he was accustomed, 'but if you think I ought to entertain him, I suppose I must.'

This was ungracious, even for Sophie, and her mother coloured a little. Susanna said, sharply for her, 'Cobie doesn't need entertaining, he entertains himself, and he does not like being treated as though he were a parcel.'

This accurate description of Sophie's handling of him did not help matters. It was her turn to colour and to show her anger by clutching Cobie in a death grip before bouncing him violently up and down on her knee.

It was one of the many wise sayings of mothers and grandmothers in those days that babies and little children always knew whether the person who was holding them was a friend or not. Cobie immediately demonstrated his mistrust of Sophie by beginning to cry, something which he rarely did, and to try to twist out of her grasp.

'Goodness me,' exclaimed Sophie, 'of all things I do detest a squalling child,' and she almost flung Cobie at Marietta.

Susanna, who had been watching Sophie's unkind treatment of her treasure, said loudly, 'I don't like that lady, she's not kind.'

'Well, really,' said Sophie. 'Have I given up an afternoon at the Van Deusens' gala in order to be pestered by *two* badly behaved children?'

'Sophie!' exclaimed her agonised mother. 'Apologise to Marietta at once. It is your own unkind conduct which has caused Cobie's distress.' For he was now howling loudly. He was always sensitive to the feelings of those around him, and the waves of dislike coming from Sophie were something to which he was not accustomed.

'Indeed, not,' said Sophie, now lost to all sense of propriety by her hatred of Marietta and her own failure to secure a proposal from anyone halfway decent. 'If you will excuse me, I will retire: it is not too late for me to visit the Van Deusens, where there will be no impudent brats to spoil the proceedings.'

She was no sooner out of the room than Mrs Hope added her tears to Cobie's.

'I don't know what has come over her these days,' she sobbed. 'She was such a pretty child, a little head-strong, perhaps, but not like this. She has been upset ever since her papa refused to allow her to visit Isabelle Tranter in Boston. He said that it was time that she settled down a little.'

Her sobs redoubled to such a degree that Marietta went over to her aunt to try to comfort her—something made difficult by her own disgust at Sophie's behaviour. The afternoon was ruined. She felt compelled to reprimand Susanna gently for her harsh—if justified—criticism of Sophie; so to Cobie's hiccuping distress was added Susanna's unhappy face.

Now Marietta was listening, her face growing whiter by the minute, to what Aunt Percival was telling her.

'It was Jack, wasn't it?' she asked faintly. 'How could he? What could possess him, after two long years of silence, to come here as though nothing had happened?'

'In fairness, I suppose that he's in Washington on business,' said Aunt Percival. 'The trouble is that you will be moving in the same circles and you are sure to meet; there's no help for it.'

'Well, I shall not speak to him, that's for sure,' returned Marietta robustly. 'I have nothing to say to him, and he chose, two years ago, to say nothing to me.'

Her words were braver than her thoughts, and she was not telling the truth. She had the most shameful wish to see him again, to throw herself at him, to tell him that he was the father of her child, the child whom she had borne in deserted loneliness, and to whom Avory had given his name when many men would have disowned him and refused to marry her.

If she could not forgive Jack, she could also not forget him.

'The Van Deusens' afternoon gala is to be followed by a reception, to which your cousin Julie and her husband are escorting you. He's almost sure to be there—and Sophie, too. I suppose that she'll be setting her cap at him again.'

Why did it hurt so much to hear Aunt Percival say that? Jack Dilhorne was nothing to her. He could marry a thousand Sophies for all she cared. He deserved her—they would make a fine double-dealing pair.

'Yes,' said Marietta faintly. 'I suppose that's a real possibility. Avory told me, before he left for the war, that there was not a man in Washington who would have her for a wife. Aunt Hope muttered something about Carver Massingham, who will be her escort to-night.'

'Carver Massingham!' exclaimed Aunt Percival scornfully. 'She must be in a bad way to be going around with *him*. He's nothing but a middle-aged, low-life profiteer. God knows, he's rich enough, but what a come-down after some of her beaux.'

'All of whom have now married other women,' sighed Marietta. 'Who would have thought it?'

'And her looks are not what they were,' said Aunt Percival cattily. There was no answer to that from Marietta because she had thought the same thing earlier that afternoon. Sophie's unpleasant soul was beginning to show on her face, and her passion for cream cakes and food was destroying her once dainty figure.

'Well, I'm not crying off myself because Jack might be there,' Marietta said briskly. 'And if I am to go, I shall have to start getting ready soon. You're sure you won't come? Mrs Van Deusen invited you.'

'Quite sure. You go and enjoy yourself, and try to forget Sophie's megrims—and him.'

Which Marietta thought, later on at the Van Deusens', was more easily said than done: particularly when she first saw Jack. He was standing by the door, Ezra Butler by his side. Jack had, in some subtle way, changed. He looked harder than the man she had known. There had been a softness about him, an easy charm, but this man possessed a cold, shuttered face. It was the face of a man of power, a face which she had seen time and again in Washington, a face like that of his brother Alan.

If she were fanciful, she would also have thought that it was the face of a man who had suffered. But what of that? Had she not suffered, and at his hands? She watched his eyes quarter the ballroom before he turned to speak to Ezra, who shook his head at him.

Was he looking for her? And, if so, why? What could he possibly want from her, after two long years? She turned away to speak to her current partner. He was a member of the Beauregard family, a man who a few years ago would not have cared to know her, for all her wealth, let alone pursue her now that she was an even richer widow. The Beauregards had no need to marry money and therefore could afford to marry for love, or to acquire beauty.

Whatever else Jack had done to her, loving him and bearing his child had made her attractive to other men. Oh, she knew that she would never be beautiful as the world accounted beauty, but she possessed something better than that: a glow of pride, of accomplishment, enhanced by fact that the severe lines which betrayed the strength of her character and will had been softened by a rare humour. Yes, she did owe Jack something—but he owed her more.

'Is that Jack Dilhorne over there?' Danvers Beauregard was asking. 'The man whose English brother made such a stir two years ago? I believe that you and the Senator were very friendly with him then, were you not?'

'Oh, yes,' she tried to reply carelessly. 'But that was then, this is now.'

If Danvers Beauregard thought that this was an odd answer he did not say so. He was still by her side, when Jack, having seen her from across the room, came over to speak to her.

He had examined her from afar, and unknowingly, like Marietta with him, had thought how much she had changed. She had become a strange, rare beauty whom even a jealous Sophie would have found it difficult to put down. Oh, he must speak to her, he must. The two lost years were as though they had never

been: but he must find out, and soon, why they had
become lost.

He reached her at last. She was wearing an amethyst
and silver gown, her rich chestnut hair was upswept
and a small tiara of amethysts and pearls nestled in it.
The amethyst-coloured gown was probably the result
of the reduced mourning after the obligatory six
months had passed since Avory's death. Indeed, in the
war, such mourning had become, for the time being,
less obligatory.

If Jack had ever thought that his passion for her
was dead, slain by her abandonment of him, the mere
sight of her standing there before him, in all her glory,
told him otherwise. If absence from her had done anything, it had made that passion stronger.

'Marietta,' he managed hoarsely, all his ready wit,
the things he had planned to say to her quite forgotten.
'At last, we may speak…'

She raised her fan to her lips before dropping it and
remarking in an indifferent voice dripping with icicles,
'Mr Dilhorne, I have nothing to say to you, and you,
sir, can have nothing to say to me. We meet, and part,
as strangers,' and she began to turn away from him.

Like Jack, it was not what she had meant to say if
she ever saw him again, but she was afraid that the
mere sight of that once-loved face was enough to set
her raging like a maenad if she were not careful. He
had let her go lightly enough, so she must play the
Roman matron to whom duty and honour were everything—and mistaken passion nothing.

To Jack this encounter was the stuff of nightmare.
She was rejecting him again, and in public, too. He

could see Danvers Beauregard's avid eyes on him. He was waiting, no doubt, for the further revelations which might follow on such an almighty snub, which was the result of—what?

Had they been alone, Jack might have said something, but Marietta's dislike of him was so plain that it drove every rational thought from his head. He wanted to fall on his knees, to clutch her hand, to ask her what he could have done to provoke such dislike, nay, hate. As it was, mindful that there were other avid eyes on them, and—for her sake—however much she had publicly demeaned him, he could not create a disgraceful scene.

He bowed, his hand on his heart, and said to her retreating back, 'I had hoped that we might discuss…'

She turned and said, 'Enough. I will discuss nothing with you, sir. If you are a gentleman, you will refrain from badgering me.'

Her words were hurting her as much as they were obviously hurting him, but she dared not trust herself to his falsity again, as much for poor Cobie's sake as for her own. Jack said no more.

'Then allow me to write to you, at least…' he began.

'*Write!*' This time when she faced him her scorn was so strong that she might have been the Medusa herself, the woman whose look could turn a man to stone. 'Pray spare me that, sir,' and she turned away again, obviously determined to have nothing whatsoever to do with him.

He turned away himself and, his face white and grim, would have left the room and the house at once, except that Ezra caught him roughly by the shoulder and said, in a hoarse whisper, 'For God's sake, man, stay. You cannot wish to expose either her, or yourself, to the mean gossip which would follow your retreat. I have no notion of what went wrong between the pair of you, but I know you to be a man of honour and of sense, and I must believe that there is something here which needs an explanation.

'From what you have said to me, you are mystified by her rejection of you. If so, there must be a reason, and a powerful one, for her to do such a thing, and to speak to you as she just did—she is no fly-by-night fool like her cousin Sophie. A man of sense—such as yourself—would try to find that reason. Think, man, think, what might you have done to deserve this?'

'Nothing,' said Jack, equally hoarse. 'I have done nothing that I can think of, and dammit, I love her still, and I fear I always will.'

'All the more reason not to give up. There is an old saying I once came across, it goes something like this, "Truth will arise, though all the world may hide it from men's eyes." Hold on to that, Jack—and remember, your father never gave up, ever, and it brought him an empire. Dammit, man, you're only after a woman!'

Jack began to laugh, his whole face changing as he did so. 'You're right, Ezra, I'm behaving like a spineless ninnyhammer. I'll find out why she has changed towards me so greatly if I have to turn the thumbscrews on a few people.'

Ezra clapped him on the back. 'That's the spirit, old

fellow. Now, let us go and get politely drunk—the other sort wouldn't do for the Van Deusens!'

It was easy to make such a decision, Jack thought, but harder to follow it up. He couldn't kidnap Marietta, or Aunt Percival, and compel them to talk to him, and if either of them saw him they went out of their way to avoid him. He came across Aunt Percival once in the street, and she immediately dashed off in the opposite direction. His own feelings of decency stopped him from pursuing her and grasping her by the arm to compel her to speak to him.

Desperate measures seemed to be necessary, particularly when he heard, through Ezra, that the word was that Marietta Grant was about to leave Washington and retire again to her farm near Bethesda—doubtless to avoid his hateful presence, Jack thought morosely.

It was while he was walking down the street where Marietta lived, after a hard morning spent in the offices of the Secretary of the Navy, that he suddenly remembered that when he had called there the little black servant had welcomed him and tried to console him. She, at least, still liked Mr Jack—although she had hinted that Marietta and Aunt Percival no longer did. If he called again to ask her whether she knew of any reason for their dislike, she might be able to enlighten him.

And if she didn't, could he persuade her to trick Aunt Percival into coming to the door in person where he might speak to her face to face instead of being abused at a distance as he had been the last time he had called?

He turned round, walked back to the Grant house and knocked smartly on the door. To his great good fortune, it was again Asia who answered and no one else seemed to be about.

'Oh, Mr Jack,' she said reproachfully. 'You know you're not welcome here.'

'But you were kind to me when I called the other day,' he said. 'Perhaps you can tell me *why* I am not welcome—it would ease my mind.'

She leaned forward and said confidentially, 'Now *that* I don't know, for neither of the Missises gossips, as you are well aware, Mr Jack. You'd have to ask them why.'

'But they won't talk to me,' said Jack sadly. 'Think, Asia, for old times' sake, would you consent to help me to speak to either Miss Percival or Mrs Grant?'

'Now how could I do that?' asked Asia, her small face solemn.

'By telling Miss Percival that there is an official at the door who is being a nuisance and won't go away. She is certain to want to dismiss him personally, and that will give me an opportunity to speak to her and try to find out what I have done.'

Asia thought for a moment. 'You was always kind to me, Mr Jack, when many weren't, me being a nigra and all, so I will do as you ask.'

'If you get into trouble through obliging me,' Jack said, 'you know that I will not see you suffer by it. You will only have to call at Mr Butler's home and ask for me.'

Asia gave him a warm smile. 'No need, Mr Jack,

I'll do what you ask. Miss Percival has a sharp tongue but she's always kind—and Miz Grant, too.'

It seemed an eternity, there on the step, until Aunt Percival appeared. The moment she saw him, she said grimly, 'I might have guessed who the nuisance was. Go away, Mr Dilhorne, you have caused enough trouble in this house,' and she began to shut the door.

Jack could not grab Aunt Percival by the arm, but he could put his foot in the door and hold it steady with his hand so that she could not shut it.

'No, Miss Percival, I am not to be dealt with as easily as that. I wish to speak to you or to Marietta, and I am determined to do so whatever it might cost me.'

'Well, you'll not speak to Mrs Grant, she's gone to Bethesda with the children so that you might not pester her further.'

'I haven't pestered her at all,' said Jack truthfully. 'I haven't been given the opportunity to.'

'Nor will you ever be,' said Aunt Percival, still grim. She had retreated behind the door, and was offering him only the sight of her head. 'I'm sure that she wishes never to see you again after you abandoned her without a word or a line two years ago.'

This statement was delivered with such venom that it shook Jack to his foundations. For a moment he was speechless, staring at Aunt Percival as though she, too, were, in truth, the Medusa who might, at any moment, turn him to stone.

Unable to believe what he was hearing, he almost stuttered, 'Abandoned her without a word! How can you say that? It was she who never replied to my letters.'

'Never a letter came from you, my man,' said Aunt Percival magisterially. 'Isn't it enough that you broke my poor girl's heart with your wickedness and then, when she found a good man to love and to care for her, God had him killed in this terrible war? She has had enough to plague her without you lying about writing her letters in order to torment her further.'

'I'm not lying,' said Jack, desperately thinking of all those weeks when nothing had come back from Marietta. He remembered, with pain, all the loving words which he had written to her, the hopes which he had had, all shattered and lost in sleepless nights and unhappy days.

'As God is my witness,' he said—and he rarely called upon the Deity— 'I wrote to her again and again—and she never replied to me, not once.'

'She could not reply to what she did not receive,' said Aunt Percival glacially. 'She tried to write to you through Butler and Rutherfurd's and nary a word came back from them—not ever.'

'No,' said Jack, his face suddenly ashen. The shock of what he was hearing overwhelmed him. 'No, this cannot be true. At least tell me how to find her in Bethesda so that I may speak to her of this, for I cannot believe what you are telling me.'

'No,' said Aunt Percival, 'you may find your own way there, but be sure that she will not receive you. She has no wish to have her heart broken again.'

He stepped back a little on hearing this, relinquishing his grasp on the door, something of which Aunt

Percival took immediate advantage. 'Good day, Mr Jack Dilhorne—and do not come here again,' she added, shutting it in his shocked face.

Jack stared blankly at the knocker and the shut door. Could he believe what Aunt Percival had just told him with such bitterness? What in the world could have happened to all his letters—and to hers? He half-moved to knock again, but he was sure that Aunt Percival would not help him, and he also had to believe that by her manner and her speech that she was telling him the truth as she knew it. Well, he would discover where Marietta was from others, and go to see her to try to plumb this dreadful mystery. His tortured mind rehearsed it and over again.

He was plodding along the sidewalk, his head down, lost in speculation, when he heard running feet behind him. He turned. It was Asia, breathless and panting.

'Oh, Mr Jack, you was allus kind to me. I was watching from the window and I saw your poor face when she told you to go. Miz Marietta's at the old Hope Farm in Bethesda with the children. Mr Butler will tell you how to get there.'

Jack felt in his pocket, pulled out several dollars and offered them to her: it was little enough reward for her kindness. Asia put her hands behind her back. 'No, thank you, Mr Jack. I liked you. I was sorry when you went away. Keep your money. This is my kindness to you.'

'And was it true that Miss Marietta never received my letters?'

Asia nodded her head. 'Nary a one, Mr Jack. I saw

her poor face when I took the mail up to her bed. She was ill after you had gone, and Miz Percival allowed as how it was disappointment made her worse. I never believed that you had left her like that, without a word, you being allus so kind. I promised Miz Percival I would say nothing to you about the letters, but you deserve the truth, that you do. I know she wrote to you, because I placed her letters on the table in the Senator's study, ready for the post. And then the Senator died and the Missises went into the country, leaving the staff behind, with orders to forward all the family's mail. They said that nothing came back from you while they was gone.'

'I can only give you my most sincere thanks for your news—although it offers me no cheer,' Jack said.

'Thanks is all I want,' Asia told him before running back to the house, arms flailing, and Jack walked back to Ezra Butler's home, still puzzling over what he had heard, and saddened by Aunt Percival's hostility.

It was now late afternoon, warm and pleasant: the day was too far gone for him to drive to Bethesda now; he could not badger her when she might be tired. The journey would have to be made on the morrow. Meantime, he would have to think most carefully of what he should say to her when at last they met where he could speak freely—if she consented to see him, that was.

All that sustained him that evening when he dressed for the Reception at the White House to which Ezra was taking him, and which he was duty bound to attend, was the thought of seeing her again and, if pos-

sible, trying to convince her that they must both try
to discover what had gone wrong.

The more he thought about his lost, loving, letters—
and Marietta's—the worse he felt.

Back at the Grants' house, Aunt Percival was having similar thoughts. For the first time in her long life
of looking after Marietta and her interests, the way
before her was far from clear.

What troubled her most of all was Jack's horrified
face when she had reproached him for deserting Marietta, and for lying about writing to her from New
York. She remembered how much she had liked him,
partly because he had seemed to care so deeply for
her darling, had made her laugh, had made her happy,
and had made her believe that she could enjoy herself
like her pretty cousins, Sophie and Julie. Her subse-
quent hatred of him for his betrayal of her darling was
the deeper for it.

She had not planned to leave Washington for Bethesda until the following morning, but she suddenly
decided that she must waste no time before she told
Marietta of what had happened. There were so many
things to think of, among them the question of Cobie,
the little boy who had made up for Jack's desertion
with his sweet good nature. Aunt Percival's face softened at the thought of him, their treasure, despite his
irregular birth.

For surely when Jack arrived at the farm—as she
was certain he would—he would discover the existence of his son, and what then? Avory had loved him,
too, and had adopted him and given him his name,

but Aunt Percival was hazy as to how legal this was in the face of Jack being his father. Suppose he tried to claim him? Yes, she must leave at once so that Marietta would have time to decide what to do for the best.

Once she would have thought such a decision easy to make, but Jack's evident distress when she had told him that Marietta had never received any letters from him had made her remember that she had once seen him as fundamentally decent and kind, not as an ogre who had treacherously betrayed a woman who had foolishly come to love him.

Seated in the carriage on the way to Bethesda, she began rehearsing again those lost days when Marietta had lived in the hope of a letter from Jack. The days when she had agonisedly realised that Marietta was pregnant and she had watched her, helpless to remedy matters.

One thing was certain: Marietta was sure to have known whether the letters were coming or not because it was she who always oversaw the Senator's mail, who inspected it each morning—and the outgoing mail, too…

And then she remembered something else, something which brought her erect in her seat, her hand to her trembling mouth, her heart thudding, her face alternately white and scarlet. The something else which had been forgotten in the turmoil of the days after the Senator's sudden death and funeral.

She exclaimed, 'No, oh, no,' and stared into the growing dusk. 'No, it cannot be true,' and she tried not to think the unthinkable, of who had taken care of the post when Marietta had first fallen ill with morning sickness... Dear God, no, do not let it be true...

What she could not erase from her recovered memory was the sight of the Senator lying dead in front of the fire in his study, of Sophie screaming above him, of the mail lying scattered and neglected on the floor... She must speak to Marietta, she must, before Jack arrived to confront her.

'Faster,' she called to the driver. 'Faster,' but he could never drive as fast as she would wish. Her dreadful thoughts would always run before him.

Chapter Twelve

Marietta, alone at the farm that evening, waiting for Aunt Percival to join her on the morrow, was remembering again what she had long told herself to forget: her happy times with Jack.

She was once more on the banks of the Potomac, laughing with him in the sun; in the bazaar where he had first shown open distaste for Sophie and his preference for her; her head on his breast when they were fleeing from the battlefield at Manassas, and finally, on their last day together, locked in his arms, happy and secure in his love.

So what had gone wrong? Had he met someone else in New York? Did he regret having made love to a plain old maid in her late twenties? All those thoughts, which had plagued her nearly two years ago when his desertion of her had become evident, were revived.

Remembering their joyful days together had made her smile; remembering those other lonely ones, when she had been awaiting Cobie's birth, made her sad again.

Susanna, happy to be at the farm, her favourite place, ran up to her and asked anxiously, 'Why are you crying, Mama? Have Cobie and I done something wrong?'

Marietta looked across to where Cobie sat on the polished wood floor, patiently building a small tower of bricks.

'No,' she told Susanna who, from the first moment she had met her, had been happy to accept Marietta as a replacement for the mother she had lost. 'No, my darling. I was thinking sad thoughts about a time before I married your dear papa. You and Cobie are my treasures, and you are both so well-behaved that Aunt Percival thinks that there must be something wrong with you!'

This mild joke set Susanna laughing, and what amused Susanna always amused Cobie, too. He looked across at them, and joined in without any notion of what his mama and his dear sister found so funny. He looked so delighted with life that Marietta went over to him to take him on to her knee to play some of the games which she remembered enjoying with her own mother, long ago.

'Bedtime soon,' she said, at which Cobie pulled a face: he thought bed a waste of time which could be better employed doing things.

Susanna said earnestly, 'Not yet—one more game, dear Mama.'

Who could resist such a plea? Certainly Marietta couldn't, and all three were soon enjoying themselves hugely when there was a bustle outside.

'Now, who can that be, calling at this time of

night?' asked Marietta, rising and replacing Cobie before his bricks.

It was, of all people, Aunt Percival, white-faced and agitated-looking.

'Goodness, Aunt, what possessed you to travel at this late hour?' said Marietta. 'I didn't expect you until tomorrow lunch at the earliest.'

'I came because it was important that I saw you as soon as possible,' said her aunt, walking forward and taking Marietta's hands in hers. 'Let their nurse put the children to bed tonight, my love. We have much to talk of.'

More than one person connected with Marietta Grant and Jack Dilhorne was in a state of distress that night.

Sophie Hope, dressing for the reception at the White House, stared at her face in the mirror and recognised an unfortunate truth. Once it had been her favourite occupation to admire herself there, but now what she could see reflected in its depths gave her no pleasure at all. Her delicate beauty was beginning to fade and, since she had started to eat to comfort herself for her lack of social success, she had begun to grow fat.

At least, though, Marietta would not be there. Her mother had told her that morning that she had gone back to Bethesda so she would be spared the sight of people being sorry for her, and having to express herself a sympathy which she did not feel.

Carver Massingham would be waiting for her at the Reception. He might be a coarse brute, but at least he was attentive, she would say that for him, if nothing else, and since no one more attractive had lately shown any interest in her, he would have to do—for the time being, at least. How hateful, though, that she was reduced to depending on him! He was middle-aged and vulgar, a widower looking for a second wife, a man of no family, made wealthy by the war, and in the new world which Washington had become since 1861, all doors were open to him. He aspired to marry Sophie Hope, whom a few short years ago he would never have met.

She was beginning to regret having burned Jack and Marietta's letters. Not because it was wrong to have done so, since remorse did not exist in her world, but because, had they married, Jack would have taken Marietta away. Then she might have married Avory, and she would not feel so bad-tempered all the time. Of course, Avory's being killed would have been a nuisance: it would have left her a widow, and missing all the fun.

She picked up her fan, and went downstairs to where her parents were waiting for her. They didn't approve of Carver and had told her so, but pooh to all that, a girl must have her beaux and he would do until a better came along. Perhaps it might even be Jack! She had heard that he was back in Washington. Who knows? She might even yet be Mrs Jack Dilhorne. That would be one in the eye for Plain Jane, and no mistake!

Carver Massingham was brooding, too, while he dressed for the reception at which he was determined that, one way or another, he would trap Sophie Hope into becoming his wife and so finally transcend his poor white origins. Marrying her would set the seal on his rise from ragged farm boy, and later minor storekeeper, to become one of the new moneyed class of robber barons which the Civil War was creating.

But that was the beauty of these United States. Only here could an able, ruthless man rise so rapidly if he were prepared to work hard and take his chances. He was certain that his rise had not yet ended—would not end, indeed, until he had reached the seats of power in the Capitol itself, and his wife, a member of one of the First Families, would be a trophy to sit beside him there.

He was as shrewd over women as he was over everything else. He had soon found out why pretty Sophie was still a spinster. She had a vicious tongue, and an uncertain temper and, as she grew older and more desperate, she increasingly betrayed them both to him and the rest of the world.

Oh, he knew that Sophie had no intention of marrying him. He was her bear, to be led and patronised, to carry her fan, to fetch her ices and lemonade until a better man came along to claim her. Alas, her reputation ran before her and better was unlikely to arrive. Give him half a chance and she would find herself married to a man whom she did not want. Then she would find out who was master and she would pay—both on her back and off it—for every careless insult she had offered to him.

He was patient and prepared to wait until an opportunity presented itself, and then this over-ripe fruit would fall into the bear's paw, and he would eat it, slowly, slowly, never mind that it had withered a little before it fell...

'Aunt Percival, whatever is the matter?' Marietta asked, nay, demanded, when she had sent the children to bed and her aunt had been given some strong coffee to drink. 'I have seldom seen you so distressed.'

She did not add that it was unlike her to treat both Susanna and Cobie with such indifference, preferring, instead of playing with them, to half-lie on the sofa. She drank her coffee as though her life depended on it, after assuring Marietta that, although she had not eaten anything since early morning, she wanted nothing in the way of a meal.

So although Cobie cried for his aunt to kiss him good-night in his bed, she refused, for once, and lay, blank-faced, in the comfortable parlour with its polished wood floor, hooked rugs, and simple furniture. Everything at the farm was quite unlike the elegant formality of Marietta's town house. It was a room for children to play in and enjoy, as Cobie and Susanna frequently did.

'First of all, Marietta, let me remind you, although I don't think that you need reminding, that Jack Dilhorne has returned to Washington.'

'Yes,' said Marietta simply, wondering what was coming next. 'I saw him at the Van Deusens' reception, but I did not speak to him other than to make it plain that I wanted nothing to do with him. I came to Bethesda because I wished to avoid meeting him again, and also to prevent him from seeing Cobie.'

'You know I sent him away with a flea in his ear, hoping that would be the last of him. Today, however, when I was readying myself to close the house before joining you here, he called again and compelled me to speak to him—which I had vowed I would never do.

'He had the impudence to claim that he had never abandoned you, or betrayed you. That, on the contrary, *you* had abandoned *him*, had never answered his letters. Indeed, he said that he had never received one from you.'

'How could he say such a thing?' exclaimed Marietta. 'I would not have thought him capable of such a gross lie.'

'Nor I,' said Aunt Percival, 'but let me finish. On neither occasion did I inform him of Cobie's existence, but I expect he will find that out when he visits you, as he surely will.'

She paused and gazed steadily at Marietta's white, shocked face. 'I fear that there is worse to come, for so you will think it. That is how matters stood to begin with. When I told him that he lied, and that you had received no letters from him, I shut the door in his face. In the moment that I did so, I saw his expression change dramatically.

'Marietta, I swear to you that I have seldom seen a man look so shocked. His look of shocked incomprehension has stayed with me all day, and made me regret that I was so short with him. I could not believe, on mature reflection, that such a look, such an expression of pain—and disbelief—could be anything other than genuine. I swear to you that from that mo-

ment on I began to consider that he might be telling
the truth. And, if he were, what could the explanation
be of such a strange event if you were *both* writing
letters to one another and yet *neither* of you received
any?'

'A trick which might baffle a stage magician,' said
Marietta drily.

'Indeed, and all the way to the farm I tried to remember what exactly had happened after he left
Washington two years ago. You see, it was always
you who looked after the Senator's mail as it went in
and out of the house, so if any letters had arrived from
Jack you would have been sure to see them—and also
to make sure that your letters went out with the post.

'And then I remembered something else. You began
to suffer from morning sickness almost from the moment of Cobie's conception. You were put to bed on
the doctor's instructions, and Sophie, of all people,
volunteered to look after the mail, did she not? She
continued to do so until the morning of your father's
death.

'So it follows that *she* would see your letters going
out and Jack's coming in, does it not…?'

'Aunt, what are you trying to tell me? That Sophie
saw our letters, and destroyed them, out of spite? That
she not only destroyed them, but destroyed our happiness, too—and made poor Cobie…'

Marietta could not go on. Her face crumpled and
she gave a swift, stifled sob. The stoicism, which had
had enabled her to carry on her life since Jack had
apparently deserted her as though nothing untoward
had happened, was under attack.

'Oh, Aunt,' she finally achieved—Aunt Percival was looking at her, herself rendered silent by what she thought she might have discovered—'can this possibly be true? Do you really believe what you are telling me? Could even Sophie be so wicked?'

'Yes,' said Aunt Percival, pulling herself together. 'If we believe that Jack is telling the truth, and I think we must, then what follows is that we know that your letters to him were placed with the outgoing mail in your father's study. There can be no doubt of that—and then they disappear, as do his incoming ones. Who else but Sophie could have handled them, and destroyed them?

'But, Marietta, I fear that I have worse than that to tell you…'

'There cannot be worse than that, Aunt. For she has destroyed Jack and me completely…'

'Oh, but there is,' exclaimed Aunt Percival, recovering her usual trenchant manner which had disappeared when she was telling Marietta of her dreadful suspicions. 'Do you remember the nature of your father's death? So sudden, when he was alone in his study with Sophie? Do you remember how extravagantly she behaved? Such screaming and such hysterics as were never seen before—and she did not even like your father, or he her. Such a how-do-you-do she made, as was never heard before.

'And where did he fall? I shall never forget how we found him—on the rug, before the fire. His hand was stretched out towards it, the poker in his hand. I think now that he must have discovered Sophie burning one of Jack's letters, and the shock was too much for his poor, weak heart. You see, my darling, if we accept that Jack is telling the truth, then everything we thought we knew changes. Yes, I believe that the Senator found her at her wicked work. What was worse, I think that she might have destroyed his last letter to you. For when Sophie left and you took over the mail again, he must, in despair, have stopped writing—as you did.'

'No,' said Marietta, 'I don't want to believe it— even of Sophie...' And then she fell silent, remembering all the dreadful words Sophie had flung at her, often in front of others, and of what both Charles Stanton and Avory had told her—that she must be wary of her cousin. Avory, indeed, had refused to have her in the house.

'Oh,' she finally said, the tears running down her face. 'If you are right, think of my poor Jack and of how much he must have suffered.' She was thinking that he must have felt exactly as she had done—betrayed and cheated, their love a lie.

'Oh, the wasted, wasted years, and, oh, my poor little boy, left without his true father and with no real surname until Avory gave him one. Oh, what must Jack be feeling, have felt? What will he think when he discovers that he has been for the last seventeen months the father of a boy whom he has never met, of whose early years he has been deprived?'

She began to wring her hands: a gesture which she had thought odd when she had seen other women doing it, but now nothing else seemed to answer, or would convey strongly enough the depths of her misery, both for herself and for Jack.

'If I know him,' said Aunt Percival, 'he will be here tomorrow and he will want an explanation. If he does not come, then it is up to you to try to see him. You must do what you have always done—the right and proper thing—and that means telling him the truth about Cobie—not that he will not know it the moment he sees him.'

'Yes,' said Marietta, steady again now that she knew the worst, for she felt sure that Aunt Percival, that hater of whim whams, that monument to sound common sense, had found the true explanation for the puzzle of the lost letters. 'Cobie is the one most hurt by all this, for all that my dear Avory tried to do for him.'

She laughed without humour. 'Ironic, is it not? For if Sophie had not driven Jack away, she might have married Avory, instead of giving me my brief happiness with him. The gods are not always unkind, except that they must be laughing at her—and at Jack and me. Oh, I know that I must take some of the blame for Cobie. I was so happy that I failed to consider the consequences which might flow from my afternoon with Jack.'

Marietta was grateful, later, that Aunt Percival had forewarned her of Jack's possible arrival and Sophie's treachery. She had had time to go to her room and try to sleep after she had wept over the past. In the morning there would be no more tears, for she must accept what had happened—and wait for Jack. She must not greet him with tears, for they might seem to reproach him.

Marietta had no doubt that Aunt Percival's reason-

ing had been correct, and that Sophie's dreadful behaviour to her over the last two years had been all the
more bitter because of the great sin which she had
committed, which had harmed not only herself, but
also Jack and their innocent little boy.

Before she slept—and sleep was long in coming—
she wondered not only where Jack was now, but what
he had been doing in the long months which had
passed since she had last seen him. Did he still love
her, as she undoubtedly still loved him?

Chapter Thirteen

Like Marietta, Jack was also remembering the past. Unlike her, he was still puzzled as to what had happened to their letters. Oh, the misery of remembering all those lovingly penned words which had never reached their intended recipient. He had to believe that what Aunt Percival had told him was true and that each of them had—wrongly—thought the other to be treacherous.

He took his misery with him to the White House. Had it not been a part of his duties he knew he would not have gone there.

The atmosphere at the reception that night was serious and subdued: the mad, hopeful ecstasy of the early days of the War had long gone, killed by death and battles lost, but the darker mood of the evening matched his own thoughts.

'We're a quiet lot tonight, Jack,' remarked Ezra wryly, 'especially you.'

'Yes,' said Jack soberly. 'I suppose there are many like me who are thinking of the dead. All wars have their dead, I know, but it means little until you have seen action.'

'It had to be fought, though,' said Ezra, who was a down-to-earth fellow, not given to much philosophising. So far as he was concerned, the war was a job to be done, like any other, and if there was benefit for him in doing it, so be it, it still had to be done.

'Oh, I don't deny its necessity,' Jack said. 'But you know that the South see it just as you do, as a holy war, and they're the worst wars of all. When they're beat, it will be a long time before they recover—or forget.'

Ezra shrugged. 'They wanted it,' he said, 'and they started it at Sumter.' Jack did not contradict him, but even that thought did not comfort him.

He was standing alone in an alcove, watching the chattering throng, when a woman's voice behind him, echoing Ezra's, said, 'You're quiet tonight, Jack.'

He turned to see Sophie Hope—for a quick glance at her left hand told him that she was still unmarried. She was being squired by a bear of a man: fat, almost middle-aged, with a hard shrewd face. He was obviously one of the new breed of entrepreneurs who were doing well out of the war. Jack thought him to be a strange cavalier for Sophie.

She smiled at him enticingly, but her youthful charm and her pink and white prettiness had faded in the two years since he had last seen her. His brother Alan had been prescient: she was growing fat and, given a few more years, she was like to become an old maid. Her once-soft mouth had a hard, petulant set to it.

'Miss Sophie,' he said politely, bowing a little. 'I trust I see you well.'

'Very well,' she said, and looked at her escort patronisingly, making no attempt to introduce him to Jack. 'Carver,' she almost snapped at him, 'pray fetch me an ice and do not trouble yourself to hurry back, I beg of you.'

He reluctantly moved away to do her bidding while Sophie turned her faded charms on Jack.

'He's Carver Massingham,' she told him carelessly. 'Rich but a bore, and a boor as well,' she finished dismissively. 'Although he has his uses.'

She was so patently telling Jack that she was free to accept his advances that Jack almost laughed. Instead, he said in as neutral a voice as possible, 'For fetching and carrying ices, I suppose.'

Her laughter at this—although she was not sure that Jack was making a joke—was consequently rather strained.

'You look worried, Jack, not quite the man you were. Were you looking for Marietta—or the widow Grant, I ought to say. She rarely goes out in public these days—so unfortunate, Marietta.' Her eyes glittered when she came out with her most cruel dart. 'One way or another, she can't seem to keep a man!'

'Now, why should you think me worried?' he countered, refusing to reply to her spite about Marietta. He was not minded to wear his heart on his sleeve for Sophie to peck at. She had become a hard and bitter woman: her sneer at Marietta was even harsher than those she had uttered before he had left Washington.

'On the contrary, I am most happy to be here—and to be entertained.'

His last sentence was a direct lie, but he thought that it was all that Sophie deserved.

His coolness made Sophie savage. How dared he look at her as though she were some ugly specimen in a mad doctor's study! Her desire to hurt him and to disparage Marietta suddenly outran her discretion.

'No? You weren't looking for Marietta, then? From all those letters you wrote to her from New York,' she began unwisely, 'I thought that— Jack! Whatever are you doing?'

Her exclamation came out as a shrill scream of fear, for Jack's face had changed dramatically on hearing her careless words and grasping their meaning. He thrust out a hand to grip her wrist so tightly that another cry of pain was wrenched from her. 'Jack! Let go of my wrist! What do you think you're doing?'

Pleasant Jack Dilhorne's expression was murderous. Sophie suddenly realised what she had unwittingly admitted. She stood, still and silent, her free hand suddenly over her betraying mouth, her own face grey.

'Sophie,' he said, his voice unrecognisable, 'to what letters are you referring? And how came you to see them? Only this afternoon I learned that Marietta had never received a single one of mine. So how did *you* know about them?' Jack's voice never rose, but became so hard that it was unrecognisable. In manner and speech he had become a twin to his formidable brother Alan. He tightened his grip on Sophie's wrist so strongly that she feared that he was about to break it.

'Jack! Stop this at once. I don't know what you are talking about. Let me go at once, d'you hear!'

'No, Sophie. Not until you tell me how you knew that I wrote to Marietta when no one else did. What did you do with my letters, Sophie? Marietta, Aunt Percival and Asia never saw them, but you have just said that you did. So tell me, what happened to my letters which Marietta never received? And to hers which never reached me? Answer me, Sophie, or it will give me the greatest pleasure to wring your neck as well as break your wrist!'

For one moment she met his hard stare and endured the pain his grasp was causing. Her head dropped, only to rise again, to show him her eyes, blazing and triumphant.

'Oh, damn you, Jack Dilhorne! Here's the truth and much pleasure may it give you! I burned them, all of them, and hers to you, so that you each thought that the other was faithless. I laughed when I watched them turn to ash. Why should that plain stick take all my beaux away from me and not pay for it? Even when I'd got rid of you, she had the impudence to rob me of Avory Grant and marry him.

'And now you're back, still mooning after her, I see. I'm glad I burned your letters. I'd do it again.'

Unseen by either of them, Carver Massingham had returned with a small tray of ices to hear the greater part of what was being said. He had done nothing to betray his presence, but had watched and listened to them, his face avid, but his pleasure at seeing Sophie manhandled carefully suppressed.

The berserker rage which Jack had never felt before

and was never to feel again, and which, unknowingly, he shared with his dead father and his two elder brothers, had him in its grip. The world slowed to a stop, until all that it contained was Sophie's white, hate-filled and triumphant face while she taunted him with her actions which had cost him Marietta, his peace of mind and two years of his life without the woman he loved, the woman whom he might, for all he knew, have permanently lost.

Afterwards, he never knew how it was that he didn't wring Sophie's neck on the spot as he had threatened. His hands were reaching out to clutch it—and then the world started again when someone tapped him on the shoulder.

It was Carver Massingham, holding the tray of ices in one hand and, having heard all he wished to hear, touching Jack's shoulder with the other to prevent him from doing the unforgivable.

'I say, Dilhorne, what in the world do you think you're doing?'

His coarse voice banished the berserker rage. Jack dropped his hands and stared at Sophie, whose scarlet wrist was beginning to bruise and to swell.

'You,' said Jack thickly, 'you…you treacherous whore,' and then to Carver, his face still avid when he heard this denunciation, 'I wish you joy of her. Buy her a padlock for her tongue and cuffs for her hands when you marry her. You'll need them.'

'Damn you, sir,' spluttered Carver, looking from one to the other and defending Sophie purely for form's sake. 'How dare you speak to a lady so?' Underneath his apparent gallantry, however, he was thinking, So *that's* the kind of thing the bitch is capable of getting up to, is it? Damn if I've not found just the hook to catch Miss Sophie with.

'A lady?' ground out Jack, looking around him, his expression still murderous. 'What lady? I see no lady, sir. Merely some poor, white trash I believe you call it here.'

'Damn you, sir,' roared Carver again, still outwardly chivalrous. 'You'll answer to me for this, Dilhorne.'

'Not I, sir,' said Jack, at last becoming aware of the stares which the scene had drawn and was still drawing. 'I've no wish to kill you over *madame* here. Ask her what she did with my letters to Marietta and hers to me, and then ban fires from your home if you're stupid enough to marry her.'

He turned to go, still shaking, the remains of the rage causing a physical nausea so strong that he felt like vomiting on the spot.

Sophie's face was ashen. She seized Carver by the arm when she thought that he was about to follow Jack—something which he had no intention of doing. His prime aim now was to deal with Sophie.

'No, I beg of you, no,' she gasped, not wishing him to learn what she had done, unaware that he had overheard most of what had passed between herself and Jack, and fearful that Jack might tell the whole room of it if he were further provoked.

Carver stared at her. Melted ice was dripping on to the tray he carried.

'What did he mean, Sophie, about his letters? Tell

me?' His voice was suddenly as cruel as it was when
he was dealing with his business rivals.

'Nonsense, oh, it's nonsense,' she replied swiftly,
trying to placate him: his face had become as unpleasant as Jack's had been. She was suddenly frightened
of him—all her usual contemptuous treatment of him
quite vanished. 'I jilted him, that's all. And now he's
trying to gain his revenge.'

'Not what I heard,' returned Carver. 'If that was
Jack Dilhorne, he left you for your plain cousin. The
jilting, if any, was on his side. What did you do with
his letters, Sophie? Burn them, to keep them away
from the plain cousin? Is that what you did?'

Mutely, she stared at him. It was hopeless to try to
deceive him: his shrewdness was a byword.

'Answer me, Sophie,' he said, putting down the tray
and trying to clean his hand with his handkerchief
where the ice had dripped on to it.

'Why should I?' she asked sullenly. 'It's no business of yours.'

'Did you burn them, Sophie? I will have an answer,
you know.'

'You will not, for I shall leave you,' she said, de-
fiance written on her face.

For the second time that night her wrist was caught
in a cruel grip.

'No, Sophie, you will stay, and you will marry me
whether you wish to or not. Otherwise I shall tell the
whole world of what you did, and that would destroy
you. There is not a decent person in Washington who
would speak to you again. Thank your God that I am

a vulgar swine who knows how to control a jealous virago.'

'You would not,' she panted. 'You would not dare.'

His cruel eyes raked her body and for the first time Sophie realised the temper of the man whom she had teased and taunted. She was trapped and knew it. She did not want him, no, not at all. She now knew how hard her life would be if she married him, but not to accept him meant that she would be ruined: and over Marietta! That was the hardest cross of all to bear.

'You leave me no choice,' she finally said.

'I seldom give others any choice,' was his response. 'And when you are my wife you will behave yourself—or take the consequences.'

He released her wrist. 'Now we shall tell your parents that we are to be married; although they will not approve of me, they have never yet denied you anything—which is your downfall.

'Look happy, my dear. You are going to be a bride at last. In order to gain a place in your world, a man has been foolish enough to marry an unattractive shrew with a fat backside. One further thing. If your cousin should ever ask you about her letters you will tell her the truth, apologise tearfully, and that will be the end of the matter. I know the Marietta Grants of this world: they have all the honour and decency which you and I do not share.'

Sophie's smile on hearing these coarse home truths was a rictus of dismay. She had given Carver Massingham his chance to trap her, and now she must pay. She walked with him over to her parents, her hand clasped loosely over her damaged wrist, and tried to hold her grimacing smile in place.

The worst thing of all had happened, for now he was her cruel master who had pretended to be her humble slave.

Chapter Fourteen

Jack could not sleep. The memory of the dislike on Aunt Percival's face when she had seen him, and the glee on Sophie's when she had taunted him with the destruction of his letters, prevented him sinking into the blessed oblivion where he could forget them.

Sophie had made him appear to be the worst kind of exploitative swine, and he had no notion whether, when he sought her out in the morning, Marietta would even agree to meet someone whom she must regard as her treacherous seducer. To her, unaware of Sophie's wicked behaviour, he was a man who had taken her to bed, made love to her, and then had callously abandoned her. It was enough to destroy any woman's love. Would it even arise from the ashes when he confronted her with what Sophie had confessed to him and Carver Massingham?

He could hardly wait for the new day to arrive when he could set off for Bethesda. He had asked Butler, before he left the Reception, to tell him exactly where the Hope Farm was, and how to get there.

His face had been so ravaged that Ezra had looked at him queerly, saying, 'It's not really a farm any more. The Senator bought it for a summer home so that he needn't spend the hot weather in Washington itself. It's not a long ride.' He gave Jack the directions he needed, while wondering what Sophie Hope could have said to distress him so profoundly.

'Take my gig,' he offered kindly. 'It will be easier than riding.'

Jack scarcely looked any better the next day. It was fine and sunny and he rose early, the marks of a sleepless night plain upon his face. All the way along the road which, once out of Washington, was little better than a track, he thought carefully of what he might say to Marietta. He wondered whether she would even believe him when he told her of Sophie's wickedness. Would she be able to credit that, since he had loved her so dearly, the last two years had been a time of great suffering for him because he thought that he had lost her—or had never really had her, or her love?

The one thing which worried him the most of all was that, even if she believed him, it was possible that she might have lost the love for him which had once moved her so powerfully that she had joyfully given herself to him on their last day together.

After all, she had been Avory Grant's wife, and he was still only eight months dead. Butler had told him that the marriage had been a happy one, and that since his death at Fredericksburg she had virtually retired from society. The night on which Jack had seen her was the first occasion on which she had attended a public event. Well, he could only try his best, and pray that God would be kind to him—and to her…

When he arrived at the farmhouse there was no one to be seen. The place lay peaceful under the sun, like something lost and out of time. He felt his presence, and what he had come to tell them, to be nothing less than sacrilege.

A black servant, not Asia, came to the door. Oddly enough he seemed to be expected, for when he gave her his name and asked to see Mrs Grant, she immediately showed him into a big, airy room which looked out on to an idyllic view of fields, hills and trees: Marietta was not present.

He paced the planked and polished floor nervously until the black servant entered and said, 'Mrs Grant to see you, sir,' before rapidly retreating—to be replaced by Marietta.

It was a Marietta whom Jack had never seen before. All the careful, formal and staid attire which Senator Hope's daughter and secretary had always chosen to wear was gone.

Her lustrous hair was unbound; instead, it was tied loosely at the nape of her neck with a broad, cherry-coloured ribbon. The long sweep of it fell down her back. She was not wearing mourning, but was sporting a simple cream-coloured cotton dress, decorated with sprigs of flowers. A broad cherry-red sash circled her waist. The skirts of her dress were full and flowing since she wore no crinoline cage beneath them. Her slippers were also bright red. Over the dress was an apron of fine cream linen trimmed with lace.

It was her face, though, which had changed the most. The severe air, which she had worn as an armour, had gone. Instead, her expression was soft and tranquil, with more than a trace of the humour which she had always possessed but had rarely revealed. Jack had forgotten her humour after experiencing the sober intensity of the women whom he had met in New York.

Strangely, this belated, and unexpected, meeting reproduced the pattern of their first one, that long-ago day in Washington. Jack was standing at the window when Marietta entered, looking out at the meadows and the trees. He turned to greet her when she slowly advanced until she was immediately in front of him.

He bowed—as did she—as though they were strangers newly come upon one another, and if Jack thought Marietta had changed, she thought that Jack had. He was more serious-looking, for one thing. There had still been something of the eager young boy about him when they had first met—and even when she had last seen him.

Now he was more like his brother Alan. There was a basic seriousness written on his handsome face, and also something wary, which was coupled with a fundamental sternness which he had never shown before. He shared something with Avory in that. This new Jack surprised her a little since he was not quite as she remembered him. From looking younger than his years he now appeared to be older than them.

'Aunt Percival has already told me that you twice arrived at my Washington home wishing to see me,' she said calmly.

Oh, dear, how banal her words were, how unwelcoming. Like Jack, Marietta was fearful that the two lost years, coupled with their lost letters, might have changed his feelings for her: that he might now no longer love her as he had once done. Aunt Percival had said that Jack's distress on being reproached and turned away had been very evident. Perhaps that simply meant no more than that he was upset at being misjudged.

To soften her words she added with a slight smile, 'And here I am.'

Jack swallowed. He had thought so much of what to say to Marietta when he saw her again, but to no avail. He only knew that, as she stood there before him in all her new-found loveliness, his own feelings for her had not changed. No, that was wrong; they had become intensified—if that were possible.

Her face was so serene. The Sophies of this world would be eclipsed by it, since Marietta's beauty was that of character which was bred in the bone and not in the flesh which cruel time would ravage and destroy. Sophie had been right to fear her, for how in the world could she ever rival this?

Marietta's smile was tender and slightly mocking.

'So silent, Jack,' she said. 'Not like you at all.'

He found his tongue at last. He would have liked to fall before her, to kiss the hem of her garment as the Bible had it, but that would be theatrical, considered, not at all the fashion in which he wished to speak to her again.

Nor did he wish to woo her with words, or deeds, even though his body was telling him that she had lost none of her attraction for him, and so he found talking to her strangely difficult. All his fine speeches, composed in his head on the journey to Bethesda, had flown away, scattered by the mere sight of her, radiant in her new-found serenity.

'You think me a traitor,' he said at last, for she was waiting for him to answer her, her expression slightly quizzical, because she, too, was finding speech difficult. Later, each was to think that it would have been simpler if they could have fallen into one another's arms and continued where they had left off on that day when they had celebrated their love in his rooms.

'A cur who betrayed you,' he continued, 'and then, mouthing false promises, deserted you, after destroying your virtue.'

'Yes,' she told him gravely. 'That is true. I felt all of those things when I never heard from you. I could not sleep for thinking of them. But I never stopped loving you, Jack, even when I married Avory, and so I told him. You see how much I cared, and thus how gravely I was wounded.'

She said nothing of her and Aunt Percival's suspicions of Sophie's guilt. That was to come. She must know whether he still felt anything for her before she assumed that he might still feel the same as she did.

'Is there any way,' Jack said, 'that I can convince you that I never stopped loving you, that I wrote and

wrote to tell you so, to speak of the future which I
hoped to share with you? It was only after months of
silence that, with all hope gone, I finally surrendered
to what I supposed were your wishes, and stopped
beseeching you to write to me. Oh, Marietta, I never
deserted you, either in mind, or body. And then I
heard that you had married Avory Grant.'

He stopped, unable to speak further for memory of
the pain he had then experienced.

Marietta put out a hand to touch his, murmuring
softly, 'So, in the end, you supposed that I had abandoned you. But, Jack, I too wrote, and received no
answer from you. What was I to think but that you
had taken your pleasure and gone?'

'No,' he said, and she saw that his face was full of
an old pain. 'And then I came to Washington, because
my duty required it, and tried to speak to you, to find
out what had gone wrong, why you had deserted me,
and then, last night I discovered what had happened
to our letters, that Sophie…Sophie…' and he choked
on the name.

Marietta took his hand and stroked it, trying not to
let her tears fall.

'That Sophie burned them,' she finished for him.
'That she destroyed the future that we might have had,
and in the doing I fear that she may have indirectly
killed my father.'

'You know?' exclaimed Jack, lifting his ravaged
face. 'How can you know? She only confessed it to
me last night at a White House Reception, when by
accident she said something to me which betrayed that

she knew that we had each written to the other. I nearly wrung her neck before I wrung the truth out of her.'

Marietta kissed the hand she had been stroking, the hand which had written to her of love and the future.

'How strange life can be, for Aunt Percival told me only last night that she saw your face yesterday after she had confronted you with our belief that you had cruelly abandoned me. She thought, for the first time, that you were not lying when you tried to tell her that you had written to me constantly. And when you claimed that *you* had never received any letters from *me*, she came here, post haste, to tell me of her sudden dreadful suspicion that Sophie, who had been caring for my father's mail because of my illness, had intercepted them and destroyed them…and destroyed us.'

It was Marietta's turn to drop Jack's hand, to put her own up to cover her face as her tears began to choke her.

'Marietta,' said Jack hoarsely. 'She destroyed nothing but paper. I still care for you and always have done, even when I believed that *you* had betrayed *me*. I will not lie to you. After I had been told that you had married Avory I met another woman whom I wished to marry, although I never loved her as I had loved you. Thank God, she refused me, although I was sorry at the time. She said that she did so because it was quite clear to her that I was still grieving for you and could not give her my whole-hearted love. It was she who made me understand that loving and losing you had destroyed other women for me.

'Aunt Percival told me, when she was reproaching me, that you had married a good man, and I know that you must have hated me for what you thought I had done. Is there anything left for me in your heart—or do you simply pity me? Is there a possibility that if I asked you to marry me you could bring yourself to do so?'

'Oh,' she said, the tears running down her face. 'Can you doubt it? You did not listen to me when I told you that I never stopped loving you, and that I didn't cheat Avory. I told him of you, of our love for one another, and he accepted it and me, and adopted Cobie. If I stayed faithful to you in my heart when I thought that you were a traitor, you may judge of my feelings towards you now that I know that you were not. Of course I will marry you.'

The mention of Cobie passed Jack by because he had heard that Marietta Grant had two children, one of them Avory's by his first wife. Perhaps, Marietta later thought, she had purposely not dwelt upon him. She did not wish to use Cobie's existence to blackmail Jack into marriage.

It was Jack's duty to kiss her tears away, which merely resulted in his mingling with hers. But now they were tears of joy which they shared together. Presently he raised his head and said, brokenly, for the enormity of what had happened was still with him, 'Shall we marry as soon as possible so that we may make up for the lost years? You had better know that I am more of a savage than I thought I was. I could have killed Sophie last night for what she has done to us. When I think of all those loving words I wrote to you which she turned into so much ash… I said that she had only destroyed paper—but what paper—'

Marietta put her hand upon his mouth. 'Shush, my darling,' she said gently. 'If Aunt Percival is right, her worst crime was to my father. But that is past, and it is useless for us to repine. Let us forget her, and think of our future together.'

He took her into his arms again and kissed her gently on the cheek. 'I almost fear to touch you, my darling. Two years ago I was too daring, too sure of myself, and of our future happiness. I tempted the gods and was taught a bitter lesson: that we may not have all we want by right, as and when we wish it. I was too greedy, and so we were both punished.'

'You were not the only one, Jack,' she said softly into his chest. 'I had to learn a bitter lesson, too. That I could not take what I wanted, as I did that last afternoon, and forget all else. I did not remember that time and chance will deal with all of us, and sometimes harshly.'

'Sophie, too, then,' he said, bitterly.

'Sophie, too,' she agreed. 'What she did to us was dreadful—what she has done to herself is worse.'

Jack thought for a moment of Sophie as he had seen her last night with her vulgar escort, and remembered the dazzling young beauty of his first encounter with her. He did not reject Marietta's judgement. Of course, Marietta was right; they must secure their future by forgetting the past.

'Come, my love,' he said tenderly, sinking on to

the settle and laying her head on his chest. 'Let us try to make up for the lost years while I tell you that this time I shall not leave you until the knot is safely tied and we are man and wife.'

'We are agreed on that,' she said, reaching up to kiss his cheek. 'The waiting will be as short as I can make it.'

Holding her, Jack thought, was almost the same as it had been before, but not quite. If they had both suffered and learned patience, they had also learned something more—to savour each moment as though it were the last without wrenching at it. Their new happiness would have a depth which the old one had not possessed. They had had to lose one another in order to learn how truly deep their love was.

Marietta slipped from his arms to look earnestly at him. 'You are still the Jack I remember, even if you resemble your brother Alan more and your old self less. I think that we have both finally grown up.'

'Which I needed to do more than you,' Jack admitted gravely. 'My father was right there: I took all my good fortune in life as my due—now I know better.'

He then told her something which Avory had said to her in almost the same words before he had returned to the Army for the last time.

'I have seen war, Marietta, and it changes a man. What was a game for me, a thing of abstract shapes on maps and plans and tables, disappeared when I encountered the realities of battle. As a consequence the bloodless shapes became men who suffered, bled and died, because Charles and I wrote and drew on paper. It was why, after I had sailed on the *Monitor*, I asked to go South, to join in the river war: I couldn't remain behind the lines and play God there. I can't forget that.'

'Nor would I ask you to,' she said gently, 'but for a little you must enjoy the calm of peace here, still far from the conflict, because I want you to meet the children for whom you will be responsible when we are married. The sooner they get to know you, the better. Come.'

Jack was greatly moved by the expression on her face when she spoke of the children. It was half-teasing, half-loving, so he immediately did as he was bid. He assumed that these were Avory's children from his first marriage, and he followed her when she led him on to the big enclosed veranda at the back of the house.

There were chairs and tables there, and another settle. A pretty, raven-haired little girl, wearing a white dress and a black sash, sat at a table writing carefully, her tongue protruding between her lips. Beside her, on a rug, a blond baby boy who was hanging on to the table leg was busy hauling himself upright to stand for a moment on sturdy legs before launching himself across the room to greet Marietta and the strange man.

He was so excited that he lost his balance, sat down and, nothing daunted, began to pull himself up again, turning his bright blue eyes on them, and offering them—and the world—a friendly grin. If Cobie had a fault, it was that he loved all the world, indiscriminately.

The little girl stood up and curtsied when she saw the stranger.

'Susanna,' said Marietta, 'this is Mr Jack Dilhorne. Jack, this is Miss Susanna Grant, Avory's daughter.'

Susanna gave him another small curtsy, and said, 'How do you do, sir? I trust I see you well.' She then turned to Marietta and asked her, still grave, 'Pardon me, Mama, but is he an uncle?'

'Yes,' said Marietta, as serious as the child. 'Yes, I think that you can safely say that he is an uncle.'

'Welcome, Uncle Jack, then,' said Susanna, bobbing yet again before she resumed her work at the table.

'And this,' said Marietta, picking up the little boy who was now hanging on to her skirts, 'is Cobie, and he is mine.'

Her face was alight with mischief when she came out with this while turning to face Jack, his child in her arms. The mischief on her face matched Cobie's, who was putting out his arms, mutely asking to be allowed to go to his new friend.

'Yours?' said Jack bewildered. 'How can that be? Any child which you and Avory had could not possibly be as old as Cobie.'

'Oh, Jack, you goose,' said Marietta, laughing at him over the top of his son's fair head. 'Look at him. He's yours. With that hair and those eyes, and his charm, who else but you could possibly be his father?'

'Mine!' Jack was thunderstruck. He did mental

arithmetic rapidly in his head. 'Of course, that after-noon! No!'

His face twisted with grief—and then he put his arms around them both. 'Oh, my darling Marietta, you mean…that on top of my apparent desertion you had to face this alone. And when I think of how I would have cherished you both…'

He fell silent and Marietta felt his hot tears on her cheek.

He took the little boy from her and hugged and kissed him—something which Cobie took entirely as his due.

'Cobie—for Jacobus, I suppose?'

'Yes—for my father—and for you. Even with you apparently gone for ever I wanted him to have at least a part of your name.'

'I cannot speak,' exclaimed Jack, who knew that he usually had a ready tongue, but the enormity of what he was hearing had silenced him.

Susanna had lifted her head from her work, and was regarding him approvingly.

'He knows how to hold a baby properly,' she said. 'I suppose that now poor Papa has gone we need a man about the house, and it would be useful to have one who is good with baby boys.'

This old-fashioned piece of wisdom, garnered from Susanna having heard Aunt Percival and Aunt Lucy Grant talking, nearly overcame both her hearers.

Marietta, realising that there was still much that she and Jack had to say which was best done out of Su-sanna's hearing, undid the veranda door and beckoned

Jack to a long wooden seat overlooking the meadows and the distant forest. Jack followed her, still carrying an interested Cobie who was busy inspecting his new playmate—he seemed to be a fearless child.

They sat down together, Jack looking around him at the kind of view which American landscape painters loved to celebrate. Even Cobie was quiet, as though he sensed that his mama and this new uncle needed a moment or two to digest the enormity of what had happened to them.

Finally Jack said suddenly, after kissing Cobie's warm cheek, 'It is not every day that one discovers that one has a family. I still feel that I would like to strangle Sophie for what she did to us both in depriving me of the first years of my son's life. How you must have suffered when you knew that he was coming, and I had apparently abandoned you to ruin, and left Cobie fatherless into the bargain. Oh, I am doubly shamed. One afternoon's heedless pleasure, for I must take the blame for that, condemned you to a living hell.'

Marietta looked at his handsome face, for his new sternness had made him even more attractive to her, and said gently, 'Oh, Jack, do not reproach yourself overmuch. I was your willing partner and must take my share of the blame, if blame there is. We could not have known that Sophie would be so cruel. Remember, I was not alone in my grief, for I had Aunt Percival to help and comfort me. She was a better liar than I could have been, and as a result of her scheming no one knows that I am Cobie's mother.

'Not even Sophie has guessed that, and I pray God that she never will. The only thing, Jack, is that he's so like you, and will be more so, I fear—no, I mean hope—when he is older.

'Before it became apparent that I was breeding, I had a convenient breakdown and Aunt Percival took me deep into the country to have my baby at the farm of a distant cousin who asked no questions of us. We pretended that I was the grieving widow of a dead war hero. Besides, I passionately wanted my coming child, for it was all I had left of you. After he was born Aunt Percival and I went back with him to Washington, saying that he was an orphan relative of hers whose mother had died at his birth after asking her to adopt him—which she legally did.

'Avory guessed that he was mine. I could not help loving him from the very moment he was born, for he is a lovable child, as you are already finding out.'

She paused to laugh at the sight of Cobie rearing up to pat his new friend's face.

'You see, Avory not only married me, but he adopted Cobie, too, and gave him his name, saying that he liked the idea of having a ready-made son— even if I were to give him sons of my own later. You must not be jealous of Avory, my darling. He was a good man, and Cobie and I helped to make what were to become the last months of his life happy.'

'No,' said Jack soberly, 'I'm not jealous of him, although how I would have felt if I had returned to find him alive, and you happily married to him, is something I am relieved not to have had to endure.

'In any case, when I thought that I had lost you for ever I tried to console myself with another woman—as I have already told you. But I ought, in fairness to her, to tell you more. She is one of the new breed of Yankee women who are making careers for themselves, like men. She was a journalist, and had decided that marriage was not for her. She and I became lovers—I tried to persuade her otherwise, and proposed to her. I even told her a little about you, for she had sensed that I had had an unhappy experience with a woman before I met her. Later, as I've already told you, she said that the real reason she refused me was because I was still in thrall to that other woman, and she would not be content to be second-best in my life.

'She was right. For good or ill you are, were and shall be the one woman for me. The one woman of whom my father spoke, and whom he found to transform his life, as I hope that you will transform mine. I parted amicably with Peggy and I later heard that she had married an older man, the editor of one of the magazines for which she wrote. I sent a letter to her wishing her well—as she had wished me when we parted. "Find that woman, Jack," she wrote back to me, "and marry her." As with Avory, you must not be jealous of her since it was that advice which brought me back to you when my duty led me to Washington. Otherwise, I might not have come looking for you.'

'Thank God you did,' said Marietta, kissing first Jack and then Cobie because Cobie looked unhappy at being left out of the caressing stakes.

'Tell me, if it does not still distress you too much, when was he born?'

'No, it does not distress me to speak of it, and even if it did, you should know the details of your son's birth. He was nearly a month early, for which I was grateful because he was already so large,' Marietta told him, smiling reminiscently.

'He came into the world on March 9th, the same day as the Battle of Hampton Roads—of which I did not learn until many months later. He was most inconsiderate because he spoiled everyone's midday meal with the speed of his arrival. One minute I was putting greens on to boil, and in the next he was on the way. He has made up for that since by being the most agreeable and happy child a mother could be blest with. He rarely cries.'

'Putting greens on to boil!' Jack exclaimed at this revelation of a Marietta whose duties, when he had known her, had been so far removed from the mundane tasks of the kitchen.

Marietta laughed a little. 'Oh, I had to do my share of the work. The Hentys were quite poor and I refused to be pampered. Besides, I liked being mindless then.'

Jack was struck by another thought. 'You say that he was born on the day of the great naval battle—around midday. How very strange. Do you remember that when we first met I spoke to you of the warship which was to become the *Monitor*? We joked about it, did we not—remember the exploding muffins? I was on board the *Monitor* on the day of the battle, as an observer for Ericsson and the Navy Department. I was busy wondering whether I should ever see land, let alone New York, ever again when the oddest thing happened.'

How was he to tell her of having seen her in the middle of the battle without sounding remarkably eccentric? He stopped to consider his words, but before he could speak again, Marietta said slowly, equally struck, 'How strange, I had an odd experience just before Cobie was born. Tell me of yours.'

Her tone was so insistent that Jack forgot all caution and continued, 'Our captain was struck to the deck and blinded. I went to help him, for I tried to do my bit in the battle. When I bent down, saying to him, "Hold on, help is at hand," he disappeared, and I suddenly thought that I saw you, lying down in bed, with Aunt Percival nearby. You were in pain, but before I could say, or see, anything more, you disappeared and I was back with Worden.

'I never told anyone of this—other than my brother, Alan, when I wrote to him a little later. You may think me mad, but I would swear on oath that that is what I saw in the middle of the noise of battle.'

Marietta's face had turned white with shock.

'Oh, Jack, you have explained something which happened to me at the moment Cobie was born, something which I have never been able to understand, and I have tried to forget. I never even told Aunt Percival of it, and I usually tell her everything.

'I was in the last agonies of birth when you suddenly appeared before me, stretching out your hand. You were hardly recognisable. Your face was black and your forehead was bleeding. You were speaking. You said, and I still remember quite clearly what it was, ''Hold on, help is at hand''—and then you disappeared.'

It was Jack's turn to look thunderstruck.

'My face *was* black and my forehead was bleeding that day,' he finally came out with. 'What you saw of me was true only on that one day because I had taken part in the battle, replacing one of the dead sailors—which explains the black of the powder on my face. My forehead was gashed and bleeding because a shell from the *Merrimac* scored a direct hit on the *Monitor*'s gun turret and a fragment of its metal struck my forehead. Fortunately it was only a fragment, or I should not be here, talking to you. How strange that you should have seen me so plainly as to be able to describe me so accurately.'

'The only explanation which I can think of,' said Marietta carefully, 'is that at a moment of great crisis for the pair of us, the bond between us was still so strong that, somehow, for a brief moment in time, we were able to reach out to one another, quite without trying.'

'That is a possible explanation,' returned Jack, 'but it goes quite against all the rules by which we run our lives.'

'True,' said Marietta, 'and it is something which we ought not to dwell on too much, except to remember what Shakespeare once said, in Hamlet: ''There are more things in heaven and earth, Horatio, than are dreamed of in your philosophy!'''

They were silent again, contemplating the mysteries of life: the chance by which they had met at all, and the providence which had brought them together again, and given Cobie back to his father.

It was Jack who spoke first. 'Some day I will tell you everything I have done both at Hampton Roads and later in the Naval War in the South—but not today. Today is a day of celebration and I simply want to sit here in peace and tranquillity, enjoying the son whom I never knew that I possessed.

'Oh, Marietta, you do realise that it is only by the merest chance that I have found you both...'

He put his arm around her again, and hugged her and his son together, the tears not far away. Presently he handed her Cobie, who had begun to protest a little at being held so tightly.

'You do understand, and it is only fair to tell you so immediately, that if you marry me you will have to leave Washington. I have bought a big empty mansion on Long Island which will be perfect for you and the children. Our life will not be easy at first, even when the war is over. Before then, I have my duties to Ericsson and the Navy Department. After that I shall take over the running of Butler and Rutherfurd's, something which I am busy arranging with Ezra in the intervals of reporting on the Naval War to the Cabinet. You will be marrying a busy man, I fear.'

'I would not have it otherwise,' responded Marietta, 'and I shall not be unhappy at the prospect of leaving Washington because it will mean leaving behind Sophie and the unhappiness which she has caused us.

Remember what Ruth said in the Bible: ''Whither though goest I will go.'' I am used to living with a hard-working man and trying to make his life easy. What I did for my father I shall try to do for you, my darling, but never at the cost of neglecting our children—those we already have, as well as those we hope to have.'

'Spoken like my true love,' said Jack. 'You remind me of my mother. Even though you do not look in the least like her, you are also of the same true metal— gold all the way through.'

'So, Cobie, darling,' Marietta said to the child on her knee, 'we shall all go to New York with Uncle Jack, as you must learn to call him, for I fear that for your sake, rather than mine, we shall have to continue to deceive the world about your origin, so you may not call him father.'

Jack nodded a sad agreement. 'All the same, I shall treat him and Susanna as I would treat my own for their sake and for the sake of the man who cared enough for you to give my son a name. Never forget that although Sophie robbed us of two years together she gave you Avory and Susanna, and made of me the man that my father always hoped I would be. Besides, the war cannot last for ever. The South is already beaten but does not know it.'

For a moment they were both sad at what the war was doing to the country which was now to be Jack's home as well as Marietta's. The moment passed, though, when the veranda door opened and Susanna ran towards them.

'Mama, Aunt Percival says, is Uncle Jack staying for lunch, for if so, she will lay another place for him.'

'He is staying for more than lunch, I hope,' said Marietta, smiling, handing Jack his son again, and bending to kiss the little girl.

'Oh, good!' exclaimed Susanna, taking hold of Jack's free hand. 'He will not be taking Cobie away with him,' she added shrewdly.

'He will take us all away with him, quite soon,' said Marietta. 'On a train to New York and then on a steamer to our new home.'

'I have never been on a steamer,' said Susanna in her old-fashioned way as they all walked into the house. 'It will be quite a new life for us, will it not?'

Jack smiled lovingly at Marietta over the top of Cobie's head, and she smiled back.

'A new life, indeed,' he said, 'and a happy one, I hope.'

*　　*　　*　　*　　*

Cobie's amazing story is in two parts,
the first to be published in paperback
in May 2001

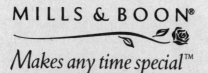

MILLS & BOON®

Makes any time special™

**Mills & Boon publish 29 new titles
every month. Select from...**

Modern Romance™   Tender Romance™

Sensual Romance™

Medical Romance™   Historical Romance™

MAT2